Whisper of Horses

Zillah Bethell

Piccadilly
PRESS

First published in Great Britain in 2016 by
Piccadilly Press
80–81 Wimpole St, London W1G 9RE
www.piccadillypress.co.uk

A CIP catalogue record for this book is available
from the British Library.

ISBN: 978–1–84812–534–6
also available as an ebook

1 3 5 7 9 10 8 6 4 2

Typeset in Sabon LT Std 12/16.15 pt by
Palimpsest Book Production Limited, Falkirk, Stirlingshire

Printed and bound by Clays Ltd, St Ives Plc

MIX
Paper from
responsible sources
FSC® C018072

Piccadilly Press is an imprint of Bonnier Zaffre Ltd,
a Bonnier Publishing company
www.bonnierpublishing.com

Part One
Inside

We did not dare go near them. Yet they waited,
Stubborn and shy, as if they had been sent
By an old command to find our whereabouts
And that long-lost archaic companionship.

Edwin Muir, 'The Horses'

1

Serendipity

It was around about the time Mama died that I started noticing the horses. Not real horses, obviously. But the statues of horses. Strong and proud figures that dotted the streets of Lahn Dan and stared stiffly ahead like they hadn't seen you looking. And on their backs, important men. Whenever the storytellers start talking about the horses, they always tell you that they carried important men. Lord this or King that. Into battle usually. Into war. If the Gases hadn't killed the horses off then the wars would have done in the end.

The day Mama died, the sky was slightly more violet than normal, the clouds fatter and blacker. The coughing had got worse – *hack, hack, hack,* it had been – and her colour more yellowy sick. I had helped her walk to the hospital at Lahn Dan Bridge and she had lain there all groans and *hack-hack-hack*s. They put her in a wheeling chair and whizzed her up to a room filled with other groaners and moaners and agey old *hack-hack-hack*ers. At least the candles and lamps in the room meant that you couldn't see her properly. Couldn't see how sick she was getting, I mean. The nurses all shook their heads and made sad eyes and one of them felt the need to put their arm around me. I knew then I'd be going home alone.

At one point Mama pulled herself up and, through the gloom, tried her best to look me in the eye, the coughing temporarily catching its own breath. Her straggly red hair tipped forward as she leaned in closer and grabbed my hand in her own bony fingers. A gentle tug, an almost invisible whisper on her lips. I pushed my ear towards her,

'. . . iiiiddde . . .' she whistled through her teeth.

'What?'

'. . . iiiiiiDDDDDE.' Frustrated, she yanked harder on my arm.

'Sorry, Mama. I don't know what you're saying. Try saying it—'

'Arrrttssiiiiddde.' Her hand dropped mine and her finger pointed itself at me. Slowly. Deliberately.

'What? Oh.' The trip flicked somewhere in my brain. 'Outside? What do you mean?'

Before she could reply her whole body flopped back onto the bed as the *hack-hack-hack*s started a fresh attack and Mama's dying body fought to keep itself still.

She lived for two more hours and never said another word.

*   *   *

To

Penny, without whom this book would not exist;

Ellie, protector of horses;

Dorn Cameo, the best horse;

And in memory of Bambi, Oliver, Autumn Butterfly and Parhelion.
May you gallop and graze in peace.

Initially, I thought that she was trying to protect me. Wanting me to go outside the hospital so that I wouldn't see her die. Sparing me the pain of her slip into the hands of the God Man.

It took some time for me to fully understand.

Walking home, I went a different route. I should have just kept along the bankment wall and scooted westwards, but for some reason I took the bridge over the Tems. Don't know why. Too many tears in my eyes. Not wanting to be home alone, I suppose. I found myself wishing for something I hadn't wished for in a long long time – that I had a father. A father to go home to. But there was no one.

It used to be a river – the Tems – so they say. One of the biggest rivers in the world. Gushing and whooshing along. Not that I'd ever seen a river, but that's what the storytellers say they did, gush and whoosh along. It started in the hills a hundred miles away and slid its way to the sea, cutting Lahn Dan in half on the way. Boats would go up and down, this way and that way, taking stuff back and forth. But all it is now is mud. A horrible, dangerous twisty line of mud. People fall in and never get out again. Robbers knock people on their heads and throw them in. That sort of thing. If you want to get rid of something, throw it in the Tems, that's what everybody says.

I walked and walked until I was well and totally truly

lost among crumply old buildings that I'd never seen before. Men and women pushing handcarts and rubbing their tiredy backs stared at me like I was a dancer in a roomful of lazybones. But still I walked and walked. I walked and walked and walked.

Until I came across it.

When I talked to the Professor about it a few days later, he told me that the part of Lahn Dan I found myself in was called Ole Bone Circus and before the Gases people would go there to chatter to each other and barter with each other to make as much money as possible. Now it sits as quiet as a dead mouse and nobody pays it much notice. All you can hear is the wind tunnelling down the different roads and the flap of people's cloaks as they hurry on past.

But in the middle . . .

In the middle is one of the statues I was talking about. A man – a prince, the Professor says – on the back of his horse, waving his hat as if to say 'Hello and welcome'. And the horse. Oh, the horse. If ever I see anything as handsome and as beautiful in my life again, I should shudder in amazishment. His neck all muscly and smooth like a rolled up carpet from the Gallery Market. His legs as sharp as Mrs Ludovic's knittering needles. His tail, slippery and silky. It was as if the prince himself were riding a king – a magnificent, majestic animal king.

Suddenly my legs stopped walking and my eyes stopped crying and, for the first time since Mama had died earlier that afternoon, I was thinking about something else. I stood there for who knows how long and just stared at the creature made of bronze. People went past and the day went past and all I did was wander around the statue and stare at it with my sore, red eyes. I don't know what it was, but something held me fixed. Its beauty and elegance. Its strength.

It reminded me of that bashed-up wooden toy Mama bought for me a longish time ago. One dull afternoon, thinking it was my birthday, she'd spent her last few pennies on it. The bashed-up wooden toy I'd lost forever.

As the sky eased itself into a darkness, I shook myself together. It wasn't too far off the Bat Shriek curfew and I was a long way from home. I raced back through the streets and over West Minister Bridge with just a few moments to spare before the sirens wailed over the city. Brushing past the moths in Dew Bee Lee Gardens, I grasped onto the ropes of the Lahn Dan High, pulling myself up and clambering across the spiderwebby mesh into our pod. *My* pod. It was only me now. I lit a candle and popped one of the dinner pills into my mouth before climbing into my sleep bag.

I didn't draw the curtains. I couldn't bear to see the shadows of moths tonight. I needed to see the stars.

2

Professor Nimbus

Early the next morning, before my head had a chance of flapping itself awake, the little stones in the pod rang *clack*. Someone was down below. It shuddered me into reality, I can tell you, and my heart dropped like a rock when I remembered that my mama was gone. I think I might have been dreaming about the horse from Ole Bone Circus. Mama and me were riding it over a field and through the streets and jumping over the Emm Twenty-five Wall. But being jolted awake made the dream disappear like water through my fingers, and within seconds of waking up only a kind of sickening sadness remained.

Clack-clack. The stones rang again and I dragged my legs out of the sleep bag and leaned against the side of the pod to try and see who was pulling on the rope. From where I was standing I could see the top of the Professor's head. He looked up and gave me a quick wave with his fingers. I waved back – not so much a greeting, more of an indication that I knew he was there and to tell him that I was coming. The Professor was a storyteller, but he didn't normally come to collect me for storytelling. Did he know about Mama?

I dusted my clothes off, gave my face a wipe with a cloth in the bucket of cold water that Mama had filled just the day before and climbed out onto the ropes, gently lowering myself down towards the ground. The mud of the Tems shone pink in the yawning morning light and Mrs Ludovic's washing was already dangling out to dry. It takes a couple of minutes to get from my pod to the ground, and by the time I'd arrived the Professor was sat on the floor, pulling his shoes back together with his tatty old laces.

'I need to find myself some more laces.' He spoke without looking up at me, his slightly greying hair bouncing up and down with each word. 'These shoes keep falling off me. If I don't get new laces, I shall lose them one of these days – you mark my words. I shall be pacing around Lahn Dan in my naked feet. People will call me the Shoeless Man and point and laugh. It's just a matter of time.' He stood up and looked at me. 'Hello, Serendipity.'

'Professor. What are you doing here?'

'I've come to collect you.'

'Collect me?'

'For storytelling. It is a storytelling morning for you today, is it not? Not a day for digging up the spuds or carrots or tending to the pigs?'

I shook my head. Like all other *Pb*s in Lahn Dan, for five days a week I had to work on the lotments or work with the pigs and goats. That usually meant trudging up to Hide Park or Gents Park to spend the whole day bent over, doubled up. All in return for a couple of potatoes and carrots and a tiny bit of goat's milk. If you were lucky. If the *Cu*s were feeling generous. 'No. No work today.'

'Then it's time to get going.' He stamped his feet to see if his shoes stayed on. 'Come on. No time to waste.' The Professor pulled his long jacket about him and started to march off, his green trousers blowing about his sticky thin legs. 'A tidy time waits for no man. Or girl.'

I ran to catch up with him; his steps were longer and straighter than mine so that I struggled to keep alongside.

'I heard about your mother, my dear. I am sorry.' He tried an awkward smile on me. 'Must feel a bit . . .' He searched for a word. 'Must be a bit strange.'

'Yes.' I didn't really feel like nattering about it. Once I started nattering I wouldn't be able to stop. Or worse still I'd start crying.

'Did you do the Goodbye Ceremony?'

'What?'

'The Goodbye Ceremony? Did you do it?'

'I don't know what you mean, Professor.'

He stopped for a moment and pulled his hands from out of his jacket pockets. I could see that his fingers looked stained and wrinkly like the muddy dry cracked Tems on the warm days.

'Did you cross the paper?'

'I –'

'They should have given you a piece of paper with a box on it. You take a pencil and you put a cross in it.' He made a sort of cross in the air with his flattened hand. 'It's the Goodbye Ceremony. It's how you say goodbye. Apparently. Reducing emotion to a cross in a box.'

My mind reached back to the evening before, and remembered a nurse standing in a hallway holding something – a sheet of paper? – but I was too upset to take in what it was. Then I left and that was that.

'I can't remember,' I said and carried on walking.

'Ah well, not to worry.' It was his turn to catch up with me. 'Say goodbye in your own way. It's what your mother would have wanted.'

We made our way along through the Shell building, around IMAX and into the big red block where our storytelling sessions were held. The foyer was crowded with children and a few other storytellers. Storytellers were employed by the Ministry to keep us busy when we weren't working on the lotments; get us up to the scratch with the rules of Lahn Dan; and teach us

11

what the world was like before the Gases. Professor Nimbus waved at a couple of them and the noise bubbled around as everyone started to climb up the echoey stairs.

'Serendipity!' I turned around to see Gry just behind me, her spiky brown hair looking even more spiky than usual. 'Sit next to me! Sit next to me, please. I don't want that horrid Bracken girl sitting next to me.'

'Just ignore her,' came Bracken's voice a few steps further back. 'Everybody does. Even her ma and pa. They push stones in their ears to stop listening to her. That's what I've heard.'

'See what I mean?' Gry's eyes half closed in pretend annoyance. 'Always sticking a pin in the ribs, she is.'

The Professor's room was on the third floor and we filed off from the rest of the crowd through the door.

'Why doesn't Gry sit on one side of me?' I suggested, pleased to be distracted. 'And Bracken – you can sit on the other side of me. That way you don't need to look at each other all that often. And if you do, then I can get in the way.'

'Okay.'

'Sounds good.'

They obviously hadn't heard about Mama. Thank the Goodness.

It stood on a base that shaped upwards like long moorland grass. Its legs were thin and breakable sticks

12

that thickened into muscle the further up you went. Its body sanded and filed and rasped into muscle that seemed to glint in the last end specks of the well-hidden sun. Its tail a proud twist falling away from its body; its neck and mane tapering towards its long elegant head.

'You like it?' Mama nodded encouragingly.

'It's lovely,' I said.

'Its ear's come off, I'm afraid.'

I rubbed my finger over the place where, at some point over the last few hundred years, somebody had accidentally or deliberately snapped off the tiny point of its left ear.

'Doesn't matter,' I said. 'I think it's lovely.'

'Saw it there in the market and thought . . . well . . . thought you might like it.'

I got down on the floor and started pattering it about as if it was moving or galloping or something, bringing it to life in my own childish mind. 'I do like it, Mama. I do. Thank you. It's the best present I've ever had.'

3

Storytelling

Professor Nimbus pulled his long thin arms from his long dark coat and stabbed it on a hanging peg on the back of the door, while the children sat down on the cold and difficult zig-zaggy wooden floor. There were usually about thirty of us; boys and girls, all different ages. Most of us turned up. The punishment for not turning up was longer shifts on the lotments, and nobody wanted that. Some older boys squatted in a corner, wiping their noses on their sleeves and quietly laughing between themselves. Towards the front, a couple of the younger ones were huddled next to each other, rocking back and forth to some little tune they were making up and playing Patty-cake Patty-cake. Us middle ones (I think we were about twelve years old) took up the middle of the floor – Bracken and Gry either side of me.

It was still quite early in the morning and the sun hadn't completely hit its peak in the window, so the Professor took his matchbox out of his trouser pocket and lit two or three of the oil lamps that were placed on shelves around the room. The room itself was always dusty. On the wall was a blackboard where the Professor would draw pictures in scratchity chalk to try to help us understand things. I think most of the dust came from that chalk. Anyway, a lot of the chalk ended up on the Professor's trousers and waste-catching coat, which always made us laugh.

Professor Nimbus grabbed his chair and positioned it right in front of us. Wiping the rusty old specs that sat on his nose with a tuft of cloth, he gave a bit of a *quieten-down-and-listen-to-me* sort of cough before slowly sitting himself down and looking around to see who was there.

'Is Fox not here? Fox? You here?'

'Taken ill, Professor,' a voice from somewhere just behind me replied. 'Wasn't well up on the lotments yesterday. Had to walk home sick and didn't get her food for the day. Must be still ill.'

Nimbus shook his head in disappointment. 'What about Enzo?' He looked towards the group of grinning older boys. 'Is Enzo coming?'

One of the boys shrugged. 'Dunno. Don't care. Don't like him anyway.'

The Professor frowned at the lad. 'One of the things you all need to understand, if you are to grow up in this modern world of ours, is that as *Pb*s – for you are each and every one of you a *Pb* – as *Pb*s, you need to get on with one another. Respect each other's opinions and space. Be able to put your trust and faith in your fellow *Pb*s. Generally –' and at this point he glared at the shrugging boy – 'try to like each other. Okay, Mathias?'

'Yes, Professor. Sorry, Professor.'

'If there is anything at all you can learn from me,' he addressed us all, 'it's that you need to stick together. Like gum. The whole of Lahn Dan depends on you. You are the backbone of this place. The workforce. Don't ever forget that.'

'Yes, sir. Sorry, sir.' The grinning boy still seemed to be apologising.

'Now.' Professor Nimbus leaned back in the chair. 'Stories. What sort of stories do you want me to tell you today?'

'Tell us about the machines again.' It was one of the older boys. 'I love the machines. Tell us about the ones that flew through the sky.'

Nimbus gave a little shake of his head and his lips tickled up into a tiny smile. 'I would have thought you'd be sick and exhausted of hearing about the flying machines by now, Dante. You know everything there is to know about the flying machines. In fact, you probably know more about them than I do.'

The boy nodded as if he agreed with the Professor's assessment.

Suddenly Gry's hand went up in the air beside me and Professor Nimbus jerked his head towards her. 'Gry. What story would you like to hear?'

'Professor . . . The crystal towers. Where the *Au*s live.' She looked around as if to see if anyone else was listening. 'Are they *really* made of crystal?'

Bracken gave a quiet *tut a*s though the question was ridiculous.

'The crystal towers? Made of crystal?' Nimbus shuffled in his seat. 'No, no, my dear. They are not made of crystal –'

'I've never been anywhere near one, you see –'

'No, that's right. You wouldn't have done. None of you would have. But no, they are not made of crystal. They are merely made of glass. Just glass. That is all. When the sun does manage to shine through the clouds, they sparkle like crystal, it is true. But only because they are made from a type of reflective glass and because they are so tall. Now there's a question for you. Who knows why the crystal towers are so tall? Anyone know the answer to that one, eh?'

The room went quiet as some of the children turned towards each other to see if their neighbour knew the answer. Both Gry and Bracken turned to me.

'The Gases,' I replied, my voice a bit of a croak from being silent for too long. 'To escape the Gases.'

'Correct, Serendipity. Correct.' Eyes fell upon me.

17

'They were built to protect the *Au*s from the Gases. Well over a hundred years ago now. You see, the further up from the ground you were, the more likely you were to escape the poison of the Gases. Well done, Serendipity.' He gave me a thumbs-up sign and I smiled back in reply. 'But the Gases are a rather maudlin subject for such an early hour. Is there something else any of you want to discuss?'.

Now that my voice had broken its croak, I spoke up clearly. 'Horses, sir.'

'What was that?'

'Horses. The horses, sir. Please tell us about the horses.'

'Ah . . .' The Professor seemed to sigh and sink further back onto his chair. 'The horses. Now that's a much more satisfying topic if ever there was one.'

'What were they like? Did you ever see one? Are there any still alive?'

'Alas, I have never seen a real horse in my life,' he said. 'I very much doubt if anyone alive has ever seen a real horse. They died out far too long ago for that. Now all we have left are pictures to show us what they were like –'

'And statues,' I interrupted. 'There are statues too.'

'Very true. The statues.'

Bracken gave a bit of a mumble beside me. 'I wish I could see a horse. All the fun stuff seemed to die out with the Gases.'

The Professor looked a vermillion miles away. 'Indeed, Bracken. Indeed.' Suddenly he jumped to attention out of his seat and clicked his fingers in the air. 'I've got it. An idea. Do you all have decent shoes on your feet? What about a field trip?'

4

The Gallery Market

We followed the Professor out of the building, back past IMAX, back through the Shell building and back towards the Lahn Dan High. As we passed the Lahn Dan High, Gry pointed up and said, 'S'funny. I can't see your mama in your pod up there, Serendipity.'

'Me neither.' Bracken came alongside us. 'Washing day, innit?'

'Hmm,' I answered, but I didn't say anything else. My face felt all scrunchy. I noticed the Professor turn back to look at me with a quizzy type of expression.

Marching on past the High, the older and middling children up front and the younger ones clip-clopping along behind, we turned onto West Minister Bridge.

'Keep together everyone. Over the river we go,' Nimbus shouted before spinning around and addressing us all. 'Now, on the left as we cross you'll see the remains of a building that was pulled down quite soon after the Gases. It was here that the leaders of Grey Britan would work out the new rules and laws that the people had to follow. It was called the Place of West Minister and –' he pointed at a particularly collapsed part of the building – 'if you look very, very carefully just there, you can see the remains of a large clock that used to sit on top of it. Can you see?'

We all tilted our necks over the edge of the bridge. One or two of the younger children climbed up on the side to get a better look.

'Anybody know what it was called?' Silence and a couple of shakes of heads. 'Nobody? Well . . . The clock was called Big Ben and it bonged every hour on the hour so that the inhabitants of Lahn Dan would know the time and could measure their lives by it.'

'It don't bong no more though, do it? Its bonging days are well and truly dusted.' An older boy with a big rolley head laughed to himself.

'No.' The Professor seemed to be sad for a few seconds before catching his senses once more. 'That's not what we're here to see, though. Our first stop is just around over there. Come on!' And he strode on over the sludge of the Tems and past the squashed skeleton of Big Ben, the rest of us following like midges.

We rounded the corner and went a little further before the Professor stopped once again and pointed. 'There. That's our first call of port.'

Strange that I'd never really noticed it before. In the

middle of the tumbledown mess of the Place of West Minister sat another man on a horse.

'Who's he?'

'Looks a weird 'un to me.' Bracken smiled. 'Gives me the shivers.'

'The man riding the horse is King Richard the Lionheart.' Nimbus was giving off a very studious air. 'He was a very brave king of Grey Britan a long time before even the times before the Gases.'

'Still looks a weird 'un to me,' Bracken muttered and Gry gave her a dig in the ribs.

'Lionheart?' a little girl with very matted hair squeaked. 'Did he have a lion's heart?'

'What's a lion?' A boy called Wedge gave a blank *scratching-head* type of look.

Nimbus carried on regardless. 'He led the people of Britan in a war called the Crusades. A big war in lands beyond the Emm Twenty-five Wall and even beyond the sea.'

'What's the sea?' Wedge scratched a bit more.

'He looks very important.' Gry was studying the figure almost as hard as I was. 'Was he an *Au*?'

'Back in the olden days – the very very olden days – there were no such things as *Au*s or *Cu*s or *Pb*s, Gry. The edges were more blurred. Yes, there were kings and queens and lords and earls. And yes there were the workers and farmers and coal diggers. But there were no *Au*s, *Cu*s or *Pb*s. Those distinctions came in after the Gases.'

'Were only *Au*s allowed to ride horses?' the girl with matted hair came towards the front of our little group. 'I think only *Au*s were allowed to ride them. I don't think they let *Pb*s ride them. They might fall off.'

The Professor sighed. 'Like I said, Persephone, there were no *Au*s or *Pb*s in the olden days. They didn't exist. Anyone could ride horses.'

'What? Anyone? Really?'

Nimbus *hmm*'d and nodded his head. 'Yes. Anyone. People think of them as being the reserve of the high-born and the rich but the truth is that horses were used by everyone and anyone. They pulled carts. They helped plough the fields. They carried messengers across the country. They gave races for fun. They did lots and lots of different jobs for lots and lots of different types of people.' *Like Pbs*, I thought to myself.

The Professor turned to stare at the statue behind him. 'Despite what the statues depict, horses weren't just used for wars and battles. Kings were born to fight in the wars. Horses were not. Which means that even though King Richard the Lionheart was a very brave man, his horse was probably braver still.'

The Professor led us up Parlment Street towards Falgar's Square, and halfway along White Hall we passed one of those scary posters of Commander Mordecai, the Chief of the Minister's Police Force. His face was splattered all across Lahn Dan warning everyone about the dangers of doing anything against the Minister's law. The eyes on the posters frightened you into being good and the long bubbly scar that ran down the side of his left cheek reminded you that the Chief of Police was not a man to be jumbled with. You found yourself going quiet and walking quicker past those posters as your blood ran to icicles.

We all sped up.

As we passed Nelson's Column, the Professor pointed to its base and said, '*Those* are lions.' Wedge looked horrified.

In the corner of the square, just up beyond the dried-up fountain, we saw another king on a horse. If horses existed today, I think the Minister would be riding one. Without a doubt. He probably wouldn't ever get off it.

'One more thing,' Professor Nimbus said, as he took us up the steps to the Gallery Market. 'There's something in here I think you should see if you want to know a little about horses.' He nodded at me. 'It's rather impressive.'

The market inside was thriving. A busy bustle of a day. The stalls were all set up with their candles and lamps to highlight whatever it was they were selling or trying to barter. We passed people selling pots and pans, raggedy shoes, hats, scarves and furry ear mittens. Useful sticks of scrap metal. Busted-up umbrellas. Dried herbs and bottled spices. Strings and wires and musty old tools. There were traders selling clippers and scissors, blunt knives and holey socks. Some sold pictures of places from the olden days, and maps of places that didn't exist any more. Others sold snapped snippets of toys and tired leathery bags. There were even some selling hot food that gave the whole Gallery Market a warm and snuggly cinnamon scent, and the Professor, seeing the wide-eyed looks of hunger on our faces, fished out a few coins and bought a couple of freshly baked wafers for us all to share. We broke them up and not a singular crumb was lost in the gloom, I'm pretty much certain of it.

'If you look on the walls,' the Professor eventually continued, 'what can you see?'

We all gave a squint. Behind many of the stalls and the people who were manning them were –

'Pictures!' A boy called Erasmus, with sticky-out ears, spoke up for the first time. 'There are pictures. Paintings.'

'Yes.'

We could all see them now. Clinging to the dark walls like shadows. Squares and rectangles and ovals of paint. Faces and places.

'You see, in the past this building was what was known as a gallery.'

'The Gallery Market.'

'That's right. We call it the Gallery Market because it was once an art gallery. A place where people – anyone, mind you – could wander in off the streets and look at pictures that other people had made using canvas and paint.'

'What was the point in that?' Mathias was getting a little fed up of the whole expedition and wanted to go back home to his bed.

'Eh?'

'A bit dull, isn't it? Staring at pictures. They don't do anything.'

'The point was,' Nimbus stuttered, 'to see things that you had never seen before. Places you might never go to. People you might never meet. To enrich your eyes and your senses with the unknown. Many of these paintings were very expensive and important – not that the Minister or the Party cares two toots for them, of course, because they serve no practical purpose.'

We wandered through to another of the halls. Nimbus headed over to an old woman with a rag stall. 'Excuse me, madam, but would you mind if I turned your lamp up just a touch? So kind. Thank you terribly much.' The Professor adjusted the oil lamp so that it was burning at its highest, before turning to face us all again. 'The reason I have brought you here is to see this.' He pointed to the wall just behind the old woman's head.

'Whoa!' The older boys' breath seemed to be sucked

away and I cannot be completely and entirely certain that I didn't make a similar flabbergasted noise myself. 'That is freezing cool.' Mathias was impressed at last.

The picture was enormous, a huge rectangle that seemed to take up the whole of the wall and tower over us. And on it was a handsome, soft brown horse, its front hooves rearing up in the air, its coat glossy. On its hind legs were white markings and its tail was like a great big thick brush. Apart from its size, the other extraordinary thing about the painting was that there was nothing in the frame except for the horse. No rider, no buildings, no trees, no fields. Nothing except the horse itself.

'His name is Whistlejacket. He was painted many hundreds of years ago by a man called Stubbs.'

'He's beautiful,' I whispered half to myself.

'He is,' Bracken murmured next to me.

'Totally,' Gry agreed, the three of us all hypnotised by this incredible sight.

The Professor came alongside and stood with his arms crossed to admire the thing for himself.

'Fantastic, isn't it?'

'It is, sir,' I replied.

'They say that the painter, Stubbs, *did* intend to paint someone riding him. But for some reason he decided to keep the picture just as it was. Empty. Pure.'

'Good. I'm glad.'

'Me too, Serendipity. Me too. I think that horses were probably at their best free of the reins of mankind. Don't you?'

For some reason I thought of Mama and I struggled to keep the thought and the feeling down in my chest. 'Yes.'

During the journey back, amongst grumbles about tired legs and sore feet, Professor Nimbus pulled me out of the crowd. Strolling along slightly behind everybody else, he put on a very serious face and started talking in a quiet difficult-to-hear way.

'There's something you need to know, Serendipity. As a member of the *Cu* class, and a storyteller for the young ones, I am entitled, under the rule of the Minister, to an assistant. Somebody to help me organise myself, to undertake research for storytelling. To keep this increasingly musty old mind in check, that kind of thing.' He waved his hand in the air as though swatting away a gnatty fly. 'Previously, my assistant was old Mrs Potts who – alas – slipped into the arms of death what must be two years ago now. Ever since then, I have managed on my own.'

Suddenly, an *Au* with perfect hair and perfect skin, clothes clean and dazzling, flew past in one of their zoomy white modpods. The sight was so rare this side of the Tems – an *Au* away from their own zone – that everyone stopped deadly still in the middle of the road to watch. As the modpod hummed away into the distance, the crowds warmed back to life and continued on their way.

'But,' the Professor carried on where he had left off, undisturbed by the incident, 'I am not getting any younger and I am at the stage where a little help might now be more –' he struggled to grasp the right word – 'appreciated. That is why I would like you to become my new apprentice.'

'Me?' I was blown back.

'Yes.'

'Why me?'

'Why *not* you?'

'Well, I don't know anything about storytelling, sir.'

'But you can learn, my dear. There is a room in the house in which I live. It is yours now, if you agree. You can move in straight away. You just need to help me put my stories into order and accompany me on any research trips. You will be a helper to me, to make my duties a little easier to bear as my bones grow ever older. I will teach you everything I know, and one day you will take my place. What do you say?'

'Er . . .'

'I have already cleared it with the Minister's office. You are, as of this moment, relieved of your *Pb* lotment-tending duties.'

'Well . . .' I didn't know whether to laugh or cry. 'I don't know. I'm not sure.'

'Besides,' Nimbus's mouth cracked into a warm smile, 'I don't much like the thought of you up there all alone in that pod of yours. Not now that your mother has joined old Mrs Potts in the heavenly sky. Come and join me. What do you say?'

5

The Telebracelet

Going through all of Mama's possessions had been hard. Sifting through them to sort out what was useful, what I wanted to keep and what I wanted to chuck on the heap – it wasn't easy. Most of her clothes were so dirty and torn that they wouldn't even have been good enough for wiping rags. Even her sleep bag and mattress had seen better days. But, lifting the mattress to see if the underside was any good, something fell and tapped onto the floor. I picked it up and held it up to the light. It was a necklace. A longish, grubby looking necklace with an oval-shaped dangly thing halfway along it. I'd never seen it before. In fact, the way it had been shoved deeply under the mattress made me think that Mama was keeping it hidden. But why? Why would she hide it from me? It wasn't the most beautiful thing in the world. The dangly bit had tiny scuffed ridges and bumps across it – like a kicked-about stone – and the chain itself was blackened with years of filthy fingers and thumbs. Not a fancy, sparkling *Au* sort of thing at all. Not the sort of thing to polish and shine up and display in a cabinet. In the end, I just hooked it over my neck and tucked it deep down under my shirt so that no one could see. I would let it dangle near my heart.

The Professor had helped me push the handcart across the river and towards the house in Bloomsbury. Along the way Gry and Bracken joined us and we all spent the afternoon setting up my tiny room. It had a bed and a table and a comfortable stuffy chair to sit on. The dirty cracked window looked out over the back of the derelict Britan Museum and I could just about make out the calls of the Oxford Street traders.

'Come up in the world a bit here,' Gry said, looking around the room. 'An apprentice storyteller. Who'd've thought it?'

'Me,' Bracken replied, tucking the bottom of the freshly made bed into place. '*I*'d've thought it. Always knew you'd do well for yourself, Serendipity. Too clever for just lotment work, you are.' She nodded her head towards Gry. '*She* thought so too, but she just won't admit it.'

'Huh.' Gry gave a glare towards Bracken.

It was the first proper room I had lived in. The first proper, rectangular room with corners and walls and cracks in the floorboards. It was exciting but also a bit scary. Trying to distract myself, I put all of Mama's things in the bottom of the chester drawers in the corner of the room. If I ever needed them, I knew where they would be.

'Nice to know they're there,' Bracken said. 'Keep it all in one place. Very sensible, that.' She smiled warmly.

'Wouldn't want to lose anything,' Gry finished, her face all soft and serious.

'That's right,' I replied before shoving the drawer in roughly and pretending to not really care about the things inside. 'Let's go for a walk.'

The work was easy. I couldn't read properly (very few people could – even Professor Nimbus could only make out a few simple words and sentences) so Nimbus would sit me down and tell me the stories. Then he'd ask me questions, like did I think that he should say A before B or should he put C before A and then come in with D? You get the idea. I was starting to learn an awful lot about the world and its history. Such as, before the Gases came, the ancestors of the *Au*s all bought in special injections to change their faces so that they looked like famous beautiful people.

'They would recreate the jeans of the famous and fill their faces up with them,' Nimbus absentmindedly muttered, the fingers on one hand pushing against the fingers on his other hand. 'Even nowadays the *Au*s talk of an Elvin Pretsley lip or an Angelica Jolly cheekbone.

With all of their money, they tried to turn themselves into other people. Very foolish.'

Another thing I learned about were the seasons. Hundreds of years ago, the sky wasn't the same purplish colour all year long like it is now. It would change as the days crept past one after the other.

Firstly, said the Professor, came winter, where the clouds were white and puffy and cold, icy snowflakes (not poisonous!) would drift to the ground. Children would play in the flakes and throw balls of snow at each other. Then they would try to make big fat men with round heads and waste carrots by sticking them in and pretending they were noses.

Next was spring, when the sky relaxed a little bit and actual *real* flowers pushed their way out of the earth. Birds would return from hiding and the trees would go from being dead woody stumps to green, leaf-covered giants.

Then came summer. All the clouds in the sky would be blown aside by the winds to reveal a blue – yes, blue – roof to the world and the people would roast in the sun and eat sweet creams, or fan themselves with paper and complain about the heat.

Finally, there was autumn, when all the leaves that grew in the spring decided not to cling onto the trees any more and the warm winds of summer started to get colder and began to blow the thick clouds back across the sky. After that it would be winter again and the whole thing would go round and round like a daft dog chasing its own tail.

'So very very different to the world we live in now,' the Professor sighed. 'All we ever have now is the one dull sky with a few speckles of dangerous rain. It must have been so much more . . . interesting back then.'

I nodded in agreement. I rather got the feeling that life, in general, was more interesting back then.

It all started a few weeks after I became Nimbus's apprentice. The Professor had asked me to take a walk to the Spitting Fields to interview some of the market people there. He wanted me to ask for stories that their mothers and fathers had passed down to them. It could be anything really. Some tiny fact about the history of the area. The people who used to live there. A scary story used to frighten youngsters at night. Anything that Professor Nimbus could incorporate into his teachings. We would sit down together, sift the details and plait the stories into our heads as best we could.

Lots of the people at Spitting Fields were helpful and I was full to the top with things to tell him. I was struggling to keep as much of it in my soft brain as I could remember when I took a route down a thin street that I don't believe I'd ever wandered before. There was nothing exceptional about the street itself but a small way down the pavement with the weedy cracks, something glinted in the afternoon dullness. My eyes swooped to it; my legs followed soon behind. There, lying as innocently as a strip of forgotten rag, was what I could only believe was a telebracelet. Having never seen one before, it was only a bit of a guess. But something told me that, yes, that was precisely what it was. A telebracelet.

Only the *Au*s have telebracelets. They talk to each other on them apparently. In fact, only the *Au*s have technology of any kind. The *Au*s have the technology and the *Pb*s have none. The *Cu*s meanwhile sit somewhere uncomfortable in the middle, only able to use technology if it makes the *Au*s lives easier. Gold, copper and lead – that's what the Professor told me. That's where the terms come from. *Au*, *Cu* and *Pb*.

I squatted down and scooped it up in my hands. It felt cold and heavy and, as I twisted it around, inspecting it, I could see that it was in the shape of a butterfly. A pretty, purple and gold butterfly with shiny inlays and delicate wings. The diamonds or rubies or emeralds or whatever they were wrapped themselves all the way down along the wrist strap until they had nowhere else to go.

My heart staggered and, just for a second I thought how pleased Mama would have been to see it. She would have been as dazzled by it as I was. She would have turned it over, holding it up to the light, draping it over her wasted forearm. She would have polished it up until it was so shiny you could see yesterday reflected in it. She would have put it against my face and said how the colours suited my eyes and how . . . But I shook the silly thoughts out of my head and quickly slipped the telebracelet into my pocket before anyone else should see it.

As I made my way down the street, I wondered if there was any way in which I could keep it for myself. Hold onto it like a special sort of secret that no one else in the world could know. Perhaps lock it away in the bottom drawer with all of Mama's things. But as I came out of the road onto another, busier one, I could feel the thing weighing very heavy in my pocket and I just knew that I should return it to its proper owner. Its proper *Au* owner.

I hawked it out again and looked at the back. Inscribed in the silvery surface was:

Caritas

1-76380

Crystal City 3

I didn't know what much of it said, but I recognised some letters and kind of worked out that the last line said 'Crystal City'. I also knew my numbers well enough to know that it referred to Crystal City Three. Crystal City Three was only a short walk further east. From where I was standing, you could see their icicle sharp towers on the violet skyline, like knives that had stabbed up through the ground. *Pb*s weren't allowed inside the *Au* compounds, but I could probably leave the tele-bracelet with one of the guards at the entrance and they'd be able to find the person it belonged to. So I started walking and after a while was knocking on the gatekeeper's window.

The *Cu* on duty slid the window back and frowned at me like I was a piece of unwanted clutter on a shelf. 'What?' he sneered.

'I found this. It was on one of the roads. Over there.' I pointed back. 'I thought I'd better return it.'

His hand came out of the window and snapped it off me. I saw that he wore the standard almost-black uniform of the Minister's Police Force and that on his shoulder he had two stripes. A constable. His face was craggy and his mouth untrusting.

'Let me see that . . .' The guard stared at the tele-bracelet as though it burned his eyes. 'Hmm. Okay.' One of his hands reached out for some sort of phone device, and his fingers started nudging rubbery buttons. 'Good. Go away now.' His free hand made a flicking gesture and slid the window shut. Behind the glass I could see him talking into the phone.

I sighed before spinning around on my heels and trudging away. Life felt so spectacularly unfair at that moment. I had done the right thing. I had put my own feelings aside. The telebracelet was one of the most amazing things I'd ever seen and yet I knew that I couldn't have it for myself. I didn't want a reward for finding it – Mama always said you should never do anything for the reward, you should do things because they were the correct things to do – but perhaps a 'Thank you' or a smile or a pat on the back would have been nice. Still. That was the way the world was built, with *Pb*s being nothing more than the dust blowing across the ground.

'Oy!'

I stopped and looked back at the constaple in his office. The window was open again and he was leaning out of it and waving me to him. His face looked even more red and contorted than before and his black sleeve was flapping to and fro.

'She wants to meet you. Come back here. She wants *you* to take it up to her. And she's top toffee, so mind your peas and queues.'

6

Caritas and the Crystal Tower

Everyone was staring at me. Their eyes were like lasers sweeping across the entire area, as though alarms were about to start screeching. *Intruder alert! Intruder alert!* I half expected armed police to rush out and throw me to the ground. But they didn't. The constaple on duty in the office must have told them I was coming through.

It was like nothing I'd ever seen. I had heard stories about grass being green before – I had only really ever known it to be a slightly dullish brown – but here it actually was green. Green enough to eat, like a shoot on a carrot. And the paths were all neat and even, clean grey stone after stone that cut through the green grass like hands chopping through smog. But the most noticeable thing was the people. The *Au*s. Every single one of them was beautiful and healthy looking. Even their clothes were perfect. Not crumpled and stained and hurried together like most of us *Pb*s, but crisp and ironed and clean and new. I felt like a sewer rat in comparison, so I scuttled as quickly as I could along the edges of the paths to the main entrance of Crystal Tower Number One. Close to, it looked like a coldfish bowl. They were something from the olden days – big glass bowls that coldfish swam in.

The hallway was made entirely of marble and my feet echoed as they *clip-clipp*ed towards the silver doors. The constaple had told me to head for the silver doors and to push the button next to them. When the doors opened I was to get in and to push the number 7. So, when the doors did open, I stepped inside the tiny room with mirrored walls and gently stubbed my finger on the number 7. The silver doors shut tight and the room started to shake a little. I felt as though I was getting heavier and I have to admit that a panicky feeling shot up my whole body and I wanted to get out of there as fast as I possibly could. Then, suddenly, I felt all light again and, before I knew it, the doors slid open and I was in a different place. I stepped out of the magic room and looked around. Some way further down the corridor, a long, thin hand stuck out of a door and waved. I waved back and walked towards it.

'Let me look at you.' The woman stood in front of me and let her eyes zoom all over my face. 'My goodness, you are pretty. Very pretty indeed for a *Pb*. In fact,' she squinted to try to take in the detail, 'I would go so far as to say that you are probably even more beautiful than any of the *Au*s I know. Your hair. And your bone structure.' She grinned. 'Pretty much perfect.'

The woman was quite old but her skin was as smooth as my own and her hair fell away from her unlined face in long bundles of thick grey. Her nose might or might not have been described by one of the other *Au*s as being a little bit Aubrey Heartburn or Elizabeth Tailor – popular choices amongst the old *Au*s, apparently – and the hands that straightened my shoulders as the eyes did their zooming were as soft and youthful as the rest of her.

'Tell me, what is your name?'

'Serendipity,' I whispered.

'Well, Serendipity –' one of her soft, youthful hands lowered to shake one of my own – 'my name is Caritas. An honour to meet you. Are you hungry? You look hungry. I know I am.' She led me through to a large, bright room filled with things I'd never seen nor imagined possible. A screen with pictures moving across it sat on a wall; a vase filled with more flowers than I'd ever seen in one place before; porcelain figurines that looked so thin and delicate that if you breathed too near you might just break them. All of it lit from a hole in the ceiling. 'I'll order us some food, shall I? Anything in particular you'd like to have?'

'Er . . .' I didn't understand.

'Oh, I'm so sorry. I was forgetting that *Pb*s have to

survive on dinner pills. Fizz, chalk dust and a bit of dried milk powder. Not one of our Minister's greatest ideas, I think.' She started tapping at a smaller screen sitting on a side table. 'I'll get a bit of everything.'

Within a couple of minutes, two *Cu*s in a uniform I didn't recognise came into the room carrying plate after plate of delicious smelling food. They laid them out on a table next to a window and my stomach did a weird squelching in anticipation of what was to come. It was like a list of things I'd only ever dreamt about or heard about in stories. There were rashers of hot, smoked, salty bacon. Crispy bread rolls to rip apart with your fingers. Asparagus tips with butter – yes, butter! Cold whole strawberries with little green crowns and bowl upon bowl of thick whippled goat's cream. Even the potatoes weren't soggy and squished like the ones I'd always had before. These potatoes were drizzled with butter – yes, butter again – and spattered with herbs. Freshly grown herbs. The smell was delirious.

'Please.' She sat at one end of the table and offered the chair at the other end to me. 'Sit. Help yourself.' I couldn't think where to begin, so I forked a couple of rashers of bacon and a brown roll covered in seeds onto the plate in front of me. I wanted to take more but I thought it might look greedy. 'Now. I believe you have something for me. Something of mine that you found.'

43

'Oh.' I pulled the telebracelet from one of my pockets and handed it across the table to her.

'Thank you. I must have dropped it during one of my little expeditions to the markets. Very clumsy of me.' She hooked the telebracelet around her wrist and pressed a button on it. It responded with a tiny *peep*. 'There. Ownership recognition.' Miss Caritas wore large, heavy pearls in a chain about her neck and whenever she moved, the light in the room bounced off them. 'Silly of me to drop it. And so very good of you to return it. I would have thought that a telebracelet could fetch a good price on the black market. Enough to keep you fed for a number of weeks. But,' she looked up at me as I stuffed soft, fluffy bread into my mouth, 'you didn't hold onto it. You brought it back. Try the strawberries,' she urged. 'They're genetically engineered, of course – grown in a warehouse somewhere south of the river.'

I picked one of them up by the crown and scooped it into the cream before biting it clean off into my mouth. It was sweet and wet and I quickly went back for another.

Miss Caritas smiled to herself, all the while her stunning blue eyes watching me. 'So, Serendipity. Tell me something about yourself. Tell me about your family – your mother and your father. Where do you all live? What do you all do?'

'Afraid I don't have any family,' I said, through a

mouthful of cream. 'My mama died recently and I've never known anything about my father. Mama never told me anything about him.'

'Oh, I am sorry – about your mother, I mean. Do you have any brothers or sisters?'

'No, miss. It's just me.' I fed a floppy asparagus between my lips, suddenly guilty that my mama had never tasted such a thing. I looked out of the window. 'Hope you don't mind me saying so, Miss Caritas, but I've never seen grass as green as that before. Everywhere else in Lahn Dan it's always brown.'

'The grass?' She laughed. 'Oh, it's not real. They wash it twice a week to keep it looking that way. In fact –' she leaned back in her chair and folded her arms around each other – 'there's very little around here that's real. Much of it is fake or pretend.' For a passing moment she looked sad. 'Fake doesn't die, you see.'

On the screen flashed images of the Minister, undertaking some ceremonial duty or other. Miss Caritas saw me looking. 'Would you like me to turn it off?'

I shook my head. 'No. It's all right.'

'It's just another of the Minister's many announcements. Nothing important.'

'I've never seen anything like it before.'

'Hmm.' She knifed some strange gooey golden stuff onto a chunk of the bread before offering it to me. 'Honey?'

45

'Thank you.' I took it and pushed it into my mouth – it was the sweetest thing I'd ever tasted. She quickly prepared me another one.

'Good, isn't it?'

'Hih his.' I spoke with my mouth full – something Mama always said I shouldn't do. 'Hih his goo.'

Miss Caritas tapped her fingers together in delight. 'Wonderful.' She suddenly jumped up, the chair squeaking away behind her as she did so. 'Come with me. Come on. I want to show you something.' She beckoned me through to another room as I swallowed the last of the bread and honey and wiped my sticky hands on the rough fabric of my dungarees.

The room was dazzling. An enormous bed, probably about three or four times bigger than the one I'd recently started sleeping in, sat in one corner, its pillows and sheets puffed and fluffy and lovely. The walls were bright white with pictures and paintings dotted about the place. One of the pictures, I realised, was of Miss Caritas shaking the Minister's hand, all glamorous and charming. And along one wall were racks and racks of the most fabulous clothes you might ever see. It was as though I'd stepped out of the normal world and into a dream.

'Here.' She pulled some of the clothes off one of the racks and threw them onto the bed. Satin and silk. Chiffon and velvet. Even the words sounded beautiful. 'This one.

And this one . . . This one too. What about this lace one here?'

'They're incredible.'

'Those ones would probably fit you. Shall we try them on?'

'What? Me?'

'Yes. Of course.'

'Er . . .' I was stuck for words again.

'Come on. It'll be fun.'

'I've never worn dresses before.' I looked down at the boots, heavy-duty dungarees and scratchity shirt that most of the *Pb*s were issued with. They looked clumsy and wrong in this beautiful clean space.

'Well, there's a first time for everything. Come on, Serendipity. Let's get you showered and wash that long hair of yours.'

The shower itself was another experience. Hot water. Can you believe it? *Hot* water. On demand. At the trip of a switch. Without having to boil up a big pan first. Amazering. When I came out of the shower room with a large soft towel around me, my hair was all damp and dangly.

'A redhead.' Miss Caritas grinned. 'I should have known. Underneath all that dirt there's a redhead. Shall we dry it?' Using a device that gave out hot air, my hair was bony dry in a matter of seconds, and for the first time in ages, it felt clean. 'There. That's better. Now, which would you like to try on first? The green chiffon? Or perhaps the purple velvet evening dress?'

The velvet dress looked a bit heavy to me so I pointed to the green shimmery one. I shyly slipped the dress on over my shoulders and Miss Caritas helped me to clip together the studs on the back.

'There.'

It felt really strange to be wearing something so light and smooth. Something you could move so freely in. Something so airy. You could barely feel it on you. The material kind of danced all over my skin.

'Come. Take a look in the mirror.'

I moved to where the long, tall mirror on the wall was and couldn't believe my eyes. Where Serendipity had been before was a person I hardly recognised. She was pretty, graceful and elegant. Sweeping pale green like I imagined a tree beside a lake might have been. All flowing and dipping.

'What do you think?' Miss Caritas's eyes were lit up and questioning.

'It's . . .' I gave a twirl and the dress swirled up. 'It's magnificent.'

'It's one of my great-grandmother's dresses. Over a hundred years old. She would wear it to parties.'

'Parties?'

'Hmm. Back in the days when *real* parties were

thrown. Parties that would roll on all night in wide chequered hallways with long marble staircases.'

I looked once again at the reflection of the beautiful girl in the mirror. 'I wish I could go to parties.'

Miss Caritas picked up another of the dresses she had taken from the rack. 'This was my mother's. She wore it when she married my father.' It was golden and a sort of satin, I thought.

'It's lovely.'

'She left it to me. When she eventually died. Along with everything else.' Her arm swept across the room and my eyes followed it. It was then that I noticed all of the photographs of the Minister. Lots of them. Dotted all over the walls. A photo of the Minister waving to a crowd. A photo of him looking deathly serious across a boardroom table. A photo of him with his arms crossed, all powerful and in control. Lots and lots and lots of photos. Like my *Pb* clothes, they looked out of place.

Miss Caritas swirled dress after dress at me, and I danced in and out of them, twisting and swaying and watching myself in the mirror. After a while I realised that the Professor was probably wondering where I was.

'I'm sorry. I've got to go,' I said, grabbing my dusty things from the nearby chair. As I lifted them, the necklace that I'd found under Mama's mattress fell out of the pocket of my dungarees onto the soft carpet.

'What's this?' Miss Caritas swooped down and picked it up.

'It's nothing,' I said, pulling my own clothes back on quickly. 'It's nothing. Can I have it back?'

She held it up, the dangly thing swinging just above her face.

'It's a necklace. My mama's. Can I have it back please?'

'It's not just a necklace.' She twirled it around in her hands. 'It's a locket.'

'A locket?'

'Very old. Needs a lot of cleaning up, though. Not expensive. Cheap, even. Pewter or some such. Costume jewellery. Nothing more.'

'What's a locket?'

She turned to me with a *really?* look on her face. 'A locket? It's this bit.' She lifted the dangly part to show me. 'You can keep pictures and photographs inside.'

'In there? There might be a photograph in there?'

Miss Caritas nodded. 'Usually. Have you never opened it?'

'No.'

She twisted it over in her hands. 'There's usually a small latch. Something to release.' She brought the locket right up to her nose. 'This one's rather rusted into place.'

I came alongside her as she held it out for me to see. I suddenly found myself getting excited. There might be a photograph of Mama inside this thing. All these weeks with the locket slapping against my chest and inside was (I desperately hoped) a picture of my mama, or even – my heart gulped – a photograph of my father.

'I just . . . need . . . something to . . .' Miss Caritas walked over to a neat dressing table and pulled out a drawer. She flicked open a small packet before coming back to me, a long pin in her hand. 'This should do it.'

She bent over the locket and scratched away at it with the pin. Tiny flakes of rust and dust fell onto the spotless carpet as she worked away at the latch. I craned my neck and squinted to watch. It felt like she was at it forever, until –

'There.' She held it back towards me. 'Open it.'

I took it from her and pulled at the locket. It was stiff and difficult, but slowly it came open and something fell out, fluttering onto the floor.

A small piece of paper, folded tightly to fit inside the locket. Not a photograph. Just some stupid paper. My heart dropped and I realised how silly I'd been. Why would Mama have a picture of herself? It wouldn't make any sense. Disappointed, I picked up the paper.

'What is it?' Miss Caritas was more interested in it than I was.

I unfolded it. The paper was covered in squiggles and words, none of which I could read.

'I don't know.'

51

'Let me see.' Miss Caritas snatched it out of my hands. 'It's a map.' She turned and straightened it out on her dressing table. 'Look.' Her fingers traced across the crumpled page to an area on the right. 'It's a map of Grey Britan. Here is Lahn Dan – see the Emm Twenty-five Wall going right the way around us?'

'Yes.' A scratchy circle going around some letters.

'And I suppose this must be the Emm Four – a very old road that took you away from Lahn Dan but which probably doesn't even exist any more.' A thin line of pencil wound its way across the sheet.

'What's that?' I asked, pointing to what looked like a couple of Hs.

'Must be the H H Bridge. Back before the Gases, the H H Bridge used to take people into Whales. That's what they say.'

'Whales?'

'It was a part of the old Grey Britan. Long dead now, of course.' She shook her head in a sort of pretend sad way. 'I don't know what *this* is, though.' A house with a star above its roof. 'Nor these.'

I stopped still and held tightly onto my breath. *I* knew what they were. It was so obvious to me. As clear as a tin in a mudflat.

'Horses.'

'Hmm?'

'They're horses. Aren't they?'

Miss Caritas peered hard at the map. 'Yes. I suppose they might be.'

Stick figures – four legs stretched out in front and behind them – covered the edge of the land just before the sea. Three of them. It looked to me like they were racing. But why would my mama keep a map of horses hidden in a locket? I didn't understand. Had she drawn the map herself? No. No, she couldn't have done. She wouldn't have been able to write the words. This map was drawn by somebody else.

'Does this mean . . .' I started, hardly knowing what I was saying. 'Does this map show that there are horses? In Whales?'

Miss Caritas laughed sharply. 'Oh, I doubt it, don't you? Horses died out with the Gases. And anyway,' she continued, 'there's nothing outside of the Emm Twenty-five. Everything outside Lahn Dan is dead.'

'But what if it isn't?'

Miss Caritas frowned at me. 'That,' she hissed, 'is the kind of talk that gets people sent to Two Swords.' She walked away from the map back to the dresses lying out on the bed. 'I suggest you put that silly map away – fanciful nonsense, that's all it is – and come and try this pink silk ball dress on. It will fit you perfectly, I'm sure.'

'No. I can't.'

'What?'

'I'm afraid I have to go.'

Miss Caritas looked a tiny bit hurt. 'Why?'

'The Professor will be worried about me.'

'Who's the Professor?'

'Professor Nimbus. He's a storyteller. I'm his apprentice. I help him to collect stories.'

'Storytelling?' Miss Caritas sighed. 'Look, Serendipity. We had fun this afternoon, didn't we? You enjoyed yourself, didn't you?'

'Yes. I did. Thank you, miss.' My eyes and mind were still on the map.

'As did I. What I'm trying to say, Serendipity, is . . . well . . . we could do it more often. Permanently, if you like.'

'Permanently?'

'I don't have a daughter. I never had a daughter. Perhaps it would be possible for you to move in here. Help me pick out my clothes and jewellery. We could go around the markets together, choosing things for the flat. You could eat real food every day. Shower whenever you feel like it. Live your life as an *Au*. What do you say? It would be fun all day every day.'

It was weird. I had only known this lady a few hours and she was inviting me to share her life with her. I suddenly felt strangely sad for her.

'But, miss . . . My mama . . . She's just died and . . .'

'I realise that. I wouldn't try to replace her. It would

be different. That's all. You wouldn't be on your own. And neither would I.'

It was a teeny bit tempting. To think that I could spend my life in this luxury, being warm and pampered and clean. To turn my back on all the dirt and sweat of being a *Pb*. To live here, high above the ground in the purple clouds.

But then I thought of the Professor and his kindness, and of Mama and her grubby face, and the twangs of guilt made any decision easy for me.

'Thank you, Miss Caritas. It is a kind offer. But I can't. I belong down on the ground.'

'Doing what? Storytelling? What good is storytelling?' I could see a spark of anger in her face. 'Storytelling is the preserve of fools who have nothing to say. It is a way of hiding from their lives. They hide behind what has gone before and think that it can tell them about things to come. You have to rise above that, Serendipity. Be beautiful. Accept your true self. Live for now.'

'Look, miss,' I replied. 'Good people are good people no matter where they live. The Professor has shown me great kindness and I feel that I owe him my loyalty.'

'You should never feel as if you owe anybody anything. It is one of the mistakes people make in life. Loyalty is just pompous folly. Never forget that, Serendipity. Pompous folly.'

'Still.' I tried to smile. 'Thank you, Miss Caritas. I must go now.' I started to walk away.

'Wait. Your map.' She picked it up from the dressing table and looked at it once again. 'You'd better not leave *that* here. The Ministry never looks too kindly on –' Her face fell and for a moment or two she looked confused. 'What . . .' she eventually began. 'What did you say your name was? Serendipity . . . ?'

'Goudge.'

A sharp sucking of breath. 'And your mother? What was *her* name?'

'Oleander,' I replied, my hand held out for the map. 'Oleander Goudge.'

She stood there nodding gently, still gripping the piece of paper tightly. Her eyes moved about like she was trying to think of something – digging things up from the depths of her mind and tying it all together.

And then she smiled.

'You know, I think you are right. This map *does* tell you the whereabouts of horses. And I think your mother wanted *you* to find the map because she wanted *you* to be the one to go and find them.' She looked about the room like she was worried someone was listening in. 'I am a member of the Minister's Security Council. Part of the Council's role is to maintain and monitor the Emm Twenty-five Wall. Keep it safe. Secure.' She licked her lips before continuing. 'There is a gap in the wall, I

56

hear. Past Stret Ham and Pearly. Big enough for men to pass through. And it's rarely patrolled. But there are plans to block it up. The Minister's men intend to do it soon. After that there'll be no way out. If anybody should want to get out of Lahn Dan, that would be the way to go. Only sooner rather than later. You understand?'

'Miss?'

'Your mother wanted you to find the horses, Serendipity.' Miss Caritas slowly handed the map back to me. 'Be a shame to disappoint her.'

As I skittered away down the corridor, I opened up the map. Miss Caritas had seen something in it. Something that had made her change her mind about the horses. I stared at it hard and my eyes danced all over it but the only other thing I could see was the signature of the person who had drawn it. Tiny and barely noticeable, it sat in the bottom corner, a shaky spidery hand. S. H. Y.

Shy.

I took the shiny room down to the ground and hurried out of the building, across the grass that wasn't really grass towards the front gate. As I went I noticed again that the *Au*s who lived here were beautiful and handsome, of course. But in truth, they all looked just the same.

7

The Beekeeper

If Bracken or Gry could see me, I thought, they'd pickle themselves laughing. Not only did I look silly but I could hardly see what I was doing or where I was going. My only consolation was that both Nimbus and Mr Tumbril – the roly-poly beekeeper – looked just as brush daft as I did. High on top of the roof of Fortnum and May Sons, we were all three dressed like weird spacemen. The hood over my head kept the bees out but made me feel hotter and drippier than a bagman at teatime. Mr Tumbril kept using his little *puff-puff-puff*er thing to keep the bees drunk and the Professor kept asking questions and nodding his head and going *mmm mmm* to the answers.

The four beehives stood next to one another looking out over the city. Only a few feet away was the edge of the building and a big tumbledown drop to the pavement below, so I made sure I kept one side of my eyes on where my feet were putting themselves.

'The hives were found in storage in the basement.'

Mr Tumbril was obviously very proud of the whole set up. 'They each represent a different time in architectural history. Roman, Chinese, Mughal and Gothic.' He gave an extra puff on his puffer as though to highlight the point.

'Mmm mmm.' Nimbus nodded his head. 'Which is which?'

'Um . . .' If I could have seen Mr Tumbril's face I'm certain it would have had a look of confusion pasted upon it. 'I . . . um . . . I don't really know. That is what they say.' *Puff-puff*. 'But what I do know is that last year we managed to produce a grand total of one thousand two hundred and forty-six jars of honey for the *Au*s. Plenty to go round.' Mr Tumbril moved on to the next hive.

'Fascinating. Isn't it fascinating, Serendipity? Almost a perfect society, a hive. Every bee with its part to play, don't you think?'

'If you say so.'

Nimbus spun around to look at me, or at least look at the front of my gauzy hood. 'Are you well, my dear? You seem a touch distracted today.'

'No. I'm okay. It's just –' I paused for the teeniest pop of time then whispered to him – 'I'm not really all that interested. In bees.'

'But we should learn about them, nevertheless. What we learn about them here today we can take into the storytelling sessions. Tell the children all about the bees and what they can do.'

'Why?'

'Eh?'

'Why should anybody know about them? If Mr Tumbril is here to deal with the bees, what is the point in telling other people about them? There's no need. Only Mr Tumbril needs to know.'

Nimbus seemed to go rigid. 'My dear girl . . . There is a saying from the old days – my father used to use it. "Knowledge is Power."'

'What's that supposed to mean?'

Nimbus was surprised at my sharpness. 'Think, Serendipity. Think. If there is one thing, one piece of advice this old fossil of a man can bestow upon you, it is to think. And to never stop thinking. Never stop striving to know everything you can. Not until your brain goes fizz or your heart goes numb. For one day, what you know might just be the most important thing in the world.' He leaned in closer to me. 'That is what it means.'

I kept my mouth quiet.

Nimbus walked over to the hive with the pointy top, brushing away bees about his head as he went. Slowly, I joined him.

Mr Tumbril and the Professor were whispering together as I neared, and I could only catch a few slips of words.

'. . . meeting tomorrow, Nimbus?'

'Yes. Usual place. Usual time.'

'I think old Mason has some news . . . homes that are going up . . . even more sinister than we imagined, I'm afraid.'

'Ahem,' the Professor gave a false sort of cough when he saw me alongside him. 'Yes. Yes. Lovely hives. Lovely. You obviously look after them well.'

Tumbril looked a bit shifty. 'They say,' he seemed to mumble (or was that the hum of the bees?), 'they say that if the bees should ever die out – God Man forbid – human beings will follow soon behind. We wouldn't have long left. Imagine.'

'A sobering thought.' Professor Nimbus cast me a quick look.

'Frightening.' Mr Tumbril reached into the hive and a fussing cloud of bees swirled up angrily past him. After a few seconds, he pulled out a sticky toffee-coloured lump of honey. 'Wait till we're in a safe place and you can try a bit of this. Young *Pb* girl like yourself, probably never tried honey before, have you?'

8

The Dream

You see, I hadn't told the Professor about Miss Caritas. I hadn't told him about finding the telebracelet. I kept it all inside as a secret. A great fat squirmy sort of secret that nibbled away at me like rust on a bucket. The afternoon with Miss Caritas had turned my mind tipsy-topsy and I started wondering about the point of it all. The Pbs and Cus – worker bees and soldier bees making sweet glue honey for the Au Queen bees to stick their world together. Was it right? Was it wrong? Was that the way the system should work or not? If I could go back to that afternoon with Miss Caritas, and if she would ask me that same question again, would I still say 'no'? Didn't every Pb and Cu – deep inside their hearts – want to be an Au? My mind was too loud, and for a few days I questioned everything that previously I'd known to be true. The Professor saw that something was wrong, so he watched me and waited, saying nothing, letting me sift my feelings myself.

And then I had the dream and I knew what I needed to do.

In the dream, Mama was holding my hand. She was well again, like in the old days when walking was easy for her and we could go up to the lotments together. Her face was smoother than I'd ever known it, her hair longer and darker than it had ever been when she was alive, her blue eyes shining. She danced over the streets with rinky-dink steps and sang songs – beautiful songs – made up of words and music I swear I'd never heard before. And her dress. It was like something from Miss Caritas's wardrobe. A slinky cream robe that seemed to flow in the breeze and rustle against her skin.

She pulled me along beside her as we skipped over bridges and down long tunnels. We skipped along the Bankment and past the Serpentine. We skipped from the first slice of daylight until the last crack of blackness filled the sky. And I felt so happy to be with her again.

Then suddenly she stopped and, turning to me, put a finger to her lips.

'Sssh.' Then the finger moved out in front of her and pointed at something.

It was a wall. A long, high stone wall.

Mama leaned in close until her breath was nothing between her mouth and my ear. And she whispered.

'Outside.'

Outside.

I awoke with my sheets half chopped out of my bed and onto the floor, my head dripping with wet. My body seemed to be making itself spring up and I found myself standing despite my legs being tiredly weak. It took me a few seconds to not fall over.

Outside.

I went over to the chester drawers and pulled out the map before stretching it onto the bed. My fingers wiggled along the strange lines and bumps before patting the horse at the end of the paper.

I was meant to meet Miss Caritas, I thought to myself. It was all meant to be. Mama's final words to me – 'Outside'. Finding the telebracelet. Meeting Miss Caritas. The map. It was all meant to happen. Like a story unfolding itself.

And then I knew.

I had to find the horses.

9

Nimbus's Promise

'It's a map.' Professor Nimbus stood over the paper. 'Where did you get it?'

It was the following evening and I'd tapped on the Professor's door a little after he'd taken his supper. The curtains were pulled over the window and the oil lamps were busy casting shadows all about the room. He ushered me in and I spread the map open on the desk with the leathery top.

'It's Mama's,' I said. 'I found it among her things . . . It shows where the horses are.' I hurried him on, keen to get to the crutch of the matter. 'In Whales. There are horses still alive in Whales.'

'Horses? Alive?' He looked at me again. 'No. No, that's not possible. The Gases killed them all off. There *are* no more horses.'

I took a deep breath. 'How do you know?'

'What?'

'How do you know there are no more horses?'

'Because . . .' He stumbled. 'Because there just

aren't.' He looked confused. 'Are there?'

'You've never seen one in Lahn Dan, Professor. That's all you can really say. But you've never been outside Lahn Dan. And outside Lahn Dan is the rest of the world.' I stared at him. 'You tell me to think, Professor. And I'm thinking as hard as I ever can right now. How do we know that everything outside of Lahn Dan is dead? How do we know?' Nimbus sat down in his armchair and turned his head to the wall, his fingers stroking his chin. 'Because the Minister tells us?' I went on. 'The Minister and all the Ministers before him? Is that how we know?' I knelt beside the Professor's chair and said, in a voice that was low enough to show how serious I was, 'I want to find out for myself.'

The Professor gave a little sigh. 'You want to leave Lahn Dan?'

I nodded.

'There . . . have been others.' Nimbus smiled a softening sort of smile. 'Others who have tried to escape over the Emm Twenty-five Wall. The Minister didn't look too kindly upon them.' He eased himself up out of the chair with a creaky cracky old man noise. 'Those caught trying to escape are sent to Two Swords. No exceptions. They are frozen to death.'

Two Swords was a name that overfilled all Lahn Daners with fear. Anyone caught committing a crime against the State and the Minister would be whippled away to Two Swords where some clever type of freezing would happen. Then their bodies would be put on display in the main building as a warning to others. Children would be taken there and made to file past the lifeless criminals. Parents would point and tut and tell any child that they thought might be getting a bit too excitable for their own good that if they carried on the way they were that they might well end up stuck for eternity in Two Swords. It was usually enough to calm them down.

'I still want to try,' I said. 'If I don't try then I'll never know, and if I never know then I'll be all crumpled up until the day I die. I think the person who drew this map tried. And I think they found out the truth.' I picked up the map and handed it back to the Professor. 'Professor,' I asked, pointing to the signature, 'who is Shy?'

The Professor took the map from me and studied it hard. 'No,' he mumbled to himself. His face reminded me of Miss Caritas's when she saw the name. 'Can it *really* be true?'

'Professor?'

There was a long silence as he twisted the tiny sheet of paper around in his hands and looked it all over. He was shaking his head. It was as if he'd forgotten I was in the same room. 'I don't believe it. I simply can't believe it.'

'What can't you believe?' My voice was trembling. 'Professor. Who's Shy?'

He looked at me with sad eyes and took a deep breath before he spoke. 'She was an *Au* girl who disappeared. One night, many many years ago.'

'Disappeared?'

'Yes. Along with a *Cu* boy whose name I can't remember. I assumed – well, everyone assumed – that something terrible had happened to them: an accident in a derelict building or some such. That kind of thing used to happen a lot back then.' The Professor frowned. 'Then years after – when you were nothing more than a baby – your mother told me something . . .'

'What?'

He shifted his weight from one foot to the other. 'That she believed Shy was still alive.'

'Alive?'

'Yes. And living outside Lahn Dan.'

A hundred questions whizzed through my mind. 'But how would Mama know about that? It doesn't make sense.'

'When your mother told me, I flicked the idea away like a firefly – talk like that could get you into trouble, you know. The Secret Police were everywhere in those days. Listening. So I never found out anything else about it. I shut my eyes and my ears to the idea. Stupidly. But –' Professor Nimbus held the map out

68

to me – 'looking at this, I can only guess that somehow she *did* get out and managed to smuggle the map back to your mother.'

I was confused. 'But why would she send it to Mama?'

The Professor smiled. 'Because Shy was your mother's best friend.'

The blood was pumping loudly around my ears. I leaned myself against the edge of the Professor's table. 'They couldn't have been friends. Mama was a *Pb* and you said Shy was an *Au*. It's impossible.'

'These things happen. It was very much frowned upon, as I remember it. *Very* much frowned upon. But these things *do* happen.' The Professor leaned his elbow up against the mantelpiece and looked around the room at the shaky flickers over the walls. He stayed that way for a minute or two, not saying a single lonely word. Then he made a sudden sucking noise and jolted himself back to life.

'Supposing,' he started, 'the Minister's Police Force don't catch you and you manage to get outside of Lahn Dan. What will you do if it quickly becomes apparent that the map is a lie? That there is nothing – no people, no trees, no birds, no horses. Nothing at all in the outside world? What would you do then?'

I grinned. 'That's obvious. I'd get back in again.'

'But what if you couldn't?' His eyes went all dead duck serious again. 'What if there was no way back in?'

I stood as tall as I could. I wanted to make it clear that I knew what I was doing and that I wasn't a tiny screaming baby any more. I was old enough to make my own decisions. Mama would have understood. 'If that happened –' I glared at Professor Nimbus – 'then at least I would know that I'd tried. And trying is the most important thing.'

'Even if it gets you killed?'

I thought about it for a moment before nodding my head. 'Even if it gets me killed.'

Nimbus sighed again and wandered over to the desk. He held the map up to the light, squeezing up his eyes to examine it. 'The house with a star over it.' He turned the paper around so I could see. 'Do you know what that means?'

I shook my head.

'Well, I do. Back in the early days of the Ministry, people opposed to its creation would put a star above their door to show that anyone in trouble could go there and hide. A safe house, if you like. Somewhere to meet like-minded people. Somewhere to go.' He paused and seemed to smile to himself. 'Of course, this is all academic. Nobody could ever get over the Emm Twenty-five Wall nowadays. It is too thick and too high. Any gateway built into it would be manned day and night by the police. It's impossible. Utterly impossible.'

I reached up and pulled gently down on the map so that I could see the Professor's face. 'Yes. But I know of a way.'

The next day, as I was getting myself ready for the early morning storytelling slot, Professor Nimbus knocked on my door and came into my room. His hands were a bit twitchy and a couple of times he tried straightening out the creases in his long, greying greatcoat with his palms.

'I've been thinking, Serendipity. In fact, I was up most of the night thinking. Before your mother passed across, I made a promise to her. I said that I would look after you and make sure you were as safe as you could possibly be.' He tried to disguise his twitchyness then by ramming his hands deep into his coat pockets. 'It's a promise I fully intend to keep. Wherever it may take me.'

His eyes flashed over the room as he pulled his coat together and perched himself on the edge of my bed. 'There is something . . . I've not told you, Serendipity. Something important that I've avoided telling you now for a number of weeks.'

I stopped what I was doing and turned to look at him. 'Yes?'

'I've not told you because I thought I could prevent it. I thought . . . hoped . . . it would all come to nothing.

71

The powers that be can sometimes be talked out of making these ridiculous decisions. I've made personal appeals at the Party headquarters themselves, I'll have you know. Made numerous requests for that particular rule to be reconsidered.'

'I don't understand,' I said.

He ignored me. 'But no. Sadly not. The Party are keen to push ahead with it regardless. Why, I've no idea. I fail to see what it is they hope to achieve from doing such a thing.'

'What?'

He looked at me with the miserable eyes that his face wore now and then, and sighed. 'The Ministry has decided that all orphaned children need to be accounted for.'

'What does that mean?'

'What it means, my dear, is that orphans are no longer to be allowed to live with other people. They are to be housed in special homes and looked after by State-appointed carers.'

'So . . . I wouldn't be able to live here with you?'

'No.'

'Where would I live?' I asked, my entire body suddenly feeling overwhelmed by a sort of exhaustion.

'They are building homes. Not nice homes, I'm afraid. They look more like prisons. In fact,' he gave another sigh, 'I think they probably are.'

I stood there for a minute or so taking it all in. First Mama dies, and now I was to be snatched away from the Professor by nothing more than some mad idea that somebody had whizzed up from skinny air. Life always found new ways to confuse you, I thought.

'So –' the Professor skipped to his feet – 'if you still wish to try to get outside of Lahn Dan and find the horses – real or not – I shan't stop you. In fact, I'm going to come with you. You see, I really don't want to see you carted away to some unnecessary jail, and I'm not too sure I want to stay in a city that hides its future hopes behind bars. So, if you don't mind, my dear, I shall accompany you. We shall make the journey together. Yes?'

Before I had time to reply, Nimbus had spun around and was making his way out through the door. 'Pack your bag,' he muttered. 'There is little time to lose. We leave tonight.'

10

Thornton Heef

Going through the drawer full of Mama's stuff was difficult. My bag was only teensy and I had to be very selective about what I was going to take with me. Whatever happened, I doubted that I would return here. I had a lot of her clothes and pieces of plastic jewellery filling up the drawer so I got it all out and went through it bit by bit, laying everything out on the bed. In the end I pushed one of her headscarves – the long purpley one with the yellowy flowers on it – and a rose brooch, which she liked to wear on her days off the lotments, into the bottom of my bag.

The Professor helped me to write Gry and Bracken's names on bits of paper and I left them on the landing outside my room with the two pairs of old shoes that Mama gave me in the months before she went. Sometime over the next few days they would start to wonder where I had got to, and they would come around to see if I was okey-dokey. They would find the shoes and realise that I'd left them as gifts for them both. Parting gifts. They wouldn't know where I'd gone of course, but I couldn't tell them. It would be far too dangerous.

We set off late in the afternoon. Me with my pack dangling over my shoulder and the Professor with a tatty old rucksack strapped to his stooped back, woody old stick for walking in his hand. He said that it might take us a couple of days to get to the wall going south, so we would have to crash out in empty houses along the way.

Lahn Dan was full of empty houses. Before the Gases, it was filled to the broom with people. The roads were chocker with modpods and bikes, trams and buses. All the houses were lived in. Nowadays, though, only *Pb*s with handcarts, *Au*s with modpods and the Minister's Police Force used the roads, and most of the houses were left all alone, cold and silent. There weren't enough people to live in them all. In the old days, Professor Nimbus says, men and women from other places would come and take pictures of Lahn Dan – all the buildings and the parks. They'd grin themselves silly and stick their tongues out and ask passers-by to take a picture for them. I've seen a photograph like that in the Professor's collection. They'd buy cards and T-shirts with Lahn Dany things on. Then they'd go back home and show all their family where they'd been and what they'd done and the things they'd bought and the family would be jealous and want to go there for themselves.

But that was a long time ago. Lahn Dan was a different place now.

After a couple of hours walking, I could feel my heavy feet dragging; the Professor was slowing to a dribble. We'd managed to get as far as Thornton Heef before the Bat Shriek sirens started their usual screechy thing. That meant we needed to get inside fast.

'Quick.' Nimbus sped up once again. 'Down here.'

We sidled off down a side street with a long line of stuck together brown houses. None of them looked lived in. Nobody was around. The Professor took us down a small alleyway to the rear of the houses and pushed open the gate of one. At the back door he tried the handle, but it was jammed shut. Locked tight.

'Blast!'

We tried a couple more of the houses before finally – thankfully – falling into one whose door hadn't been locked.

It was dark and musty smelling. Like the dust had been gathering itself up for many many years and waiting for this moment to tickle someone's nostrils. And it was cold. Terribly cold. I thanked the God Man that I'd packed my floppy, sloppy brown jumper, and dug it out of my bag.

Strange how much space people had in the old days. Nimbus walked through what must have been a kitchen, through a long room with a table, to what would once have been called the sitting room. He pulled the curtains together and, perching his wizardly old legs on the edge of a soft, fluffy chair, lit his oil lamp and adjusted it so that we could see the darkness retreating into the corners of the room.

'Have you brought your dinner pills?'

'Er . . .' I reached into my bag to get them.

'Don't worry.' He popped open his own rucksack. 'Save them up. We're going to need them at some point. But tonight –' his hand pulled something out from his bag with a *ta-dah* – 'we'll eat real food.'

In his hand was a small loaf of bread.

'Bread?'

'And . . .' another dip into the bag, 'honey!'

'Where did you get that?'

'Old Tumbril spares a bit of a pot every now and then. He's a good man, old Tumbril. A good sort.' The Professor took his knife and sliced up the bread.

'You didn't tell him where we were going, did you?'

'No. No. Don't worry. Everybody thinks we're off on a story-finding mission around Lahn Dan.' He levered some of the honey out of the jar and onto the bread. I grabbed it and gobbled gutsily. 'The Minister's office has given me five days' leave.' He took a bite of his own honeyfied bread. 'Not that I'm going to be back in five days, of course.' He gave a snorting laugh and some wet crumbs shot out of his mouth and onto the floor. 'Oh. Excuse me. With any luck we'll be well on our way to Whales by then. Well on the way.'

We ate in silence for a while, the stickiness of the honey making it difficult to speak. Then, after wiping my fingers on my dungarees, I decided to broach something that had been bothering me for a while now.

'Professor,' I asked, 'if my mother was given the map by Shy, why didn't she use it? I mean, why didn't Mama get out of Lahn Dan herself? Wouldn't she have tried to escape?'

The Professor stared at a point somewhere on the opposite wall and thought, his forehead wrinkling. 'I don't know. Perhaps . . .' A flash of doubt crossed his face. '. . . perhaps she didn't trust it. Perhaps she wasn't sure it was true.'

Later on, I took a wander around the house. Everything looked untouched. Caught in a moment when the Gases came and trapped the house in a bubble of time. An unmade bed with the sheets pulled back; a sink full of dishes waiting to be cleaned; a pair of socks draped over a radiator. It told the story – the tiny story – of people whose lives had changed one awful day, never to return to the house in which they lived. (It could have been worse, of course. This could have been one of those houses where the skeletons were still sitting at the dinner table.)

There were photographs of a man and a woman – fairly young – spotted about the place. He had a helmet of blond hair and dimples on his cheeks when he smiled. She had long dark hair, a chin that pointed straight out of the photos and eyes that caught light like marble. There were pictures of them both on a boat, the man holding up a fish and smirking. Pictures of them dancing together at some party. Pictures of him wearing a funny hat and holding a rolled-up piece of paper. Pictures of her standing proudly next to a yellow modpod, arms crossed all cool and cocky. Lots and lots of pictures. Of dead people.

'A long, long time ago.' Professor Nimbus had followed me up the stairs and was standing in the doorway. 'It's all so old now. So dated. We're probably the first people to have set foot in this house in well over a hundred years. Imagine that. Look at all this.' He slid a book off one of the shelves and held it up. It had a picture of a baby on the front. '*The New Mother's Handbook*.' Nimbus shook his head before pointing over to a small cot at the foot of the bed. 'Glimpses into people's lives. Like sparkles of sunlight on water. They flicker and then they're gone.' He gave a long sigh. 'We'll sleep on the chairs in the sitting room tonight, my dear. We won't use the beds up here. It seems somehow . . . disrespectful.'

I found myself nodding.

11

The Emm Twenty-five Wall

The next morning we set off decent and early after the Bat Shriek announced the end of the night. Before we left, the Professor straightened up the chairs – slapping the cushions so they were back to being good and fluffy – and cleared away any of the messiness we'd made. Then we slipped out of the rear door and got on our way, packs on our backs.

It didn't take us all that long to get to the centre of Croy Don with its tip-tiled weed-smattered streets and smashed-up shiny buildings. Something I'd noticed on our journey was that the number of people seemed to dwindle the further south we went, and Croy Don was particularly deserted. A couple of street trudgers hawking their goods, a spittle of *Pb* men and women and children stuttering by, but not a great deal more. Even the Minister's Police Force were hardly to be seen tapping their beat.

As we pushed on and the day grew warmer – Professor Nimbus had removed his coat and shoved it into the top of his bag – the people lessened and lessened until, by the time we were coming to the other end of Cools Dun, there wasn't a single sole soul to be seen. There was nobody.

'Eerie,' the Professor whispered.

'Mmm,' I whispered back. The silence in the road was so strong that it made you feel as if anything more than a whisper was forbidden and that our footsteps were a nasty intrusion. Even the bump of my rucksack against my back sounded like a punch of thunder in the air.

But on we pushed, out of the city and into the countryside. The brown, dead countryside, with fallen stumps of diseased trees and long rotted hedges. Scars left behind by the Gases.

On we went. Towards the wall.

The afternoon nudged itself towards the evening and we rested up for a while in an abandoned cottage a few hundred yards off the main road. The Professor said that we should try to get across the wall during the night-time – we'd be less likely to be spotted by any guards on duty. So we slept a little and swallowed down the last of the bread and honey. If the Bat Shriek sounded then we didn't hear it. It was as though the Minister's reach didn't quite extend that far, even though we both knew that it did.

When darkness spread itself all over the sky, we trotted out as quietly as two human beings could. Two cardboard silhouettes against the misty blueness. Two cardboard silhouettes on a magnificent quest.

'After we are through the wall,' the Professor spoke with a deliberate lightness that I knew was for my benefit, 'we will go a few miles before turning west.' He wrestled with something in his pocket. 'We will use this.' A circular lump of brownish metal was clasped in his hand.

'Er . . . What is it?'

'It's a compass, my dear. It tells you what direction to go in. Look.' He stopped to show me. 'If I turn this way . . .' The little dial inside it wobbled a bit but stayed where it was. 'And if I turn that way . . .' The Professor spun and the little dial still remained pointing in the same direction. 'You see?'

'Delirious.' I grinned. 'Is it magic?'

The Professor shrugged his bony shoulders. 'I don't know. But it seems to work.'

Our tired feet slapped on the cracked tarmac and it was all I could do to struggle down a yawn. We forced ourselves up over a ridge when –

'Look!'

There, in the distance, we could make it out. Not more than a mile or so away. Running from left to right for as far as I could see. The wall. Glistening stone at least ten times the height of me. Suddenly the Professor crouched, pulling me down with him. He put his finger in front of his lips.

'From now on, we must be incredibly careful. If we are caught it's Two Swords for the both of us, you understand?' I nodded. My mouth felt dry. 'We must be as quiet as possible. We'll keep ever so slightly off the road and when we get to the wall we'll edge along it until we find this hole that you believe is there.' He looked up, his eyes scanning the area. 'I can't see any lights. But that doesn't mean there's no one there. The police could be sitting in huts with no windows for all we know. We must be careful. We must try to be invisible. Come on.'

We ran over to the field on our left before making our way up and across it towards the wall. It was harder going and once or twice my feet trippled over the difficult uneven earth and old ropey roots. The night was cold and seemed to be getting colder so I tugged my jacket with the rip in the sleeve tighter round me to keep the cold outside and my fear well and truly inside. I think I was more scared than I had ever been before.

Eventually the hill levelled out and walking became easier. I forgot how tired I was feeling – the blood that was rushing around my body seemed to be keeping my limbs awake. As I got nearer I could see that the wall had been built right across the road, cutting it dead. It looked a bit like the wall had simply sprung out of the ground one day without a care for whatever it was disturbing. Road, field, tree. Whatever.

It was silent, the night like black cotton wool drowning out all noise. When we arrived at the wall, Professor Nimbus turned nervously to see if anyone was watching us before running his hand across the stone. I did the same. It felt warm. It had sucked up the heat of the day and was still clinging to it.

'We must act as quickly as we can. Do you have any idea exactly where this gap is? Where did the market trader tell you it was?'

I shrugged guiltily – I still hadn't told him about Miss Caritas. 'I don't know. All I know is that it's somewhere near this road.'

'Let's go left.'

We worked our way along, the wall on our right. Nimbus's hand dragged over the stone, feeling for a gap that his weak eyes couldn't see in the dark. We went quite a distance over the field but found nothing so we retraced our steps back to where the road met the wall and headed off in the opposite direction. A small copse of barely breathing trees sat a few hundred yards away, and we forced our way over the dried mud towards them. Every now and then a little piece of the cement between the stones would flake off under my hand and for a second or two I would get excited, thinking I had found the start of the gap. But it was never anything more than just a tiny crumble of dust, and the Professor would give a little *hmmph*.

'If there is a way through it must be further along than we imagine. We might have to go quite a way before we find it. It could be a mile or two in either direction. I don't think this gap –'

yyyyyyYYYYYYAAAAAAAAAWWWWWWWWW-Wwwwwwww.

A vicious light from the copse smashed the night apart and a siren screamed out, rattling my bones to a standstill. Then another light shone out from behind us and another from the road at the top of the hill.

'STAY WHERE YOU ARE. DO NOT MOVE. I REPEAT, DO *NOT* MOVE.'

The rumble of a modpod, and the light in the copse started to judder as it made its way towards us. They had been hiding in the trees. My heart slithered. The Professor grabbed hold of my sleeve and pulled me towards him, his mouth fallen wide open at the sheer horror of it all.

'No,' he mumbled, his face getting paler by the second. 'No. No. It can't be.'

The modpods stopped just feet away from us. After a few seconds their rumble subsided and the door on the modpod that had been hiding in the trees hissed itself open. Out ran three, four, five police men pointing guns. They stood either side of us, rifles at the ready. It was like some sort of weird dream that I desperately wanted to wake up from. The men all dressed in their almost black uniforms looked cold and stern and unjolly. Like they would easily shoot you and wander away without winking.

Then out walked Mordecai.

I recognised him straight away despite never having seen him in the real flesh before. Commander Mordecai, Chief of the Minister's Police Force. The man in front of us was smaller than on the scary posters dotted all over Lahn Dan, but his eyes stared with a solid intensity that made me want to look away. The Professor held me tight. Then Mordecai turned and called back to somebody still sitting in the modpod.

'Is this her?' His voice fitted his face.

Slowly, out of the modpod, a woman stepped. She moved more gingerly than the men and she had to ease herself down the ramp to the ground, a thick stick helping her to keep her balance. Behind the bright glare of the modpod's light, I could only just make out her shape. It looked rather out of place here in this field filled with modpods and uniformed men.

'Yes. That's her.'

I recognised the voice.

It was Miss Caritas.

'You.' Mordecai's finger pointed straight at me. 'What's your name?'

I swallowed before I could say anything. 'Serendipity, sir.'

'Serendipity?'

Miss Caritas's voice went up a tone or two. 'She's just a nasty little *Pb*, Commander. Better keep a close eye on her. A weasly little thing, she is. Probably do or say anything to worm her way out of trouble.'

I didn't understand. What was going on? None of this made sense.

Mordecai marched towards me, his eyes bitter and hard. 'You'd better not lie to me, girl. If I find out you're lying I'll –'

'She's not lying. She does not lie.' The Professor released my arm and took a step forward. 'Her name *is* Serendipity.' He turned to face Miss Caritas who was looking cruelly amused by the whole scene. 'And what, pray, madam, is your name? Are we to be told –'

Suddenly Mordecai slapped the back of his hand across the Professor's face. The Professor stumbled to one side but managed to stop himself from falling over completely. Stunned, he levelled his spectacles back on his nose.

'Quiet!' Mordecai growled. 'How dare you talk to an *Au* like that?' He walked around us, his moonless eyes scanning us up and down. 'Nobody has the right to talk to an *Au* like that. You should show more respect. You're a disgrace to your class, Pro*fessor*.' He said 'Professor' like it was poison rolling around his mouth. 'You're *both* a disgrace. Guards.' He addressed the police men with the guns. 'Put them in the locker. Let the Minister decide what to do with them.' He turned and went back to the modpod.

The man standing behind me poked me in the back with his rifle and shoved me onwards. Without thinking, I tucked the locket with the map deeper into my shirt, hoping they wouldn't see it.

One of the modpods was a transporter, designed for carrying people across Lahn Dan. Its rear end lowered, revealing a dark, unwelcoming interior with benches running along the inside walls. Both the Professor and I were marched towards it. As we passed her I could see the thin, unkind smile on the lips of Miss Caritas.

'It could have been so different,' she whispered. 'Silly girl. Too late now, of course. Far too late. Silly, *silly* girl. I suppose I should have known. You can't turn lead into gold.'

12

The Minister

Neither of us said very much as the pod prattled its way along the very same roads we'd just been walking over, back towards the centre of Lahn Dan. We simply sat next to each other on the hard wooden bench, trying not to fall every time the pod hit a bump. My heart had dropped about a hundred or so feet in my chest and all I wanted to do was to roll over and give myself up to the tiredyness in my legs and sleep for a thousand years.

As we came over the Tems and twirled east, the Professor finally turned to me and asked, 'Serendipity. Who was that *Au*? Did you know her?'

So I told him. The truth, I mean. About how I came to meet Miss Caritas and how she helped me find the map. After I spilled my beans out, he just looked at me with sadder than sad eyes.

'*Au*s are a strange bunch, Serendipity. They have lives that are a million miles away from our own. So many of them are too afraid to die, and without death everything lacks purpose. To those *Au*s there is nothing more than the moment. The now. A ridiculous lack of history and future. We know, you and I, that death is just another part of life, and that after we are gone there will be others to carry the world onwards. That is why the *Au*s will always be weaker than us. Because they believe they are everything.'

We were kept in the modpod overnight. It stopped moving at some point and I slipped into a sleep, waking in the very early hours with a horrible, unmovable neck and my hair all matted up.

'Where are we?' I croaked.

'I can't quite tell,' the Professor replied. The modpod only had a thin strip of window near the roof and it was impossible to see out of it. 'But I do know that we're not at Two Swords. I think we're somewhere on the east of Lahn Dan. Yes. East Lahn Dan.'

Suddenly, there was a swarm of voices outside the pod and a scuffle of feet, before the door started to hum and let in the bright morning light. Armed police stood in front of us and the one who looked as though he might be in charge proved that he was by ordering us out.

'Up the steps and inside, now.'

We were forced into a building that I'd never seen before, along some wide, open, *clip-cloppity* marbled corridors into a room with massive tapestries and paintings dangled on the walls. At the far end stood Mordecai, his hands clasped behind his back, his face as solid as steel.

'Leave the traitors with me.' He nodded towards the guards who promptly saluted him and turned on their heels. 'I hope you slept well,' he sneered. 'The Minister has put his breakfast on hold in order to deal with your case, so be appreciative.' He strode to an enormous door and pushed it open. 'Come on. Move.'

I remember a time when I was a lot younger – when Mama had just started allowing me to wander around on my own – walking into Falgar's Square. Just past Nelson's Column, by the dried-up fountains, a pigeon fluttered and landed, cleaning itself under its wings, picking off lice. Everybody froze and stared at the bird, it was such a rare thing to happen. *A pigeon? In Falgar's Square? Impossible.* But it really was there, as solid and real as the day itself. Not a toy or a ghost, but a real-life pigeon. After preening and fluffing itself up, it strutted around, wondering what everyone was looking at, before coming to its senses and flapping off to safety.

As I tottered my way into that room with the Minister sitting before me, I felt a little bit like that pigeon. All eyes upon me – and the Professor, of course. Everybody shocked at what they saw. I wished that I could just flap my wings and fly off too.

'Horatio Nimbus. Good grief.' The Minister was sat behind a magnificent wooden desk, his elbows resting on it, fingers interlocked. His face was fatter than the pictures and government flyers depicted, and his hair greyer and thinner. 'It's been a long time.'

'Easterbrook. I mean, Minister.'

'How long has it been now?' The Minister's eyes rolled up into his head as he tried to think it over. 'I don't know. Can't work it out.' Suddenly any sign of warmth seemed to drain from his face. 'A pity we meet again on such terrible business. Such a shame.' He got up from behind the desk and walked slowly around it. 'Commander Mordecai tells me you were both caught trying to escape last night. That you were looking for some imaginary crack in the Emm Twenty-five Wall.' The corners of his mouth seemed to lift up in slight amusement. As he got to the front of his desk, he perched his bottom on it. 'Is that correct?'

'Minister, we were simply on our –'

'Is that correct?'

Professor Nimbus looked at me before speaking again.

'We were simply trying –'

'Is. That. Correct?' The Minister's face was as deadbolt as could be.

The Professor nodded.

'I see. So you were trying to escape. Why? Are you not happy in Lahn Dan? Are you dissatisfied with what the State has done for you? The people of Lahn Dan have good lives under my Ministry. *Pb*s have full access to food pills and drinking water in exchange for their physical labours. The *Cu*s help keep order and educate the new generation. The *Au*s keep the system running. It is a perfect society.' As he spoke, bees seemed to buzz into my mind. 'I really don't understand what would possess you to attempt an escape. It's such an anti-social, selfish thing to do. In Lahn Dan, everyone has a role to fill. To run away is to . . .' he made a kind of flicking motion with his hand, 'is to wave everybody else away with thought-lessness. It's just not decent.'

'We were going to search for the horses.' I found myself speaking out in this large echoey room, and my voice took me by surprise. 'It was my idea.'

'Horses? Ha!' He rolled back and forth on his desk with spiteful laughter. 'There are no horses, girl. There's nothing beyond the wall. Everything outside of Lahn Dan is destroyed. Especially the horses. You must be simple-minded. What *is* your name, anyway?'

'Serendipity, sir.'

Nimbus seemed to lean forward. 'Serendipity. She's Oleander Goudge's daughter.' He said it like it meant something.

The Minister scrunched up his forehead and stared at me and, for a few seconds, the air hung heavy like a storm cloud. There was thunderous silence as he surveyed me before shaking his head.

'Like I said, there's nothing outside of the Emm Twenty-five Wall.' The Professor crumpled beside me. 'The reason why the Emm Twenty-five Wall was built by my predecessors in the first place was to protect the inhabitants of Lahn Dan from the horrors of the outside world. To keep you all safe. What is so wrong with that? Is there anything so bad about trying to keep the people of Lahn Dan safe? Eh?'

'No, sir.'

'No. Of course there isn't. Sometimes people need to be protected from their own curiosity. What good would it serve Lahn Dan if everybody could come and go as they pleased? Lahn Dan would just fall apart. Can't you see?'

I managed to keep myself from speaking.

'With respect, Minister –' the Professor was busy staring at his own feet – 'if horses did exist, then they could be used to help Lahn Dan rebuild itself. They could be used for –'

'Are you not listening, Nimbus?' The Minister's face was horribly sour again. 'There. Are. No. Horses.' The Professor went quiet. An embarrassing void filled the room. 'Get that into your history-addled brain, if you can.'

It was awful. The Minister didn't even believe that

horses still existed. The whole idea was ridiculous to him. And it had been dug in deep, six feet down. There was no way on earth or in the universe that we were ever going to persuade him that horses might – just might – exist.

'Ahem.' Both the Professor and I turned as Commander Mordecai coughed to intervene. 'What shall we do with them, sir?'

The Minister gave a gigantic sigh and his eyes flickered to me for a moment. 'Treachery is treachery, Mordecai. No two ways around it. Anybody caught fighting the system by trying to escape . . .' He paused. 'You know the law. *Anybody* caught fighting the system that seems to work for every other Lahn Daner will be taken to Two Swords and frozen into submission at a time and date of the State's choosing.'

'No. Please.' Nimbus took a step towards the Minister. 'Freeze me. Not the girl. She still has a great deal to offer the State.'

'Oh, do be quiet, Nimbus. You always were such an inflated fool.' The Minister stood up and walked back to behind his desk once more, sitting himself down on his chair. 'You shall both be driven from here to a place where you shall await the execution of the sentence. Now take them away.' His eyes lowered to something on his desk and didn't lift back up again.

13

To Bucknam Place

We were thrown into the back of a different modpod, one even darker than the first. It grumbled before moving off and we steadied ourselves on the benches.

'You know the Minister?' I asked. My mind was all dazey with the past few minutes and it latched onto something to say. 'He knows *you*?'

It was hard to see the Professor's face in the gloom, but I could tell that it was turning sad. '*Knew. Knew* would be more correct. I knew him many *many* years ago. Back in the time before the Party had managed to get hold of him and twirled and twisted him into the leader they needed him to become. Back in the days when he had a semblance of a heart.'

There was silence for a moment. Then I remembered something.

'You told him who Mama was. Why did you do that? Did he know her?'

More silence. Only a slight snuffly sound from the opposite corner of the speeding cell seemed to break the thick black monotony. The modpod bumbled over a hole in the road and the jolt shook Nimbus back to life once again.

'It was just a thought,' he muttered. 'A hope that he *might* just have known her. A pot in the dark, that's all.' But something in his voice didn't jangle right.

Suddenly, before I could push the questions a little more, something ran out from the opposite corner and brushed against my leg. I shrieked. It felt like a giant rat, like one of the ones that you'd see scuttling around the old sewerage pipes along the Tems looking for dropped crumbs and rubbish to nattle up. I shivered and pulled up my legs without thinking.

A thin wispy voice came from the corner of the pod: 'Mouse! Come here.'

There was somebody in the pod with us. I munched up my eyes and could just see a shape in the corner. It was either a small man or a boy. And jumping up onto his lap was the furry thing that had tickled my legs.

A mouse?

'Hello.' The Professor's weary eyes could see less than even my own. 'Is there somebody there?'

But there came no reply, and for the rest of the journey the person in the corner sat silent, the rat on his lap snorting and yawning and puffling now and then, as though tired with the whole business.

*   *   *

97

The daylight was harsh again as the door lowered on the modpod. The Professor put his arm around me and squeezed my shoulder as we were made to walk down the ramp. Police with guns waved us on towards a pinkish building.

'Where are we?' I whispered.

'I believe . . . Yes. It's Bucknam Place. This is Bucknam Place.'

Bucknam Place was the headquarters of the Minister's Police Force. Sectioned off with fences and wires, it was usually impossible to get anywhere near it. Down the end of a long pink road known as the Mall, it was a massive multi-windowed police station with a tremendously open courtyard in front.

'And you!' a voice barked behind us.

'Awright, awright. We're comin. Keep yer hair on.' Out of the modpod came a boy a year or two younger than me. His hair was spiky and sticking up and his face was smeared in dirt. In his arms wriggled a bundle of hard fluff. 'We know the drill.'

'Hurry up.'

'Yeah, yeah.'

He came up behind us. The Professor tried a smile at him but the boy ignored it, stroking his horrible-looking dog instead.

Inside the building, the corridors were like tunnels. Huge tunnels that could probably accommodate modpods going up and down on either side. But there were no modpods going up and down, just police men and women, uniformed and armed, chattering and serious-faced – all of them with somewhere to go or something to do. None of them looked at us.

'Up the stairs. Move it.' The soldier alongside us waggled the tip of his gun up and down. 'All of you.'

At the top of the stairs, an officer with a thick moustache gave the one with the gun a dull nod and unlocked a gate. Through we marched, into an area with blacked out windows. There were a number of rooms with solid metal doors and numbers on, and as we passed them I could hear shouting and crying coming from behind some. It made my blood run away.

'Here.' The police man stopped outside a door with the number 7 on it. He pushed it open. Beyond it was something I hadn't really expected to see. Instead of a drab, sparsely furnished cell with grey walls and nothing much else, there was a room that had once been brightly coloured and beautiful. Soft, satiny wallpaper had been scratched from the walls and hung now like layers of flaking skin. Golden mirror frames with crackled glass dangled uselessly. Thick, rich luxurious carpets had been kicked and scuffed and worn away into hopeless patches over the years. An intricately carved dressing table had been overturned and smashed up along with shapely bottles of expensive perfume. And a giant wardrobe with tarnished wooden panels stood guard against a wall. In the centre of the floor, a bed larger than any bed I'd ever seen before or since – even Miss Caritas's – sprawled itself over the room, striped silky drapes falling from the posts at each corner, veiling the grubby sheets. 'Get in. You'll stay here tonight and get moved first thing in the morning. All of you.'

The boy with the dog rattled up and squinted beyond us. 'What a dump.'

'Shut up, kid.'

The man shoved us in and clanged the door shut.

'Kings and queens used to live here,' the Professor stuttered. 'Bucknam Place was home to the kings and queens of Grey Britan.' You could tell he was nervous. Whenever he was anxious or nervous about something, Professor Nimbus would chatter away like he couldn't control his teeth. 'That's always been the rumour, anyway. They would rule the whole of Lahn Dan and Grey Britan from this very building. I'll bet there's a crown or two floating around here somewhere. That would be interesting to see.'

The boy pushed past us like we weren't even there, clumping towards the bed, where he put the mangy dog on top of one of the flattened pillows. 'There you are, Mouse. You rest there for a bit.' The dog licked itself before settling down. I could practically see the fleas leaping off it.

'Er . . . excuse me.' I stepped forward. 'There's only one bed and three people. I don't think your . . . dog . . . should be lying on the bed.'

The boy looked at me with a puzzley expression. 'Three people can't share one bed. It don't go. There's *one* bed, there's *one* dog. That goes. You do the maffs.'

'So where are *we* going to sleep tonight, then?' For some reason I put my hands on my hips and looked at him straight on. 'I mean, there's nothing else to sleep on. Should we all just sleep on the floor?'

The boy wandered over to the broken up chester drawers and started rootling around inside. 'If you like. I don't plan on being ere that long meself.' He pulled a bunch of dirty old clothes out of the drawers and dropped them all over the floor, discarding everything like he was searching for something in particular.

'Anyway.' I felt pretty annoyed by the boy and wanted a bit of a diggity at him. 'What sort of a name for a dog is Mouse? If you ask me he looks more like a rat. A rat that's never learned to clean itself properly. Mouse! Ha! Ratty, more like. Stinky Ratty . . . thing.'

The Professor cast me a tutting kind of glance before offering up his hand to the boy. 'Horatio Nimbus. Good to meet you. And you are?'

The boy looked at the Professor's hand like he'd never

101

seen one before. It took a few seconds for him to pull his eyes away from it and to face the Professor fully for the first time. 'Tab. They call me Tab.'

'Hello, Tab.' The Professor lowered his hand back to his side. 'And this is Serendipity.'

'Hmmph.' The boy went back to his emptying of the drawers. 'And you got the nerve to say my dog's got a funny name,' he mumbled so I could barely hear it.

'What?'

'Nuffin, nuffin. Go back to sleep.'

'So, Tab,' Nimbus was chuntering on to avoid the awful silence of our dreadful situation, 'what brings you here?'

'Eh?'

'What have you done to be brought here?'

'Oh.' The boy's eyes never stopped their search. 'Y'know. The usual.'

'The usual?'

'Yeah.' He abandoned the chester drawers and moved over to the wardrobe, flinging the doors open and mussling up the stuff inside. What *was* he looking for? 'The usual.'

The dog on the bed gave a wet snort and we all turned to look at it.

'You do know what is going to happen to us, Tab. Don't you?' The Professor's voice became all fatherly and soft. 'They have told you, haven't they?'

102

'Eh?'

'We are all to be taken to Two Swords. You've heard of Two Swords? It's where they freeze criminals and put them on display.' As he said it, it sent a shiver along my back. 'That's what they are going to do with us tomorrow.'

The boy looked up from what he was doing.

'Nah.'

'I'm afraid so, Tab.'

'No such thing as Two Swords.'

'Yes there is.' I was getting more irked by the second. 'I've been there. Lots of times. Haven't you been there? People all frozen to death. It's horrible.'

The boy seemed to smile. 'Nah. They're just wax models from the olden days.'

'What?'

'They're not real people. Just a load of old dummies. Made out of wax.'

'No, no. That's not right. Is it?' the Professor stuttered.

'Yes it is. Where you been living? Under Earl's Caught?' He climbed back into the wardrobe and pulled out a shiny neck tie. 'Might be useful.' He rolled it up and stuffed it into his back pocket. 'The Minister just pretends to freeze people. Thinks it scares everyone into doing what they're told.' He reached up to the top of the wardrobe. 'Seems to me, if you say something loud enough and often enough people start believin it.'

'I don't understand,' I said. 'So what happens to all the people who break the rule of the Minister?'

He had clambered back into the wardrobe so his voice sounded all stuffled. 'There are prison camps. In the north. There's one in Hen Field. We've seen the prisoners, smashing up rocks for the Emm Twenty-five Wall.'

'We?'

Either he didn't hear me or he chose not to answer, just kept banging around in the wardrobe.

'Prison camps?' The Professor looked as dumb-foundled as I felt.

I didn't know whether to laugh or cry. At least we weren't going to be frozen stiff. Smashing up rocks didn't seem too bad compared to that.

Nimbus and I sat on the edge of the bed. 'Two Swords is a lie?' He still couldn't climb over it. 'Incredible.'

'It's a good thing, isn't it?' I asked aloud. 'All those people everyone thought were dead. They're still alive.'

'Yes. Yes. It's just . . . incredible. Utterly incredible.' He shook his head. 'I feel so foolish.'

Soon after arriving, a guard came to the room and ordered me out. On my own. I stopped at the door and looked nervously back at the Professor who gave me a *you'll-be-all-right* sort of smile, though his eyes said something quite different.

The guard marched me along the long, wide corridors that peered out over the rooftops of Lahn Dan, and eventually down some worn stone steps to a door that looked as though it didn't go anywhere.

'In there,' he growled. 'And show some respect.'

The door slammed behind me.

It was dark inside, with a single lamp dangling from the middle of the ceiling. The light from the lamp didn't stretch far, the walls were still smothered in darkness. As far as I could tell there was nothing else in the room.

'Walk forward.' A voice suddenly came from opposite me and made me jump. 'Come into the light.'

There was something familiar about it.

'Walk forward, I said.'

I shuffled forward until I was standing almost directly under the lamp.

There was a long silence.

Eventually the voice spoke again. 'How old are you, Serendipity?'

'Twelve, I think. My mama says I'm about twelve.'

'And where is your mother? Why aren't you at home with her?'

I tried to block the light out with my hand so I could see the person asking the questions.

'Mama's dead,' I said. More silence. 'She died recently.'

The man stepped forward slightly and I nearly fell

backwards. It was the Minister. He looked as cold and as dead-eyed as he had earlier that morning.

'I'm going to give you a chance. A chance to save yourself from Two Swords.' He looked me up and down. 'Give me the information I want and you can go back to living your life.'

I thought hard, wondering what information I could possibly have that the Minister would be interested in.

'Why is Nimbus trying to escape? I want to know precisely what he's up to. All his little meetings with his storyteller friends. Everything. Tell me everything you know about Nimbus and you can walk free.'

A flash of whispered conversation between Tumbril and the Professor passed through my mind. What were the storytellers up to, and why was the Minister so bothered about them? I shivered. The room was cold, but that wasn't it. The Minister was asking me to betray the Professor. The man who took me in when my mama died. The man who gave me a chance when I could have just been left alone to rot. The man who chose my dreams over his own life in Lahn Dan.

The Minister wanted me to sell the Professor to save my own life.

'No.'

'What?'

'No. I won't do it.' I was suddenly angry. 'Two Swords is a lie. Everything's a lie. I'm not going to help you.'

The Minister frowned and his eyes twitched. We both stood there silently for a while as he plotted his next move.

'I think . . .' he started. 'I think, perhaps, you need to sleep on it.' He strode across the room, brushing past me, and banged hard on the door. 'Think it over. Come to your senses.' The door creaked open. 'This is your one chance, Serendipity. Your *only* chance. Don't mess it up.'

'It won't make any difference,' I shouted. 'I'll still say the same thing in the morning. So don't bother asking.'

The door squeaked shut behind him and I was left on my own in the room.

When the guard pushed me back into cell number 7, the Professor rushed over to me.

'Are you all right, my dear? What was that all about?'

For the splittest of seconds I thought about telling him. I didn't want another big squirmy secret rusting away in me. But then I stopped myself. It wasn't right. Wasn't right for the Professor to know that betraying him was the key to my freedom.

'Oh,' I muttered. 'Nothing for you to worry about, Professor. Nothing at all. Just a mistake.'

'If you say so, my dear.' He smiled, though his eyes were saying something different again.

14

Escaping

Sometime around the middle of the day we were brought dinner pills and water. Tab snapped his pill in two and gave half to the dog – who gobbled it up in a nano-second – then vamooshed back behind the wardrobe.

'What's the point?' I half grumbled to myself, crunching into a square of what I now knew to be fizz, chalk dust and dried milk powder. 'We're going to be locked away in a prison camp for the rest of our lives. Breaking up rocks. We're never going to get outside. We're never going to find any horses.' I was nattering now to distract myself from what the Minister might have in store. If I didn't betray the Professor what would he do to me? 'All we're ever going to see now is a strip of Lahn Dan sectioned off with a razor-wire fence. Nothing more.'

The Professor patted my arm. 'Don't despair. Until the very moment you stop breathing, don't despair. There might still be a way.'

'Mouse! Come on, boy. Mouse. Come on,' Tab called.

The dozing rat-thing spiked to attention and scuttled off the bed and behind the wardrobe, from where his master's voice had come.

Then silence. The Professor and I looked at each other.

'What's going on?'

We both got up and peered around the back of the wardrobe. Both Tab and the dog had gone.

'What on earth . . . ?'

Then I saw it. A door in the wall, half open. I could feel a cold draught coming out of it.

'He's found a tunnel!' I cried.

'A tunnel. Of course.' We both pushed the wardrobe a little further forward so that we could fit behind it. 'The kings and queens would have had escape tunnels built all over this place. In case enemies tried to capture them. Clever boy.'

I pulled the thin wooden door further open. It was covered with the same wallpaper as the rest of the room so that people wouldn't know it was even there. Beyond it was a dull blackness where the air felt chilly. In the distance I could just make out the shady outlines of Tab and Mouse – one feeling his way along the tunnel, the other *tip-tapping* his tiny claws just behind.

'Tab, my boy!' the Professor shouted. 'Wait for us.'

In a way, I was more annoyed by Tab finding the tunnel than I was by his rudeness beforehand. The Professor seemed to be impressed by him – *clever boy* and all that – and I was suddenly overwhelmed by a sickening feeling of jealousy. How dare he come along and interfere like this? I felt all tipsy-topsy.

The tunnel wasn't as dark or narrow as it first appeared. But it did smell. It was obvious that nobody had been down it for a long time so it had a bit of a soggy whiff about it. The walls were made of lumpy stone and the floor was gritty and uneven. Little slits of light shone out from other unopened doors in other rooms.

After a bit of scrabbling about, we caught up with Tab and his scrubbing-brush dog.

'Wha you doin?' He turned and hissed at us. 'Go away.'

'We're coming with you.'

'Go away. Leave us alone.' The dog started to sniff at the Professor's feet.

'But you might need our help.' The Professor bent over and stroked the ball of fleas on its head. 'We can help you escape.'

'I don't need no one to help me escape. I can do it on me own.' He continued slowly making his way along the corridor. After a few feet, the passageway twisted to the left and Tab disappeared once again. We raced around the corner and caught up with him.

'Look,' I said, in a brick of a voice, 'we're coming with you. Like it or not.'

He stopped moving and stared me straight in the face.

'You wanna come with me cos you can't escape on yer own.' He smirked. 'That's right, aint it?'

'Oh, shut up. You're just an idiot.' I wanted to scream.

The Professor poked me with his finger. 'You're right, Tab. We don't know our way out of here. Whereas you do.' At that, the boy seemed to swagger. 'It's very impressive.'

'Yeah. Well. Been ere before, aint I? Knew there'd be a secret door somewhere.'

'You've been here before?'

'Oh yeah. Undreds of times. It's like a game.'

The Professor and I looked at each other.

'And you've escaped? Hundreds of times?'

'They catch me. I escape. Cat an mouse, aint it? Fing is, they aint worked out all the tunnels yet.'

'So what happens now?' I asked, hoping he wouldn't have an answer.

'Depends where this partiklar tunnel takes us. But what I do know is –' he looked around to check nobody was listening, even though there was nobody in the tunnel with us – 'that we got to get out before any of the guards goes and notices we're gone.'

With that he scampered off, virtually on tippy-toe. The Professor gave me a mischievous little wink.

As it happened, the passageway led to the underground modpod parking area. We found ourselves looking out at the rows and rows of transporter pods through a grille in the wall. They reminded me of Mr Tumbril's bees – big, fat, metallic bumblebees. A couple of police men strolled past us, but nobody noticed the three faces – four, I suppose, if you counted the scruffy mutt – peeking through the slits in the duct.

'Oddly quiet.' The Professor adjusted his spectacles on the tip of his nose. 'Not many of the guards around.'

'Watch it,' Tab warned. 'Might be a trap.' He started pulling at the grille, but the Professor tapped him on the wrist to stop him.

'I'm sorry, Tab. But how are we supposed to get out of Bucknam Place from here? Isn't there some other tunnel that might lead us outside? If we go back and retrace our steps, mightn't we find such a tunnel?'

'Maybe. Maybe not.' Tab scowled at the Professor like he was badly drawn or something. 'Are you a spy?'

'What? Oh, goodness me, no. What makes you think I'm a spy?'

'You talk like one. All sort of . . .' He waited for the right word to land on the platform of his brain. 'Fancy. Like you don't understand.'

'Stop being ridiculous,' I cut in. 'Just how are we meant to get out of here?'

Tab pointed at one of the modpods.

'What? A modpod?'

'Yeah. Why not?'

The Professor shook his head. 'But I can't drive one of those things.'

'No,' said Tab. 'But I can.'

Tab and the Professor heaved the large metal vent out of the way and we scuttled as silently as three human beings and one dog possibly can across a cavernous old car park. When we came alongside the modpod, Tab tried one of its doors. It was unlocked, so we all climbed in, Tab positioning himself in the driver's seat.

'Pass me that.'

'What?'

'The hat. Give it to me. You lot better keep low.'

I picked up the hat that was hanging from a hook by the door and threw it onto his head.

'Very fetching.'

'Hmmph.' He pulled it down properly and straightened it in the mirror. 'You oughta hold Mouse. Keep im quiet.' He grabbed Mouse and shoved him onto my lap. It wasn't pleasant. I didn't want to hold the stupid dog, and it didn't want to be held by me. But I did it anyway because the thought of the awful thing starting to bark and getting us caught was worse than the smell and the roughness and the fleas rolled into one. I tried patting it on the head but it wasn't having any of it.

Tab pushed a button and the vehicle roared into existence.

'Keep down. And keep quiet.'

He lowered a lever and pushed some pedals with his feet and the modpod eased itself away. Crouched low in the seat, Tab looked ridiculous dressed in the oversized hat, manhandling the far-too-big-for-such-small-hands wheel. But – I had to admit – he looked as though he knew what he was doing. He spun the wheel around in one direction then the other and I felt the modpod going up a long ramp. A few seconds later, it started to slow, and Tab made one of the darkened glass windows slide down.

'What's up?' a voice from outside asked.

'Buncha dissidents down in Full Ham. Aincha heard?' Tab put a bit of a growl in his voice to make himself sound older than he was. 'Gotta go scoop em up.'

A moment passed before the modpod lurched forward again and Tab tossed the hat off his head.

'S'awright now. We're out. You can get up.'

The Professor and I stretched ourselves. We were whooshing along the Mall, police men wandering by not paying the slightest chunk of attention to us.

It was amazering.

Tab was only just about long enough to reach the pedals, but he seemed to be driving along like a professional. He slowed when he thought it sensible, and accelerated when he thought it possible. And Mouse seemed to realise that his master was doing something good so he started yapping and barely let up all the way along the flyover that led out to the west.

That ride in the modpod was one of the most strangely joyous things that I'd ever experienced in my life up to that point. It was also one of the scariest. All the time we were zipping along the roads, getting further and further away from our captors, I was worried that we might get pulled over or chased by the real police pods. But nobody did pull us over and nothing did chase us. Instead we just made our way out from the centre of Lahn Dan to the endless suburban wastelands of the west. Slowly, steadily, surely. To the wall.

The modpod was not fast. It tittered along, but not at any great rate. Perhaps it hadn't been fully charged up, I don't know. But I found myself kicking my legs to try to make it go faster.

It took a surprisingly long time for us to get out towards the wall, and as we passed Hee Throw the sun behind the dull purplish sky was lowering itself as if it was too tired to fly so high. Like a withered, wrinkling balloon fed up with being played with.

'So,' the Professor asked. 'How do we get beyond the Emm Twenty-five Wall? Is there a hole that you know of?'

'Aint no holes in the Emm Twenty-five.' Tab concentrated hard on the road ahead. 'The Minister and his men wouldn't allow it. Coupla gates here and there, but no one can get through them.' He swivelled the stick thing between the seats. 'Not normal people, anyway. Minister's not stupid enough to leave gaps in the wall.'

The Professor and I gave each other a look. We were both thinking of Miss Caritas.

'So how do we get across it then?' I asked. 'If there are no gaps?'

Tab tapped the side of his nose. 'That's for me to nose and for you to find out. Firstly,' he grabbed the wheel with both of his tiny hands, 'we come off this main road.'

The wheel spun hard and the pod lurched off the deserted old motorway and onto a weed-riddled side road. I struggled to hold onto Mouse as we bounced our way down the derelict tarmac.

'Steady on.' Nimbus held onto his specs, just catching them before they shattered on the floor of the pod.

'Hold onto yer bones, old fella.'

'You don't know what you're doing, do you?' I cried at the boy with the too-small hands and too-short legs. 'You're just making it all up as you go along.'

'Got you outta Bucknam Place, dint I?' He sounded hurt. 'Wern complainin then, were yer? Happy to come along then, eh?'

Tab yanked the wheel to the right one more time and we found ourselves pottling along an even narrower, bumpier piece of road. Empty houses, long since abandoned, stood guard either side of us, but there was not a single sole soul to be spotted.

'There it is.'

About half a mile ahead of us we could just about see the wall, blocking out the rest of the world. The night seemed to be charging in now and in the murky gloom it was hard to pick out any detail from such a distance. Tab killed all the lights in the cabin and we rolled slowly onwards. After a few hold-your-breath minutes he eased the pod to a standstill and switched the buttons off. We all sat there for some seconds, just waiting and watching. Mouse jerked his head from Tab to me to the Professor and back again, wondering what was going on.

Suddenly Tab leapt up and opened the side door with a hiss. Mouse had skittered out before the Professor and I knew what was happening.

'Come on,' I whispered and virtually dragged the Professor with me.

The air outside was still, perfectly still. Not even the teeniest slice of wind blowing across the dead of the evening. And it all seemed so quiet. Eerily quiet. Too quiet. My mind skipped back to the night before. It had been too quiet last night too, and Miss Caritas had spooked out of the darkness to scare us. It felt so familiar. Was it going to happen again? Were the police going to blaze us all senseless with their bright lights and frighten us into standing statue still?

We all kept to the side of the road, tucking ourselves against walls and tripping over risen-up paving stones. We turned left then right then right again, Tab leading the way. He had the look of someone who knew where he was heading.

Suddenly, a beam of light shot out over us from some distance behind. It was a police modpod. Its moany rolley siren started up and the flashy red light on top turned round and round.

'Quick!' Tab shot off like a peashooter, sweeping Mouse up in his arms. 'They've spotted us. Run!'

Tab led us down a lane. The houses were thinning out; pretty soon we were going to be in open ground where the police would find us easy pickerings and start popping us off one by one with their long-distance rifles.

'Where are we going, Tab?' the Professor gasped.

'Here.' Tab stopped in front of some rusted and rundown vehicles from the olden days. He slid his way past one and pointed towards the ground. 'This is our way out. And if we act quick enuff they'll never suspect a fing.'

It was one of those circular metal doors in the road that you see everywhere but nobody ever uses. A manhole cover, the Professor said they're called.

'The sewers,' Nimbus muttered to himself.

Tab bent over and started tugging on the small metal hooks. He managed to strain it a centimetre or so out of its hole. 'Givvas a and.' He gurned up at us. 'I carn do it on me own.' I grabbed onto the hooks with my fingers and the Professor helped push the thing out of the way with his foot.

Looking down into the hole I could see the top of a ladder that seemed to taper away into the blackness beyond.

'It's a bit dark down there,' I said nervously.

'Lucky I brought this then.' Tab reached into his pocket and pulled out a small stick. He clicked a button and a light shot out of the end of it. He switched it off again as quickly as he could, worried that it might just give the game away. 'This partiklar tunnel goes about a mile the other side of the stupid wall. We can climb out there and get well away fore the stupid coppers have stopped scratchin their stupid heads wonderin where we all got to.'

'You've used this tunnel before?' I found myself asking.

'Undreds of times,' he grinned. 'Undreds and undreds of times.'

With one arm holding onto Mouse – who had been surprisingly quiet since we'd all got out of the modpod – and the other holding the rungs of the ladder, Tab

119

lowered himself down into the shaft of darkness. 'Last one down pull the cover back over,' he ordered, before disappearing into the gloom below.

'You go next, Professor,' I urged.

Nimbus stood still and straight and looked me in the eye. 'I'm not going, Serendipity.'

'What?'

'I'm not going.'

'I don't understand.'

The Professor stepped forward and grabbed me by the shoulders. 'My dear. I've come to realise that my work here is not finished. In fact, I now see that it has barely started.'

'But the police . . .' I looked behind Nimbus but no one was coming; the lane was as empty and dead as it was a minute or two before. 'If they catch you they'll throw you into one of the camps. Or kill you. You won't be able to get away.'

The Professor smiled. 'You underestimate this bag of bones, Serendipity.' His hands squeezed my shoulders and I wanted him to say that he was only joking and that he was coming with me and that we were going to escape together. But he didn't. 'We storytellers are a tight bunch, you know. I have many friends who will protect me and together we might just be able to show people the truth. Open their eyes to the things that they see every day but are too afraid to notice. The lies, the deceptions. I owe it to all the Grys and Brackens that grace this city. Every single one of them deserves to know the truth.' He hugged me and I hugged him back.

'Be careful, Professor,' I said, remembering what the Minister had asked of me.

Nimbus slipped his hand into his coat pocket and brought out a heavy round lump of metal. He pushed it into my hand. 'Take this.'

I looked at it. It was the compass. 'But –'

'It may prove useful. Keep the dial pointing to the N and walk towards the W. That's the general direction. Follow the Emm Four – but whatever you do, keep off the road. You will be too exposed on the road itself.' He sighed. 'I do not know what is outside of these walls. I cannot help you once you get out there. But I'm sure Tab will help. I can tell he has a good heart.'

'You're really not going to come with me?' I felt like my body had been dipped in icy water.

His smile became wider and I felt some of my fear thaw. 'This is your dream, Serendipity. Dreams are things that you have to reach and stretch for. And your dream is a good dream. The best dream.' He stood back from me.

'But Professor –'

'No buts, Serendipity. I'm afraid you don't have time for buts.' He cast a glance over his shoulder. 'They're not that far away. Anyway, I've every faith in you. As far as apprentices go, you knock old Mrs Potts into a cockled hat.'

I found myself grinning.

'On top of which, you survived Lahn Dan without your mother. And if you could survive Lahn Dan without your mother, I'm certain you'll survive the rest of the world without me. Now go, my dear. Find those horses.'

I scrambled down the ladder, my rucksack on my back, and looked up as the Professor pushed the manhole cover back into position. A pale crescent moon of blue light waning; the man in the moon fading from view.

At the bottom of the ladder, Tab stood with his light stick glowing. Mouse skittered around on the floor at his feet.

'Where's the ole fella?' he asked.

'He's not coming,' I replied.

Tab shrugged before moving off down the long dank bad-smelling tunnel. 'Huh. Probly just as well. He'd only have slowed us down.'

Part Two
Outside

15

The King

Climbing out on the other side of the wall, the night looked no different. The sky was the same rumble of bruised blue, the horizon just a silhouette. Tab and I pushed the cover back into position and then turned to see exactly where we were.

The road we were standing on was nothing more than a cracked strip and on either side of it were swathes of emptiness.

If this was the rest of the world then I wasn't sure that I wanted it. At that moment an enormous part of me just wanted to climb back through the sewer into Lahn Dan and into my cosy bed. I wanted to slip back into being the person I was just days before – an innocent storyteller's apprentice. How silly I'd been for thinking I'd needed to escape. But now it was too late. I could never ever go back. I was a fugitive. I was on the run.

'Let's go.' Mouse ran alongside Tab, his head turned to hear his master's voice. The idiotic little thing seemed to dote on him.

'Where are we going?'

'To find my people, of course.' He gave a *doh* slap on his forehead to remind me just how stupid I was. 'You comin?'

The glow was coming from a city of tents, hundreds and hundreds of them flapping in the night breeze. Fires flickered between them and, as we approached, I could hear the beat and screechy blare of music being played. Horns and pipes, strings being strummed over the thud and the thump of a drum. And voices. Whooping and laughing and screaming.

'Is it a party?' I asked as we passed line upon line of old-fashioned two-wheel modpods – the ones you see in old pictures with people sitting on top of them.

'They're smugglers.' Tab shrugged. 'Every night is party night for smugglers.'

Smugglers?

The outer edges of the tent city were deserted, but as we zig-zagged through, a youngish man emerged out of one of the tents and yawned, stretching his arms awkwardly upwards as he did so. Peeling open his eyes he spotted us passing nearby.

'Hello, Tab. Got caught again, didya?'

Tab said nothing, just grunted and nodded in response before carrying on towards the noise at the centre of the camp.

'Don't think the King is best pleased,' the man continued. 'Better go and see him and be all apologetic like. Who's yer friend?'

Tab turned a little as he walked. 'Not a friend. Just someone.'

As we skipped our way around a couple of small dying fires, I came alongside Tab and poked him on the arm.

'That's not very nice, is it?'

'Wha?'

'Saying I'm just someone.'

'Well you are, aincha? Everyone's just someone. Stands to reason. Or doncha understand English?'

'That's not what I'm talking about. Anyway,' I let my voice dip into a whisper. 'Who's this king he was talking about?'

'*The* King. King Billy, of course.'

'Who's King Billy?'

He rolled his eyes. 'You don't know nuthin, do ya?'

'No. I don't think I do.'

'His Royal Highness King Billy is king of all the smugglers. He's our Commandeer in Chief.' Tab looked nervous and stared straight ahead. 'He's the one who's gonna fetch me a right clunker for getting meself caught.' He gulped. 'Again.'

'Tab, Tab. Come here, my lad.' The music stopped suddenly as we entered the ring of jumping, swinging people. I looked around at them all as we made our way through. The clothes they wore were bright and colourful even in the dimness of the night. Reds and greens and yellows and blues that clashed happily against each other without a care. Shirts and blouses, all shiny and silky. I looked at Tab and noticed for the first time that even his blue top was quite a different thing from the stiff, uncomfortable overalls of the *Pb*s. More like something an *Au* would wear. Staring closer at the people I could see pictures on their arms. Dark swirls and patterns that had been scratched into their skin, weaving their way up their sleeves. They all seemed to have them.

'Here he is, everyone. Come on, my lad. Come on up here.' The man was sitting on a chair on top of a low platform. He wore a plain wooden crown on his head and his face was craggy and hairy, like a war had been raged across it and both sides had lost. 'Come on. Don't be afraid.' He waved towards Tab in a warm and inviting way, beckoning him up to the throne.

Tab edged forwards gingerly, the crowd parting as he went. I noticed Mouse close on his heels, his stubby tail wagging like a blind man's stick. As Tab climbed up onto the stage, the King stood up out of his chair and grabbed Tab by the shirt with both hands, lifting him clean off the ground and into the air.

'How many times is it now?' the King growled.

'I've lost count. Is it eight? Nine? Twenty? A hundred? Can you even remember yourself?'

Tab's legs dangled a couple of feet off the platform and he tried to speak even though his chest was being squeezed tight against his own shirt. 'Six. Or seven. I think, Yer Royal Ighness.'

'Six or seven, is it?'

'Yessir.'

'Tell me, Tab. Do you like getting captured? Do you like putting our little set up at risk? Is that it? You like risking the livelihood of every member of our community?' Mouse started yapping up at the big hairy man. 'Or perhaps it's this horrible little ball of fleas that gets you snatched each time.' The King kicked Mouse off the end of the podium like a piece of rubbish. I ran over to the dog but he just flicked himself back onto his feet and carried on with his unstoppable high-pitched barking.

'No, sir. Not Mouse, sir,' Tab croaked. 'All me own fault. Every time. But . . .' He seemed to pause to try and suck in his own breath.

'But what?' The King frowned hard into Tab's face.

'But . . . I always manages to escapes, sir. Dun I?'

The King stared frostily at him. Then, eventually, his eyes softened a bit. 'Yes. Yes you do, Tab.' He slowly lowered him down to the ground. 'Every single time they capture you and every single time you escape.' He smiled, then rubbed and scruffled the top of Tab's head with his large hand. 'You're our own little Houdini, aren't you?' The King laughed out loud, then turned to the crowds of people standing before him. 'Come on!' he shouted. 'We need some music to celebrate the return of our own little Houdini!'

Everyone seemed to sigh as one and the drumming and tootling started up again with limbs and bodies swaying and bouncing in time with the music. It was strange and exciting both at the same time. Perhaps even a touch scary-looking. I had no idea who this Houdini was, but the very mention of him seemed to evaporate any tension in the air.

To one side I could see a long table of food piled up like mountains all the way from one end to the other. Breads and meats and strange-coloured fruits and vegetables I'd never seen before in my entire little life. It smelled delicious.

'And who's this?' The King peered down at me and I suddenly felt smaller than Mouse. His eyes burned me with their stare. 'What's your name?'

'Serendipity. Sir.' I found myself gulping. 'I escaped with Tab. And Mouse. Under the . . . er . . . wall.'

'Want to become a smuggler, do you?'

'Well . . . er . . .'

The King clicked his fingers and one of the guards

standing just behind the King's throne came forward. The King spoke loudly into the guard's ear. 'Prepare a tent for this one. She looks fit to collapse. And fetch some new clothes. She needs to shake off these miserable London rags.' He pronounced Lahn Dan oddly. The guard retreated and the King clicked his fingers once again. This time a female guard stepped forward, holding a silver tray with expensive-looking glasses on. The glasses were half filled with a ruby liquid that slopped from side to side as she moved. 'Give our two little fugitives some wine. I think they deserve it.' Then he turned back to face me. 'Drink. Eat. Dance. Then sleep. Tomorrow is a different day.' The King returned to his throne and the female guard handed Tab and me glass each.

We slipped off into the crowd towards the table of food, Mouse forever tagging on behind Tab. I lifted the glass to my nose and sniffed the wine. It made my nose spasm. I wasn't sure if it smelled nice or not, so I started to lift it to my lips, to see if it tasted nice or not, when Tab slapped the glass clean out of my hand and it tumbled onto the blackened earth at my feet.

'What did you do that for?' I turned, stunned.

Tab threw his own glass down. 'Don't drink that. It don't do you no good. Everyone's grumpy in the morning because of that stupid stuff. They shake and shiver and moan about their stupid heads. Here.' He scooped some

131

juice out of a bowl with a small plasticky cup. 'Drink this instead.'

I swallowed it down. It was soothing and beautiful.

'Apple juice,' Tab said, scooping some up for himself.

'What? From apples?'

He looked at me like I'd gone doolally. 'What else is apple juice gonna be made of?'

'You mean it's made from *real* apples?'

The expression on his face was like that of a cat who'd fallen out of a tree. Shaking his head he decided to just ignore me. 'Better than that stupid wine rubbish,' he spat. Then, in a whisper, 'All adults are idiots.'

Drinking the juice made me realise just how thirsty and hungry I had become. All the excitement and fear had pushed it to the back of my mind but now, stood here watching these strange people dancing and laughing, my body pleaded with me to eat. Tab must have felt the same way because, almost as one, we launched ourselves into the piles of food that adorned the long wooden table.

I stuffed myself on meats and breads and cheeses and fruits and things I couldn't even name. When I looked up at Tab and saw that he had juice dribbling down his chin and onto his clothes I laughed for the first time in days. Tab gave me yet another look that said 'Are you mad?' but it didn't even matter, I felt that happy.

I watched the dancing for a while but before too long my eyelids were flickering shut. A kindly woman with a big smile but very few teeth showed me to the tent they had kept free for me on the edge of the camp. I thanked her before climbing inside, zipping myself in and falling fast asleep.

16

A Good Heart

I awoke to find new clothes stacked in the corner of the tent. They were colourful and neat and I happily changed out of my heavy dungarees and into the fresh, light trousers and top. The boots left for me were solid and untarnished. They were cherry-picker red with laces that went up through lots and lots of little holes. I tried to read the label that stuck out at the back of the boots, but all I could piece together were the letters *DrM*. I pulled them on and hooked my fingers through the laces to tighten them up.

The camp outside was silent now. Silent and empty.

The sky was the same monotonous violet it had always been – no different to the sky above Lahn Dan, and I gave my head a shake, thinking how silly I must have been to imagine it would suddenly change colour the moment I stepped beyond the Emm Twenty-five Wall. We were, after all, only a mile or two away.

The tent city looked dead in its emptiness. Only the

canvas flapping gently in the morning breeze told me that it was part of a breathing, living world.

I worked my way around the tents. The silence was picked away by the occasional sounds of snores and yawns and bad-head groans coming from inside them. Tab had been right about the wine, then.

When I did come across Tab, he was working hard. Slaving away, to be honest. Sweating. He and two young men – one slight, the other lumpen – were carrying out boxes and packages from the back of a bloated modpod.

I sat a short distance away on a patch of brown grass and watched them as they worked – none of them seemed especially pleased to be doing it. Eventually, after a lot of moanings and groanings and to-ings and fro-ings, the modpod sped away and the three of them wandered off in different directions.

'Hey,' I called out to Tab. He looked up and nodded his head without smiling. 'What was that you were doing?'

'Heaving.'

'Heaving?'

'The King's put me back on heaving duties.' He continued walking and I strolled along behind. 'Moving all the stuff about. Taking it from ere and putting it there. Meaningless work. Says he don't trust me on smuggling trips any more.' As he walked, his finger picked at slivers of wood caught in his trousers and shirt. 'Stupid, really.'

He stopped walking and sat down on a tump of earth a little away from the canvas city where life was slowly starting to crack out of the triangular fabric eggs. I sat down beside him. It was then that I noticed that Mouse was nowhere to be seen.

'Where's . . . your dog gone?' I didn't want Tab to think that I'd paid enough attention to him to correctly remember his dog's name.

'Restin. Somewhere. Or getting scraps off anyone who shows an interest. Treacherous little so and so he can be.'

We both remained silent for a while, watching the drinkers and dancers from the night before crawl back out into the dull light of morning, their eyes squinting, limbs aching and heads sore.

It suddenly struck me that all through that morning and during the previous night's revelries, I'd not seen any other children.

It felt a bit like suddenly realising that your left shoe had disappeared. It was obvious but for some reason only noticeable the moment you noticed it.

I fished up the point with Tab who gave me a dull, uninterested look.

'What about it?'

'Well . . . er . . . why?'

He shrugged his shoulders and stared down at the

ground, his hands playing with the clumps of earth between his feet. 'No idea. You're right, though. I think I'm the youngest smuggler in the crew.'

There was a touch of the swagger in his voice, so I quickly tried to cripple it.

'And the *least* successful.'

His eyes flicked up at me. 'No need for that.' He sounded hurt as his fingers crumbled the dry mud beneath him. 'No need for that, at all.'

I shifted uncomfortably. 'So what about your parents?' I asked. 'I've not seen them yet.'

'Neither have I,' he replied. 'Never met them.'

'What? You don't know who your parents are? That's awful.'

'Is it.' His voice was flat and what should have been a question certainly didn't sound like one. 'I just don't think about it.'

'But it *is* awful,' I said. 'Everybody needs to know about their parents.'

Tab threw a stone as far as he could. 'Okay. Tell me about your parents then.'

'Eh?'

'Let's hear all about them. Must've been a marvellous pair to have one as perfect and spotless as you.'

'Hold on –'

'Go on. Tell me about them.' His eyes were as cold as steel. 'I'd *loooove* to hear about them.'

I stared back at him. I needed to make a point. 'My mother died recently.'

If I thought that statement would make Tab ease off, I was terrifically much mistaken.

'Everyone dies,' he replied, looking hard at me till I turned away. 'Even Princess Serendipity will die in the end. What about your father? Is he dead too?'

I kept my mouth shut. Mama had never told me anything about my father. She would mutter jokey stuff and chuck away comments like rubbish, but she'd never sat me down and told me anything about him. And I didn't ask. It just wasn't what we did. We lived our lives without my father and we didn't really question it. Neither of us. We rolled along merrily enough on our own.

'Was that ole fella yer father? The creaker who left you to fend for yourself? The one you deserted last night?'

I felt like swinging a fist at Tab's idiot face. What did *he* know? He knew nothing. All he knew about was heaving boxes around and getting himself caught by the Minister's Police Force. His brain was probably riddled from rabies or something that his fudgey little mutt had given him. That or rotten innards from drinking too much apple juice. I wanted to scream and shout at him and poke him in the eye.

I bit my tongue and said nothing.

138

'Can I ask you a question?' Tab's voice was as quietly angry as I was feeling. 'Why were yer escaping? Whadya done in Lahn Dan that was so bad you had to escape? Hmm?'

'Nothing,' I replied. 'We hadn't done anything.'

'Wha? Nuthin?' Tab shook his head disbelievingly.

'No.' I found the words difficult to form. 'We left because . . . because I wanted to look for something.'

'Yer father?'

'No. Not my father.'

'Wha then?'

I waited a second, unsure whether or not to spit out my secret to this boy so totally against me. 'Horses.'

'Horses?' His face didn't split into the mocking smile I'd imagined it would.

I nodded.

He nodded.

'They're as good a thing to go looking for as any,' he agreed, his face serious.

We sat there for a few minutes watching the world come slowly alive. Tab's reaction to what I'd said about finding the horses surprised me and I started to think about what the Professor had said just the night before – *I'm sure Tab will help. I can tell he has a good heart.* It was at that particular moment – a vaguely foolish explosion of a moment – that I decided to put my trust in him.

139

'There's something I want to show you,' I said, pulling the locket out from inside my shirt. 'Something my mother left to me.'

I clicked the latch on the locket and took the map out, unfolding it and flattening it with my hand. Tab looked at it with squinty eyes.

'Wha is it?'

'It's a map.'

He twisted his head to get a better look. 'Wha's it show?'

'I think,' I began, 'it shows where you can find horses.'

Tab pointed at the horses drawn on the map. 'Here?'

'Yes. This is an old road – the Emm Four. Do you know it?'

'Course I know it,' he barked. 'It's one of the roads smugglers use to get to some of the small towns. There's loads of good stuff still in some of them towns. We go along, borrow things –'

'Steal them, you mean?'

Tab ignored me and continued. 'We borrow things, then we smuggle them into the city and sell them all to the posh people. Them *Au*s. Pay good money for partiklar things, the *Au*s. Love their little nicker-nackers, they do.'

Part of me wanted to argue the borrowing/stealing point with him further, but a more sensible part stepped in and told my mind to forget it. It wasn't important. Not any more.

'The horses are in a place called Whales. Just over this bridge.' I showed him. 'Have you ever been to Whales?'

He scrunched his face up and thought. 'No . . .' He gave his head a tiny shake. 'No. Don't fink I've ever been there. Wha's tha?' He poked his finger at the house with a star over it.

'I don't know, but the Professor says it may be somewhere safe to go.'

'Nice.'

'Good morning, Tab. Serenity.' We both jumped at the tall figure in front of us. It was King Billy, escorted by some of his guards. 'How are you both?' His eyes squinted down at the map I was holding. 'What's that you've got there? Something interesting? Something we could sell?'

Tab leapt to his feet. 'Good morning, Yer Royal Ighness. No, no. Nuthin interesting at all.' I crumpled the map up in my hands. 'Jus a rubbish piece of paper from the olden days. Wouldn't fetch a penny. Shoppin list or summat.'

'Oh.' The King looked disappointed. 'Pity.' He looked much older in the daytime and his hair fell clumsily away from under his cobbled together wooden crown. His robes were slightly stained and his hands were rough and gritty-looking.

He turned to me. 'I trust you slept well, Serenity. All good smugglers need their sleep, you know.' I didn't

141

know what it was – it might have been a glint in his eye or the twist of his lip. It might have been the way his head gave a tiny hardly noticeable jerk as he addressed me, or even just the tone of his questions. But something – something – told me that King Billy didn't really like me.

'Yes,' I replied. 'Thank you, sir. But my name is Serendipity.'

He frowned. 'I wouldn't be too worried about your name, girl. It shows an unhealthy obsession with one's self. Never good to be too concerned with one's self. Especially around here.' And with that off they all went, shuffling through the rubbish-strewn landscape like brightly coloured beetles in search of food.

17

Flight

The evening passed like the one before with the smugglers partying and dancing and fighting and singing. It was all an enormous clashing of light and colour and noise – especially noise – and I felt overwhelmed just watching. In the early hours I fell into bed and instantly dropped off to sleep.

It was a little later that something tapped on the sides of my tent, jolting me awake. Then came a snuffle along the edge of the tent.

'Hey.' A voice hissed through the fabric at me. 'Wake up.'

The snuffling stopped and I could hear the tiny patter of tiny feet on hard ground and a slight grumble in the back of an animal's throat. Then a bark.

Mouse.

'Shut it, you stupid dog. Keep yer stupid muzzle shut.'

Tab.

He tapped on the side of my tent again. 'Wake up. Come on. You gotta wake up, now,' he hissed.

I whizzed down the zip on the tent to find him standing outside with his finger on his lips, showing me that I needed to be quiet.

'What is it?' I whispered.

'You need to get yer stuff and come with me.'

'What? Now? But it's the middle of –'

'Before they come to get you,' he fizzled, his eyes wide with worry.

I looked at him. He was carrying a bag over his shoulder as if he was going somewhere. Mouse nuzzled up against Tab's leg, his little tongue lolling out of the side of his mouth.

'I don't understand.'

'No time to understand. Get yer stuff and come with me. I'll explain on the way.'

For some reason – the look on his face or the fact he was carrying his possessions on his back – I realised I needed to wriggle on. Something serious was happening.

I pulled on my boots and stuffed all of my stuff into the rucksack before squirming outside. Tent City was dead again. Just a mass of poles and fabric. Not another soul to be seen. Mouse skittered about my feet like I was his long-lost best buddy and Tab pointed into the distance before crouching away.

I followed, crouching too. 'Where are we going?' I asked, perhaps a tad too loudly. Tab turned and frowned, his finger once again waving in front of his lips. So I nodded and shut my trap, plodding on softly behind him.

Once we'd cleared Tent City, Tab tugged at my sleeve and we squatted down behind a greying fallen tree that had probably not erupted in leaves for well over a hundred years. Tab's eyes darted around before his mouth hissed into my ear.

'The King has guards that patrol the outer areas. We need to wait until the next guard has passed before we can escape.'

'Escape? Why are we leaving? Why do *you* need to escape?'

'Shut up, will yer.' He pulled Mouse close to him and clamped his hand around the dog's nose. The dog seemed quite happy for him to do it, his tail wagging as if it was just a strange game that they were playing.

The minutes passed like hours and we both struggled to keep our breathing as silent and invisible as possible, which was difficult when every breath we let out made a puffy white cloud that floated up above us into the raven black sky.

Then the guard came past, not paying attention to the slightest thing, humming to himself and kicking stones away from under his feet. His hands were deep in his pockets and his eyes seemed miles away; if any enemy had made some sort of attack at that moment he would have been totally dumbfoundled and overcome.

Dead before he knew what had happened. So it was no surprise when he shuffled past us, the tune still rattling around his head – a whistle half-forming on his lips – and disappeared slowly into the darkening distance.

'Now.' Tab crawled over the tree trunk and pattered off, Mouse on the ground alongside him.

I crept along, slightly slower, my eyes straining on the daydreaming guard. After about thirty yards I came alongside Tab, who looked across at me with strangely angry eyes.

'We need to get a bit of distance between us and the camp. There's a village not too far away. If we hide away there tonight, we should be okay.'

I nodded, suddenly trusting him and his scruffity dog.

The moon gave little light and we stumbled our way across dodgy turf and abandoned roads for a good hour or so until we made out the silhouette of houses and long-dead street lights. As we edged into the village, Tab nodded towards me and we slipped into an old bus shelter, tucked away from the pavement, holes worn through the corrugated roof. We sat on the wooden shelf-like bench and caught our breath.

'Why?' I asked. 'Why are we running away?'

Tab reached into his bag and tossed his dog a piece of something or other. Mouse chewed it down in no time whatsoever.

'The King wanted to return yer to the Minister.' Tab didn't look at me. 'Said he'd pay a good price to ave yer back.'

'What?'

'The King thought he might get a modpod or two out of him for returning you.' I noticed his eyes darting up at me. 'Tha's what he said. Said the Minister's Police hardly ever leave Lahn Dan but that last night two of their modpods came out looking for something. He thought they might have been looking for you.'

'I don't understand. Why would the Minister pay to have me back? I'm nothing. Just a *Pb*.'

Tab shrugged. 'Dunno. But I listened in. The King and the people on the Council thought it was best to have you returned. It might have benefited them in some way. Tha's what they said. Keep the Minister's Police Force off their backs for a while.'

I didn't know what he meant. The last couple of days had been a rush of happenings and my mind was finding it hard to take everything in. I watched Tab as he tossed another titbit to his dog.

'Thanks,' I muttered. 'You didn't have to help me, but thanks.'

'S'awright.' He patted Mouse on the head. 'Dun matter.'

The night was pitchy black again. And cold. I pulled my jacket around me and repositioned my bottom on the bench.

147

'Look, Tab,' I said. 'You'd better get back. Before anyone notices you're gone.' Mouse was sniffing my boots. 'If you go now you'll be back before anyone else is up. You can sneak back into camp and into your tent and nobody will know any difference.'

'Not going back.' He sounded sulky. 'Not ever.'

'What?'

'Don't wanna go back. They can all go jump as far as I'm concerned.'

'But . . .' I started. 'But they're your family.'

'Family! Huh. Buncha stupids, that's wha they are. Buncha thieving stupids. Besides,' he tickled Mouse under the chin, 'the King said he'd chuck Mouse over a cliff or drown him in a bucket if I slipped up one more time. I didn't like that. I didn't like that at all.'

I sat and watched him in silence for a while, his eyes focused on his filthy, wiry mutt. Mouse's stubby tail wagged left and right like a blur as his master's fingers stroked him. Each dependent on the other.

'So what will you do?' I asked eventually. 'Where will you go?'

His shoulders jerked up and down awkwardly. 'Dunno,' he said. 'Thought I might go along with you for a bit. Be nice to show Mouse what a horse is. He'd like that. Be nice to see one for myself, for that matter.'

18

Tab's Path

The rest of that night we slept in an empty cottage on the edge of the village and in the morning we downed a couple of food pills each. I was just packing up my bag when Tab rushed into the room.

'Sssh,' he insisted. 'Can you hear that?'

I stopped and listened. In the distance I could just make out the sound of an engine. It was getting nearer.

'It's a two-wheeled modpod,' Tab whispered even though the sound was still a long way off. 'A smuggler's motorbike.'

We went down to the sitting room and peered out of the front window, hiding ourselves behind the dusty curtains. The roar got gently louder until, a few minutes later, the 'motorbike' came along the road. I noticed the rider was helmetless as he pulled up on the road outside the cottage, the engine still running beneath him.

'Tab!' he shouted and I could make out that he was the yawning boy from the camp. 'Tab!'

'It's Hunter.' Tab got up as if to go outside but I tugged at his shirt.

'Don't! It might be a trap.'

'No, Hunter's cool. I trust him.' He pulled my hand from his shirt and went out to the hallway. I could hear the front door opening up.

'Over here.'

Hunter waved and smiled as Tab came out towards him, and he switched off his engine. It was a feeling of guilt and awkwardness that drove me outside in the end.

'Hello.'

'Hello,' I replied, still not entirely convinced that he could be trusted.

Tab turned to look at me. 'He says that the Minister's Police Force were out again last night.'

Hunter nodded. 'Federico – one of the outlookers for King Billy – he got close and overheard a couple of them talking. Said something about wanting to find the girl and the old man. He wasn't too sure what they were on about.'

'Old man?' I said, my heart suddenly filling my body. 'They said "old man"?'

'Yes. Old man.'

They were still looking for the Professor! I couldn't believe it. That meant they hadn't captured him that night. They still thought he had escaped like Tab and me. I felt like throwing my arms in the air and dancing and hugging Hunter.

'That's fantastic.'

Hunter gave me a slightly odd look. 'Thought I'd better let you know,' he started absentmindedly, 'so you can try to avoid them. They seem to be sticking to the main roads.'

'What about the King?' Tab asked. 'How's he feel?'

'Bit cheesed off. I don't think he'll ever take you back now, Tab. Think you've done for yerself as far as the King is concerned.'

Tab looked a little sad but tried shrugging his shoulders in an attempt not to. 'Fair enuff.'

'Thought you'd head out this way,' Hunter continued. 'No one reads your mind like I can, Tab.' He ruffled the top of Tab's head before Tab tried patting his hair down again.

'You're not going to tell on us, are you?' I looked Hunter straight in the eye.

'What? No, no. I'm not gonna go lemongrassing you up.' At that moment, Mouse scuttled out of the house and skidded to an ungainly stop right at Hunter's feet. 'Mouse, boy! The worst dog in the world. How are you, eh?' He bent over and scratched the dog's rough fur with the tips of his fingers. Mouse panted like an idiot and kept turning around to try to position Hunter's fingers in the place where, at that very second, the fleas were most bothering him. 'You look after your master now, Mouse. He needs looking after, does young Master Tab.'

Tab's face fell. 'You going?'

'Got to. Can't stay long. Someone'll start wondering where I've got to otherwise. Here.' He leaned back over his bike and pulled up a large sack. 'Come to give you this.' He shoved it coarsely into Tab's hands. 'Leftovers from last night's party. Thought you might need some, now yer out on yer own.' He turned to look at me. 'Well, you know what I mean.'

'Thanks. Thanks a lot.' I thought I saw Tab's eyes starting to fill with tears, but not for long.

'We're going to –' I began, but Hunter cut me off.

'Don't tell me. If I don't know then I can't say, can I? And if I can't say, then nobody'll find out. And then . . . well . . . you're safe, yeah?'

Tab nodded.

Hunter grabbed him by the shoulders and they stood face to face.

'You take good care of yerself now, bruv. Eat well, wash yerself properly – all that sort of guff. They say there are good people living out to the west and to the north. Not like around here. Remember that. And also remember,' his hands seemed to squeeze Tab's shoulders, 'that you know where I am. If you need me. Ever.' It was Hunter's turn to blink back tears. 'Yeah, bruv?'

He pulled himself together and patted Tab's shoulders in a jokey, joshing sort of way before turning back to the bike and climbing on. He twisted a key and the engine roared loudly into the silence.

'Take care.'

He winked at us both and the bike rolled off slowly out of the village.

Tab seemed in a huff. He marched on ahead of me; even Mouse was finding it tricksome to keep up with him. As we passed through the dead countryside and into another small collection of houses and rusted down modpods, I caught up with him.

'What's wrong?' I frowned at him. 'Why're you in such a moodle?'

He frowned right back at me. 'Eh?'

'You're in a moodle.'

'Yeah, well . . . I didn't like the way you nearly told Hunter we were going off together to find yer beloved horses.'

'Well we are, aren't we?'

'No.'

'But we're walking together now, aren't we? You're walking with me.'

'No. *You're* walking with *me*. *I'm* the one in front. *You're* the one scratching along behind.' He tugged the bags tighter over his shoulders. 'Feel free to push off whenever you like. Toodle pip.' He stretched his legs and put more distance between us.

'Don't you want to find horses?'

'No,' he called back. 'Don't think I do.'

'Oh, don't be such a baby!'

Then he stopped and turned to me and I could see in his eyes that it wasn't horses he was thinking about. His eyes were drooped and sad and I realised that that was probably the way I'd looked just the other night when the Professor turned back and left me to get out of Lahn Dan without him.

Everything in Tab's life had changed just as suddenly as everything had changed in my own. Like a rabbit caught in a deadlight. He was stunned and he didn't know what he was saying. He was just lashing out at the person standing nearest to him.

'I'll help get yer to the Emm Four,' he said, without any feeling, his heart not really meaning it. 'Then I'll probly go me own way.'

19

Bikes

'You ever ridden one?' Tab asked, eyeing the bikes in the dusty shop window.

I'd seen *Cu*s in Lahn Dan riding them, of course, their legs pumping up and down as they whirred along. But I'd never ridden one myself. No *Pb* ever had, to my knowledge. So I just shook my head.

'Wanna learn?'

Before I knew it, Tab had picked up a bumpy piece of debris from one of the smashed up houses nearby and was running towards the glass.

'No!'

Too late. The glass stuttered into a squillion slices and fell to the ground. I looked around nervously to see if anyone was rushing out at us, but the village was completely dead. As the sound of the tinkling glass faded, the only noise that could be heard was the *patter-patter* and *yap-yap* from Mouse and Tab's out of breath puffing.

'Come on.' Tab knocked the spikes of glass out of the window frame and climbed into the shop.

'You can't do that.'

His head peered out. 'Why not?'

'Well . . . it's stealing.'

'Who from?'

'What?'

'Who would we be stealing from? Nobody lives here any more. Everyone's dead.'

'That's not the point.'

'Oh. What *is* the point then?'

I shifted from foot to foot. 'It's just wrong. Those things don't belong to us. They're not ours to take.'

Tab sighed. 'And if we don't take them? What'll happen to em then?'

'Er . . .'

'Nuthin. Tha's what. Nuthin. Which is a pity, cos these bikes were made to be used. Whoever made them in the old days made them to be used. Not to sit getting dustier and dustier in a shop window. The bikes're ere. *We're* ere. And we *need* to get away from ere. Tha's all you need to know. End of. Now come on.'

I shook my head and muttered, just loud enough for Tab to hear, 'Once a thief, always a thief.'

Admittedly, the first time I fell off, I didn't feel like getting back on again. Tab laughed out loud as I wibbled over to one side and the bike seemed to twist away from under me. My arm scraped along the rough

156

of the road, and my leg got stuck under the pedal. It hurt.

'Not like that. Like this.' Tab wheeled around me like I was some sort of useless idiot, giggling as he did so.

After the fifth and sixth fall, I found myself getting madder and madder and desperately wanting to beat this hunk of metal that was making me look so foolish. It only took a couple more slips and I was away. I was cracking it. I pedalled and pedalled, turning the handlebar as gently as I could. I cycled up the road and came back down, speeding more speedily than I'd ever sped before. Tab looked on in amazishment as I swooped past him, swerving just in time as I approached.

'It's easy!' I called out.

'Yeah, yeah. Very good.' He sounded a little deflated. 'Now you've got to learn how to use the gears.'

'Gears? What are they?' The wind was racing past.

'Turn the lever. On that side. The one near the middle.'

'What?'

'The lever. On that side.'

'You mean this one here.' I lifted a hand to point and felt chuffed that I could cycle one-handed.

'Yeah. That one. Click it forward.'

I shoved the stumpy lever forward and the chain clunked awkwardly beneath me. The whole bike jerked and my legs suddenly found it difficult to pedal. I wobbled from one side to the other before falling again.

Tab snorted.

'You did that deliberately.' I stood up and wiped myself down. 'You ruined it for me!'

'Don't be bonkers. You just have to learn to ride *properly*, that's all.'

Mouse barked as if he was laughing too.

20

The Valley of the Wolves

The hills were tricky. My legs strained and ached as I forced the bike up over them. And there were more hills now. More and more of them. Little ones and big ones. Hills with sweeping, snaking roads that made it awkward not to have to put your foot down on the ground every now and then to stop yourself tumbling over. Hills with weeds pushing themselves up through the tarmac, trying to grab hold of the wheels of our bikes, trying to trip us up. Lots and lots and lots of tricksy, exhausting hills.

Going down the hills was a simple matter, though. We'd freewheel down them as fast as we could, Mouse sprinting alongside, the air brushing our faces. Sometimes I'd lift my feet off the pedals and stick my legs out to the sides as I accelerated downwards, balancing the bicycle beneath me.

It was at the top of one longish hill at the edge of a dense wooded valley that I heard Tab's brakes screech behind me just as I was about to let it all rip. I pulled my brake tightly and turned to look at him.

'What?'

His eyes were scanning the valley ahead of us. 'I know this place. I been ere before.' He rolled over to the side of the road and stared at a crumbling wooden sign that had been stuck on a post shoved into the ground. 'I can't read very well, but I know what this says.'

The letters on the sign had been sprayed on in a purplish colour many years before and were fading away. It took all of my reading skills to piece together the two words that were still readable.

'*Beware . . . W.O.L.V.E.S . . .* Wolves?'

Tab nodded. 'Yeah. Wolves.' He looked back at the wood that lay beneath us. 'This is the Valley of the Wolves.'

'You mean . . . wolves live down there?'

'That's what they say. After the Gases, the animals in Lahn Dan Zoo were set free. I don't know what happened to most of them. Probly died. The story might not even be true, fer all I knows. But the wolves . . . the wolves they came out ere. And people say they live –' he pointed – 'down there.'

I was suddenly smacked in the chest with a sorry sense of hopelessness. Behind us were smugglers who wanted to sell me back to the Minister; modpods filled with Lahn Dan police men were swooping around the whole area like flies, hoping to hunt us down; and now wolves were standing in our way, teeth all shiny and hungry and ready to gobble us up. The world outside the wall was proving to be every teensy bit as dangerous as the world inside it.

'There was nothing about wolves on the map,' I said, trying to wish the whole wolf thing away. 'My mama's friend drew nothing about wolves.'

'I been thinking,' Tab looked at me with quizzing eyes, 'about that map.' He repositioned himself on the seat of his bike. 'Are you sure it's real? It just looks like summat someone's scribbled on a piece of scrappy paper to me. Are you sure it shows you that horses are in Whales?'

I gave him a hard stare back. 'Of course it's real. My mama left it to me so it must be real.' But secretly inside I was wondering the same thing. What if it wasn't true? What if Mama had been holding onto the map for no other reason than it reminded her of her best friend? What if I'd got out of Lahn Dan, put the Professor at risk and broken Tab away from the only family he knew for a piece of tatty pointless paper? It was all too horrible to think about.

It was Tab who broke the silence in the end. 'Don't spose it matters.'

'What?'

'Well, if you can't turn around and go back to summat then yer might as well just push on and try to get to

161

summat else. Stands to reason. No use looking behind yer all the time.'

And it was true. Neither of us had anything to go back to. So why not chase a dream that might turn out to be as fake as the plastic people at Two Swords? I had, after all, nothing but the air in my lungs to lose.

Annoyingly, Tab could say the right things at the right time, and part of me wanted to throw my arms around him whilst another part wanted to thump him one.

'Is there another way around?' I asked. 'Can't we just go around the wolves and get to the Emm Four?'

'Maybe. Problem is it'd be a long long way. And I mean a *long long* way. Be easy to slip into the fingers of the Minister's police.'

'But we can't just go whizzing through the wolves.'

Tab fiddled with the gears on his bike. 'Why not?'

'Well, I'd've thought that was obvious.'

'Look, I've never seen a wolf, have you?'

'Of course I haven't.'

'That might be because they don't exist any more.'

'But you just said –'

'Listen, *you* might believe everything that everyone tells you – that Minister of yours did a very good job of that – but *I* don't. I grew up with smugglers and I know what bilge they all chat.' He pulled a squinted-up face. 'Wolves? Bah! Load of old crab. Nuthin down

162

there but rats and ants.' He pushed off and started pedalling down the hill, calling over his shoulder. 'Trust me.'

The road leading through the wood was weirdly quiet, like the wind couldn't bring itself to blow its way around the trees, and even though it was only the afternoon, the whole area was packed in with a kind of evening gloominess and a slight mist drifted around us. The trees lining the roads were nothing more than bare brown sticks that stuck out of the ground like rows upon rows of soldiers standing to attention. The only sound that I could hear was the whirr and whoosh of our wheels. Tab pedalled up ahead of me with Mouse lolloping alongside, and every now and then I cast my head backwards to see if I could spot any wolves. Each time I looked I could see nothing but the broken tarmac along which we had just cycled. If anything, I was a little disappointed.

After a while the trees thinned out and the outskirts of a town began to appear. All towns followed the same pattern as Lahn Dan, I was beginning to realise. Every single one of them. Exactly the same pattern, over and over and over again. Firstly you had the trees and the fields that hovered around the edges, holding the town in position and stopping it from spilling too far away from itself. Then come the farms and the barns, dotted on the dying breaths of hills, the first signs of human interference. Suddenly the ground flattens out and the factories and warehouses, shops and glass buildings erupt out of it.

Tab let his tyres skid to a sudden stop, and I slowly rolled alongside him.

'See! What did I say? No wolves. We're outta the woods and we didn't see a single wolf. Told you there was no such thing as a wolf, didn't I?' He had a relieved, smug look stapled to his face. 'I *knew* all that stuff they said about wolves was rubbish. I just *knew* it.'

'So what happened to the animals that escaped from Lahn Dan Zoo all that time ago?'

'Dunno. Musta just died out, I guess. Who cares? Come on.'

The town was as deadly quiet as every town and village we'd ridden through or seen from a distance, and the buildings jutted up against the sky, just like they did in Lahn Dan. Crowding you in like giants, staring hard down at you, like they'd like nothing better than to squash you and to kick your remains under the pavement.

We cycled uphill out of the centre, past some scruffy-looking shops. The mist was thickening fast now, and everything was beginning to look hazy – the edges of buildings no longer sharp and pointy but blurred and difficult to pick out. We rolled to a stop outside a large church and took swigs from our water bottles.

'Getting dark now,' Tab said, screwing the top back on his. 'Better find somewhere to kip soon.'

I looked up at the church. The long-dead clock face showed the time at which it gave up the goat, its bells clanging to an end. The tiles on its roof were all buckled and broken and cracked, the walls all mossy and blackened. It gave me the shivers. There was something creepy about it. The headstones in the churchyard were long and grey and scattered about. I pointed them out to Tab.

'S'funny,' he said, screwing his eyes up tight to try to see. 'I always thought people had statues of angels made for them when they died. That's what yer see in other churchyards.'

'What?'

He pointed at the headstones. 'All the dead people in that one had statues of dogs made. Weird.'

'Dogs?' I strained my own eyes to see.

And then one of the headstones moved.

And then another.

Tab looked at me – his mouth like a cave – and I looked at him. They weren't statues of dogs at all. They weren't statues of anything. They were wolves. Real, breathing, living wolves.

'What were you saying about them dying out, Tab?'

165

Slowly they came out of the churchyard past the gate that had been ripped off its hinges. One by one. Three. Four. Five. Six of them. Their yellow eyes staring as they padded all the way around us until we were surrounded.

Mouse barked. Tab scooped him up and clamped his hand across the dog's muzzle. 'Sh'up, you stupid mutt. Dya wanna get eaten?'

Tab was scared. I could tell. So was I. We stood there with our bikes and watched them as they circled us. Never rushing. Always staring. Softly. Softly. Taking their time.

'Wha're we gonna do?' Tab whispered. 'I don't like this one little bit.'

'Just stay still,' I whispered back. 'Don't do anything.'

'But . . . they're going to eat us, aint they?'

I didn't answer. I stood iced to the spot as the wolves kept revolving calmly around us.

Suddenly, a snort and a growl came from the church-yard and another wolf strode out. This one was much much larger, with a beautiful coat of thick, silvery fur and eyes that gleamed bright in the quickly dimming light. It moved so gracefully. So elegantly.

'He's the boss,' Tab gabbled on nervously. 'I can sorta tell. He's the boss wolf.'

'Sssh. Keep quiet.'

The silver wolf came to the line of wolves and goggled

at us, twisting his head one way and then the other. Weighing us up.

It was at that point that something jangled inside my head. It was something the Professor had once said in a storytelling session many years ago when I was tiny. Something I hadn't forgotten.

'Don't be scared,' I said to Tab.

'Eh?'

'I said don't be scared.'

'Well, that's easier said than done, aint it?'

'If he sees you're scared, he'll attack. The Professor told me. Sometimes, if they think you're not scared, animals will leave you alone.'

'The Professor?' Tab sighed. 'Excuse me for not getting too excited, but when was the last time that dotty old brainbox had to wrestle with a wolf?' He shuffled Mouse tighter under his arm. 'If they *do* start eating us, can I just say it was nice knowing yer.'

'Look, just listen to me. Stare the boss wolf in the eye. Tell yourself you're not scared and stare him in the eye.'

Tab picked up on the seriousness in my voice. 'Okay.'

The silver wolf watched us straighten ourselves up. It was hard peering directly into the eyes of something so dangerous, knowing that the tiniest slip could make everything worse. But both Tab and I stood there and tried our hardest to look as strong and as brave as we could. After all, there was nothing else we could do.

The mist wisped across the scene and time seemed to stand like a statue. The wolves stopped moving and I think I stopped breathing.

'Gurrraa.' One of the other wolves roared and bared its teeth, making me jump slightly.

'RRRooooohh.' The silver wolf roared even louder, and the first wolf seemed to skulk off back to the churchyard, its head bowed low.

My hands were white around the handlebars of my bike, but my face remained still. Unswerving.

'Wha's going on?' Tab spoke out of the side of his mouth. 'I'm staring so hard, me eyes are weeping. Wha's happening?'

I didn't answer. I breathed in deeply and filled myself up to my fullest, my cold eyes fast on those of the large silver wolf.

Suddenly, another one of the wolves turned and peeled itself away from the circle, slowly padding through the gate towards the church. Then another did the same. Then another. Like grey angels drifting back into the graveyard.

'Are they –'

'They're leaving us alone,' I said, hardly able to believe it. 'They're going away.'

The last two walked alongside each other – their bodies solid walls of muscle and fur – following the others.

There was only the silver left.

'You sure he's not just saving us for himself?'

I glared hard, my heart more alive than ever, my head more determined. I kept telling myself that I was strong and I was brave and that I was *definitely* going to see the horses. No matter what. Nothing was going to stop me.

The silver looked from Tab to me then back again. A small grumble from the back of his throat, and then . . .

He walked away. Steadily and deliberately he joined his pack without turning to look at us.

'I don't believe it.' Tab was still talking out of the side of his mouth.

'Come on,' I said. 'He's let us go.'

'Yeah, but –'

'And we'd better show him respect by going right now. Not too quickly, though. We don't want them to catch on to just how nervous we really are.'

Tab dropped Mouse to the ground and we both started to push our bikes slowly away. The wolves in the churchyard paid us no more attention as we worked our way gently out of the town in the dying light of dusk. As we went, I began to think how dignified and noble some animals were. Creatures of honour.

So unlike many humans.

21

The Dragon

When the rain started, I panicked.

'We need to get inside somewhere.' I waved at Tab. 'Somewhere safe.' The first few drops had started to hit the road and the rumble in the darkening clouds directly above us suggested there was a great deal more to follow.

'Safe?' Tab asked. 'It's only a drop of rain.'

'But the rain is dangerous.' We were out in open countryside and there were no houses nearby. 'We need to hurry! We need to find somewhere to hide.'

'Calm down. It's not going to hurt you.'

'But it's poisonous! Back in Lahn Dan they sound a siren whenever it rains so that people have time to get inside before it starts.'

'Whoa . . .' Tab took his hands off the handlebar and held them up, palms towards me. 'Slow down, will yer. The rains haven't been poisonous for years. Loads and loads of years.'

'Rubbish!' My eyes were scanning about for somewhere

we could protect ourselves. 'If we don't get out of the rain, our skin will start to blister and bleed and before we know it we'll be dead. Come on! We need to get to safety.'

'Dint you hear me? I said the rains stopped being poisonous a long time ago.' Tab's hand reached out and grabbed my wrist. 'I've been out in the rain undreds an undreds of times. Thousands of times.' He spoke in a soothing, quiet way that made me listen to him. 'I aint never come out in blisters or nuthin. The rain is safe.'

'How can I trust you?' I wanted to pull my arm away from him, but I didn't.

He snorted. 'Blimey, if I thought I was goin to come over all bubbly-skinned and sore, I wouldn't be hanging around ere now, would I?'

A drop of rain splashed onto my forehead and I flinched. Then more drops. They came suddenly, heavily, hitting the ground and my head and my arms and my face. And Tab's too. And we both just stood there and let it happen.

'Remember all the lies the Minister told you?' He grinned. 'Well, that rubbish about the rain – it's just another one of them. Just another one of his stupid, sorry lies to keep everyone in their place. The rain is safe. Trust me.'

The heavy clouds above unleashed themselves and, for the first time in my life, I let myself get soaked. It was a strange feeling. All those years in Lahn Dan, avoiding rain like madness and then . . . this. My clothes got drenched and heavy and started to stick to me, but the rain didn't care. It kept on pouring out of the sky and covering the whole world in water. And it really didn't matter. Not one tiny bit.

The rain wasn't dangerous.

I looked at Tab and he was laughing. 'What?' I smiled back.

'You.'

'What about me?'

'Oh. Yer know. Just you. You and yer funny little ways.'

I nodded, holding my arms out to catch the rain and wondering what other things about this world I'd always got wrong.

The following morning, we had our first sight of the Emm Four. We rounded a corner and swooped over a small hill and there it was. A line of old concrete, lifted above the ground on pillars, as though it felt too special to be on the ground with the rest of the roads.

We slipped down the hill and rode straight under it, coming out on its other side.

'So,' I said. 'You've got me to the Emm Four. I suppose this is where we say our goodbyes, is it?'

He looked down at his feet where Mouse was panting

and did a sort of shuffling back and forth on his bike. 'Thought I might come with you a bit further. Just for a while, anyhows.'

I had a bit of a secret smile inside. 'Okay, if you like.'

'I aint asking permission.' He scowled and pedalled off like a scolded rat.

At lunchtime we pulled off the road and onto a sort of embankment, valleying down to some old metal tracks buried in grass and weeds. Mouse was finding the travelling hard going, collapsing next to us, his little sides going in and out and up and down as he struggled to regain his breath. He didn't even lift his head as Tab dug out the slices of ham and hunks of bread that we were going to devour for our lunch.

'Apple juice?' Tab asked, pulling a plastic container from the sack.

I took the bottle from him and, popping open the top, put it to my lips. It tasted like a perfect sweetness as I gulped it down.

'Hold on,' Tab croaked as he tried to snatch the bottle back off me. 'There might be a load of it left but we'd better try an save it. Won't do to go wasting our supplies.' He took the bottle and just let his lips be rinsed by the liquid.

Some picky rain had sputtered out hours before, and

my clothes were starting to dry in the midday warmth. The purple clouds looked ever so slightly less purple here, and the grass on the slopes of the embankment was the teeniest bit greener than it had been just a few miles further back. If I wasn't very much mistaken, the sunshine felt a tiny bit warmer too.

I ripped apart a roll with my fingers and shoved a slice of ham inside it before taking an enormous bite. After a busy morning pedalling, my stomach was grumbling like a bad dream, and all I could think of was filling it up as much as possible to keep it happy.

'I don't fink –' Tab mumbled with a mouthful of bread.

'I know you don't. That's your problem.'

'Seriously, though, I don't fink Mordecai and his men are gonna stop lookin for you yet.'

'Really?' My heart did a nosedive.

'You're like a bird what flew the cage and they're scared you're gonna start singing about it. Stands to reason they'll wanna put you back as fast as they can.'

I shrugged. I didn't know anything. That had been made startlingly clear over the last few days. Everything I had assumed to be the truth had been stripped away to be nothing of the sort. Only the memory of Mama stayed true. So it struck me as pointless to guess anything about the Minister's men and their ways.

'We'll see,' was all I could think of saying in between bites of ham roll.

I finished the sandwich, dusting crumbs off my hands, before breaking off pieces of biscuit with chunks of chocolate sticking out and lying back on the grass, watching the clouds softly pass by.

'I hope the Professor's okay,' I half murmured to myself. 'I wonder what he's up to right now.'

'Probly doing sums or summat.' Tab leaned back onto his elbows. 'Seemed the sort. All specs and clumsiness. Ancient. Had it.'

The countryside undulated away in all directions and we both just lay still for a few minutes, letting the turn of the world hold us in place with our thoughts.

Then we heard the noise.

A long screech. High-pitched and glass-smashingly scary.

'What was that?' Images of wolves and modpods flooded my brain. I sat upright. Whatever it was, it was far off to our right.

Mouse straightened up, ears pricked. Tab eased himself slowly into a crouching position, his hands automatically slipping things back into the sack.

The noise sounded again. Nearer this time.

'What is it?' I asked once more.

But Tab wasn't looking at me. He was staring into the distance beyond me. 'Look,' he said, his face like a slapped haddock.

I turned to see where he was pointing. Some way off,

175

over a number of hills and rooftops, came a billowing cloud of smoke. And it was moving in our direction.

'I don't understand,' I quaked.

'It's . . . it's a . . .' His hand shivered as he pointed. 'It's a . . . dragon.'

'What?'

'A dragon! It's coming this way.'

'But dragons . . . They don't exist any more. Do they? The Gases would've killed them off. Yes?'

Tab's eyes met mine. 'You've got a map showing where horses are. You're looking for horses even though they're supposed to have died out. The wolves are still as alive as they ever were. So why not dragons? Perhaps they still exist too.'

'But . . . were dragons even really real? I'm not sure they were even real in the first place.'

'I don't know what's real or not. All I do know is that there seems to be a dragon flying over the ground towards us.' He gulped. 'And it's going to be here soon.'

It was true. Smoke was still streaking away in the distance and the rumble that went with it was getting louder.

'Let's hide.' I scrambled up but Tab pulled me back down to the ground.

'No. Too late for that. It'll see us moving off. Better to stay still and hope it flies by without even noticing us.' Tab grabbed hold of Mouse and clung onto him

176

like his life depended on it. 'Come here, boy. Stop strugglin.'

The smoke moved smoothly along and above a nearby slope. The sound of the dragon puffing and panting got louder and louder and then it came into sight. A dark blue, sleek metallic-sided creature, scraping along the bottom of the ridge, its tail a long, brown squarish tube with glassy scales.

I stared harder at the dragon. No, they weren't glassy scales. They were windows.

Windows?

Suddenly the creature squealed a terrifying squeal, its whole body slowing, fighting against its own momentum.

'It's seen us!' Tab whimpered. 'It's spotted us! Run!' He dropped Mouse and scooped up the bag, stuttering to his feet before launching himself away from the monster below.

The dragon screeched and jolted to a stop just as I, half sprinting myself, noticed the wheels. Wheels beneath its torso, sitting on the tracks that ran along the valley floor. Metal wheels.

'Wait!' I stopped and turned back. 'Tab, wait!'

'Come on!' I could hear him behind me getting further and further up the bank.

'No, stop!' I shouted. 'It's not a dragon. It's a train.'

'I said come on!'

'It's a train!'

He twisted around to see. 'Hold on. That's a train.'

'I know.' We both stood still and watched as the 'dragon' hissed, the smoke from the funnel now fluffing out and floating haphazardly about the ridge. 'I said that.'

Then a man jumped out of a little black opening in the front half of the train.

'Hello!' He was waving towards us whilst behind him another man – older than the first, judging by his movements – climbed gently down the ladder and onto the side of the track. 'Hello!' the first man called again.

'Should we scarper or should we stay put?' Tab muttered out of the side of his mouth, his eyes upon me.

'Er . . .'

'Hello there!' The men started to walk up the ridge towards us.

'Stay put. I think.'

As they got closer I could see that the first man was young and slight with a brush-like moustache perched under his nose and black hair swept back over his head. The second man was thicker set and a bit rougher-looking, with a rug of curly grey hair under which sat tiny eyes. Both were wearing soot-covered overalls that reminded me of *Pb* clothes back in Lahn Dan, and, for the splittiest of split-pea seconds, my heart ached to see Gry and Bracken again. Even just to hear them arguing.

'Good afternoon! It's not very often that we see

anybody this far out east. Very rare actually. Very rare indeed. Not common at all. Especially youngsters like yourselves. You heading somewhere?' It was the younger man who did all the talking.

'West,' I said. 'We're going west.'

'West, eh?' Mouse had pattered up to the man and was sniffing about his feet. 'Hello, little chap. You heading west too?' He bent over and gave Mouse a tap on the head.

'Where you from?' It was the second man who spoke with a voice that sounded much the same as he looked. Gruff and gargly, thick with clotted cream and rolley-hilled syllables. His tiny eyes seemed suspicious and his brow furrowed with doubt. 'Ain't no settlements out this way as I know of. So where'd you come from?'

'Lahn Dan,' I replied. 'We've both come from Lahn Dan.' I cast Tab a look.

The first man pulled himself back up as Mouse moved over to sniff the feet of the second man, who promptly ignored him. 'From London, eh? Fascinating. Absolutely fascinating. Tell me, who rules London nowadays?' He said Lahn Dan the weird way that King Billy did. 'Is there a King or a Queen? We don't get much news out of London nowadays. What about your parents? Have they come with you?'

I shook my head. 'The Minister rules Lahn Dan. He's not very nice.' I could feel Tab's eyes burning into me.

'And no. Our parents aren't with us. My mama's dead and Tab's never even met his mother or father.'

'Oh, I *am* sorry.' An awkward silence. Suddenly the young man lurched forward, his hand extended. 'Sorry, I've not introduced myself. My name's Wessex. And this is Mr Trott.' The older man grunted and frowned even harder.

I reached up and lightly touched the younger man's hand. 'Serendipity,' I mumbled. 'Serendipity Goudge.'

'Delighted to meet you, Serendipity.' He turned to face Tab. 'And your name is Tab, I take it?' Tab nodded but either refused to shake the man's hand or just didn't realise that that was what he was meant to do. Either way, Wessex's hand dropped to his side pretty quickly. 'So, how far west are you travelling?'

I fiddled awkwardly with the buttons on my jacket. 'As far west as we can.'

'Oh?'

'To Whales.'

'Wales, eh? Long way to go, isn't it? What's in Wales? Family?'

'No, sir.' I cast another look towards Tab. 'Horses, sir.'

The older man gave a critical little sniff, but the eyes of the younger man lit up. 'Horses? In Wales? Really? How do you know?'

'I was told, sir. Someone in Lahn Dan.' I thought it

best not to mention the map quite yet. It didn't seem right.

'Well, well.' Wessex stroked his chin. 'Horses, eh? I can show you a horse if you like.'

My heart shot up. Had I heard him right? 'Sir?'

'It's not real,' he quickly added, and my heart shot back down. 'Goodness, no. Not real. But it is very interesting. I think you'll like it. The railway line runs straight past it – we always see it from the train, don't we, Trott? Ever ridden on a train before?'

'No, sir.'

'Then you're in for a treat. Grab your things and we'll stuff them in the coach.'

The two men lifted the bikes into the coach behind the steam engine and propped our bags onto velvety red seats. Peering down the carriage I noticed boxes of old tins and tubs, some types of food that I recognised – like tinned potatoes and rubbery red beans – and others that I didn't. There were other more industrial-looking things too – rotary blades and long metal arms and big shiny scoops for machines of some sort.

'Been stocking up,' Wessex said when he spotted me staring. 'Essentials for back home.'

It was decided that Mouse would be safest shut inside the coach. The engine itself had no doors and Mouse could easily have skittered out which, when the train was moving, Wessex explained, would not be a good thing. Tab reluctantly agreed and the scruffy mutt was locked inside. I half expected to hear him whine and bark, desperate to get back to his master. But instead I saw him bounce onto the soft scarlet seats and curl himself into a sleepy ball. I think all that keeping up with the bikes had finished him off.

We climbed the ladder into the cabin of the engine, Trott's untrusting eye watching us all the while. The first thing that struck me was how unbearably hot it was – hot like a swoop past the sun. I felt like dropping on the floor. Tab noticed it too and he huffed and puffled and rubbed the sleeve of his shirt over his head.

'Yes. It is a bit hot. Takes some getting used to, I'm afraid.'

Behind us, coal was spilling out all over the floor. Lots of it. Lots and lots and lots of it. I thought back to the Professor's sorry hearth with its meagre lumps sparingly used on the half-hearted flames. What he would give for such a hoard.

'Steam up yet, Trott?'

'Not yet, sir. Lost some power when we stopped.' His eyes darted back accusingly at me and Tab. 'Need to build it up.'

The two men reached around, picked up scruffy shovels and starting throwing coal through a small hole, beyond which a fire was roaring away like the end of the world. They twisted from left to right, their tops swivelling back and forth as they scooped up the coal and threw it into the stove before going back for more. The fire grew brighter and angrier.

'Want a go?' Wessex held up his spade to Tab who gingerly took it from him and attempted to take over where the young man had left off. Unfortunately Tab stabbed hopelessly away at the coal, making far too much of it spill out onto the floor and getting very little of it onto the spade.

'Not like that. Like this,' Trott growled. 'Get more on your shovel, boy. Get a real great load of it in at once.' Trott demonstrated. 'We'll never get moving again if we leave it to you.'

Tab handed the spade back to Wessex who smiled warmly at him before filling the firebox with even more fire.

After a few minutes, they threw the shovels aside and Wessex pulled onto a lever. 'Here we go.'

Slowly – inchingly slowly – the train eased forward and then, a jerk as the engine tugged on the carriage behind. I thought I could hear Mouse bark but quickly forgot as the train gathered speed. Hissing and puffing, you could barely hear yourself sneeze, and the wheels beneath turned quicker and quicker, the *rat-a-tat rat-a-tat* rhythm getting faster and faster.

'Good, eh?' Wessex shouted, looking like a little boy who'd just found a ball.

And it was. I'd never stood anywhere quite so filthy and noisy and hot and airless before, and the countryside rolled past like a smudge and the train itself felt like it could rattle itself to pieces at any moment. But it was fantastic. Exciting. Exhilarating. The thought that we were moving faster than I'd ever moved before – even faster than the modpod out of Lahn Dan – made me oddly light-headed.

'How fast are we going?' I eventually barked at Wessex as Trott fed the train's glaring red mouth with more coal.

'What?'

'How . . . fast . . . are . . . we . . . going?'

He leaned across me and tapped a little dial. The pointy hand inside quivered a bit. 'Sixty. Sixty-two. That kind of thing.'

'Sixty?'

'Miles per hour, yes. Good, isn't it?'

I nodded and turned to look at Tab, expecting to see my excitement mirrored on his face. But instead he looked pale and petrified, his arms clinging desperately to a pole running from the floor to the ceiling.

'You all right?' I mouthed. He shook his head and shut his eyes tight as though hoping to make everything go away.

*   *   *

The train slowed to little more than a roll.

'There it is.' Wessex pointed.

'Where?'

'Over there.'

It wasn't clear. The grass had grown up too high but I could just about make it out. A weirdly thin and wiry shape, curving around to the squarish head. Not exactly *healthy* horse shaped, more *starving* horse shaped. As though the horse hadn't been fed for a month or two and you could see its ribs prodding out of its belly.

'It's called the Uffington Horse.'

Tab leaned forward. 'The uffing puff horse?'

'Uffington,' Wessex corrected him. 'Been there for thousands of years. They say it was carved into the ground by a local tribe to show that the land belonged to them. Not much use now, of course.' His eyes looked sad.

'They must have loved horses,' I spoke mostly to myself. 'They must have loved horses to have cut one into a mountain like that.' I felt like I'd felt all that time ago in the Gallery Market, seeing Whistlejacket. Amazed and happy but also a bit sad that Mama wasn't with me.

Wessex nodded. 'You're right, Serendipity. They must have done. Worshipped them probably. Thought them on a par with the highest of gods.'

Who was the God Man? I imagined him a ghostly king, peering down at us all from the clouds. Was my mama up there with him? Could she see me now? Did she still click her tongue when I forgot to wash my hands?

22

Ashdown

Not that far from the Uffington Horse, Trott made the train slow down and let it totter itself to a stop just past a road bridge. As the engine gave its final dying lurch, Tab's arms seemed to miraculously separate from the stick of metal about which they'd been wrapped for the last hour or two.

'There we are.' Wessex grabbed a dirty rag and started wiping his hands. 'This is where we get off.'

Trott tugged on a few things and threw water into the firebox before straightening up the shovels and the supply of coal.

I looked outside.

'Where are we?'

'A few miles north of Ashdown.'

'Ashdown?'

Trott spun around to glare at me. 'His Lordship's ancestral home, of course.'

Lordship?

'Don't forget Mouse.' It was only the second time

that Tab had spoken since boarding the train. 'He'll be scared left alone back there.' His voice seemed to stutter and squeak.

Trott clambered down the ladder with Wessex close behind. They lowered both Tab and me to the ground and the cool air hit my face for the first time in however long. Wessex walked back to the carriage and popped open one of the doors.

'Out you come, chappie.'

Mouse jumped out, his tail quivering like a twig in the breeze as he skittered happily around the young man's legs. He didn't even seem to notice Tab who, obviously feeling a bit put out by the attention Wessex was getting from the flaky mutt, stepped forward and called out to his dog.

'Oy! Mousie.'

Mouse stopped suddenly, looking as though he was thinking hard about who his master was, before scampering over to Tab's feet. Tab bent over and gave Mouse a tiny tap on the head. 'You awright, boy?'

'We'll leave all this now, Trott.' Wessex indicated the carriage full of supplies behind him. 'Let's get back to Ashdown and get tidied up.'

'Yes, sir.'

'And besides.' He turned and grinned at Tab and myself. 'We have guests.'

Trott tried unsuccessfully not to sigh. 'Yes, sir. Of course, sir.'

Some steps to the side of the bridge led up onto the road above and there, sitting on the verge, was a modpod. I recognised it – I had seen pictures of them before, but to see one in the shiny metal flesh was something else altogether. A car. A really, really old car from the beginning of time. It had a soft, floppy roof, a running board, a spare tyre fixed to its backside and large, glarey lights that looked a little like shocked opened eyes. And it was pitchetty black, glossy and solid-looking – not like the weak and white plastic modpods that *Au*s drove back in Lahn Dan. They always had the look of something that would snap in two if they went over a dodgy manhole cover. But this . . . this was built to last. And it *had* lasted. A couple of hundred years by my reckoning.

'Nice wheels,' Tab whistled, sounding like he was merely repeating something that he had heard somebody else say.

'You like cars, Tab? Know much about them?' Wessex pulled the driver's door open and gestured to everyone to get in. Trott eased himself old-mannishly into the passenger seat, while I climbed into the back and waited for Tab and Mouse to join me.

'Er . . .' Tab hesitated. 'I wouldn't say I was an expert, you know . . . but . . . er . . . yeah. Yeah, I like cars.'

189

Mouse leapt onto the seat beside me as Tab got in next to him and slammed the door to.

'That dog is going to make a right mess of the upholstery, sir. You do realise that, don't you?' Trott cast yet another critical glance over his shoulder at us. 'Filthy paws like his. Take weeks to get the leather buffed up nice, it will.'

'Oh, don't moan on so, Trott.' Wessex started the engine up and the car rumbled beneath us.

'Two hundred years old,' Wessex tossed the statement over his shoulder to us. 'Bought by my great-great-great . . .' He quietly counted in his head. 'Yes, that's right, my great-great-great grandfather. Each generation has tried to take good care of her. Got a bit neglected around the time of the Gases, of course. Bit of rust, and all that.'

'*Her?*'

'Yes. Her. Old Gussie. That's what we call her.'

Tab gave a wrinkled-face sort of snort and looked at me with 'They're mad' eyes. I slapped him hard on the legs.

'Whadya do –'

'I think it's lovely,' I spat out as swiftly as I could to smother his protests. 'Giving your car a name. Very . . . nice. Old Gussie. I like it.'

The car seemed to speed up as we wheeled down the narrow lanes, our bodies jerking from one side to

190

the other as Wessex twitched the wheel in his hands, negotiating bend after bend.

'My great-great-great grandfather christened her. It's stuck ever since. Trott does most of the maintenance on her now, don't you, Trott?' Trott didn't answer. 'But she takes a lot of love and attention and, as you can imagine, we have to be careful about how we use the petrol. We can't just go –'

'Look out!'

Both my voice and the truck came from nowhere. Wessex spun the wheel hard to avoid hitting the large, white modpod and it swept past us, bumping badly along the verge before crashing down into the ditch on the opposite side of the track. Wessex managed to hit the brake just in time as a rickety wall made out of slate hurtled towards Old Gussie. He pulled the car back onto the road with just the slightest of scrapes to the front and a terrible-sounding screech from the tyres.

As the car shuddered to a halt, all of us sat there for a second or two, stunned at what had just happened. I looked down at my hands to see that they were shaking and I could see that Tab's hands were quavering too. Trott's mouth was as wide open as his eyes and Wessex's fingers were white with fear as he hunched over the steering wheel. Only Mouse seemed unfazed by the incident and he jumped back up onto the rear seat and sniffed at his master's face, licking enquiringly.

'Everyone . . . everyone okay?' Wessex turned to look us over. 'Anyone hurt?'

I shook my head. So did Tab.

'You all right, sir?' Trott pulled his lips back together. 'You all right?'

'Yes . . . yes . . . I'm . . . But wait –' Wessex pulled the door open and started to climb out of his seat.

'No! Don't!' Tab cried, fixing us all to the spot. 'It's them!'

I twisted my neck, which felt horridly stiff, and looked out of the back window to see the transporter that we'd only just managed to avoid. Steam was rising out of the buckled front end and one of the rear wheels was spinning slowly, inches above the ground.

'What?' Wessex looked confused.

'It's them,' Tab repeated. His eyes stared imploringly at me. 'The Minister's men.'

I looked again. Tab was right. It was one of the Minister's modpods from Lahn Dan. A second, sudden spasm of panic ran up through my chest.

'But they might be hurt.' Wessex seemed to shrug off his confusion. 'They need help.'

Wessex nodded to Trott and Trott popped open his own door, stepping out into the country lane.

'Serendipity!' Tab clawed at my arm. 'We need to get away.'

Wessex and Trott were marching up to the truck when –

WHOOSH.

The two men were knocked backwards as the front of the vehicle erupted in a tornado of flame.

'We've got to help them,' I cried as I scrambled out of the car. 'They're trapped inside! We've got to help them!'

'But . . .'

I ran up to the transporter. Through the cracked glass, I could just make out the driver, his head leaning to the side, blood trickling down his forehead. I reached towards the handle to open the door but it was too hot. Looking around I could see the thin oily rag hanging out of the back of Wessex's overalls. I grabbed it and put it over the handle before yanking hard. One pull, two pulls, three pulls and it opened up. The driver started to fall out and I tried to catch him but he was too heavy for me and knocked me over, the two of us rolling clumsily to the ground. Wessex and Trott meanwhile had picked themselves up from the ground and lifted the driver off me.

'There are more in the back!' I scrambled up and raced past them to the door at the rear. 'They'll be trapped.' I jerked hard at the door handle but nothing happened. I tried again – but nothing. The fire from the engine was raging even harder now and the smell of burning plastic was choking the air in the lane. Wessex and Trott had dragged the driver across the tarmac, and

I punched, kicked and pulled the door handle until my knuckles were raw.

And then it dawned on me. A lock in the driver's cabin. A button to be pressed to release the locks on the doors. I ran back to the front and was greeted by a wall of tremendous heat as I sprang through the open door and into the driver's seat.

'Wait! What are you doing?' Wessex shouted up at me.

Smoke was starting to billow into the cabin, making me cough. My hand searched along the dashboard for any button that I could find. It was red hot and the tips of my fingers felt like they were being roasted off. The windscreen cracked then cracked again as the flames outside licked and flickered over it and the mirrors to the side started to drip with molten plastic. As the smoke got more and more thick and it got harder and harder to see, my burning hands dipped under the steering wheel and found it. A button. I pushed and felt it click. A second or so later I could hear a whirring noise coming from behind me. I'd done it! I'd opened the back door to the modpod.

Stumbling down from the truck, retching from the black smoke, I noticed Trott run to the slowly opening rear as Wessex continued to drag the unconscious driver to the other side of the road.

'There's no one there,' Trott called towards us. 'There's no one in there.'

Part of me felt pleased. Pleased that there wasn't anybody injured – or worse – in the back of the truck. But another part of me was annoyed. Cheesified off that I'd just risked my life for an empty modpod.

'Look!' Tab had got out of the car and was pointing at the modpod. We all turned to Tab before looking back at it. The fire had blistered its way through to the driver's cabin. Where I had been sitting just a few seconds before was a thundering mass of flame.

'We need to get away. Quickly,' Wessex shouted at us all. 'Trott, start the car up. You two,' he looked towards Tab and then me, 'get in.' He pulled the driver's body awkwardly around to the passenger's seat and pushed him in as Trott, Tab and myself clambered into Old Gussie. Shutting the door on the car, Wessex tapped on the roof, and positioned himself on the running board.

'Go, go, go!'

Trott's foot hit the floor and the car lurched forward. Not half a second later, a gigantic explosion seemed to lift us off the tarmac and throw us further along the road. Trott swerved to control the vehicle, before stabbing at the brakes with his feet. Wessex stumbled and fell from the running board, rolling a little towards the slate wall.

For a moment everything was still. All that could be heard was the roar of the fire behind us and Wessex picking himself up from the ground.

'I'm sorry, sir,' Trott called through the window. 'I'm sorry about that. I didn't mean to do it, sir. Are you all right, sir?'

Wessex was dusting himself down. 'I'm fine, Trott. I'm fine.' There was some annoyance in his voice – not for what had occurred, I thought, but for Trott's over-bearing concern. 'Don't worry.'

'Is he dead?' Tab jabbed a finger at the man slumped in the passenger seat.

'No.' Wessex leaned in through the open window. 'But I think we'd better get him back to Ashdown as quickly as possible.'

'You as well.' Tab nodded his head towards my hand and I looked down at it. The skin on the palm was black and swollen and it was only then that I realised I was in a lot of pain.

The road that seemed to wind from the gates to Ashdown House itself passed exquisitely lined trees on sentry duty for what seemed like miles. Suddenly a wall of hedgerow loomed up in front of us like the Emm Twenty-five Wall – only greener. Wessex steered us through a small gap in it before weaving left then right, then left again. On either side of us the hedgerow blocked out most of the sun, so he switched on the big, glowy lights to see where he was taking us. Meanwhile, my hand throbbed in and out of hot agony and I bit my tongue to try to keep it under control.

'What is this?' Tab asked, his eyes swerving from one window to the other.

'Maze,' Wessex replied. 'Security. Only a handful of us know the route through.'

'Security? Against what?' Tab looked nervous.

'Raiders.' Trott was the one to answer, and the way he looked us up and down for the millionth time that day made us realise that that was precisely what he thought we were. Raiders. Come to help ourselves to whatever we could get away with. Best not to tell them that Tab was a smuggler, I thought to myself.

We turned sharply left then another left then a sudden right until, eventually, the darkness of the trees opened up and a house stood slap-bang on display in the middle. It was grubby white with wet-weather weathering and dusty-looking windows dotted evenly about its face. And it was big. Big enough to house lots of families and their dogs.

Old Gussie rolled around the wide crunching circular driveway and stopped outside the tall steps to the front entrance. A youngish woman came running down the steps and opened up the driver's door.

'Oh, my!'

'It's all right, Molly.' Wessex straightened out of the driver's seat. 'Nothing to be alarmed by. We have some

197

guests, two of whom require some immediate medical attention. Ask one of the boys to cycle down to Dr Buxton's house, there's a dear. Tell him to come as soon as he can.'

The young woman ran back inside and Wessex waved us out of the car.

'Welcome to Ashdown.'

Tab gave a little whistle as he stared up at the stately home in front of him. 'Must costa fortune to keep this place runnin.'

Wessex smiled but Trott glared hard.

'You watch yer tongue, young un. Have some respect.'

'I was only –'

'I'm afraid Tab does just tend to say the first thing that catapults itself into his head.' I tried to soften Trott down a bit. 'It does get on your nerves sometimes.'

'Oy.'

Wessex grinned to himself as Trott gave a dismissive *tut* and helped him lift the Minister's police man out of the car. With an arm over each of their shoulders they carried him up the steps, Tab and I following close behind.

'Whadya wanna go say that for?' Tab spat.

'Because it's true, perhaps?'

'What? I get on your nerves? Cheers. Thanks for the vote of confiduns.'

'Look, Tab. Mr Trott doesn't seem to like us very much for some reason.'

'Yeah. Miserable old sod, aint he?'

'So,' I continued, 'it might be better for you to keep some of your ideas to yourself. Just some of the time. Just until he knows he can trust us.'

'Hmmph.' We got to the top of the steps and Wessex pushed the large oak door open. 'But what about *him*?' Tab said, pointing his finger at the slouching body between Wessex and Trott. 'What are we going to do about him?'

'I don't know.' I shook my head. 'The thing I don't understand is, where were the rest of them? Why wasn't there anyone in the back of the modpod? What –'

'Whoa!' Tab's eyes widened as we entered the enormous hallway, and I elbowed him in the ribs to try to shut him up. He took the painful hint and swallowed down whatever he was about to say. I wished I hadn't done it – my hand hurt at the sudden jolt and I tried to wince it away.

The hallway was beautiful – far more dazzling than Bucknam Place. A colossal dark wooden staircase seemed to roll down into the room, spiralling a little as it got to the bottom. Paintings of darkly impressive men and women were hung on the walls, and wooden panels gave the hallway a slight echoey feel. Even the floor beneath us sounded clipped and important. Suddenly a door to the left flew open and in rushed another young woman. She had long, blonde hair that

199

seemed to float behind her as she walked, and she was dressed in a flowing, dreamy sort of dress that brought a small rustling into the room. Her face was thin and sculpted with smooth, pale skin and her fingers were long and delicate. Back in Lahn Dan, I thought to myself, she would be an *Au*.

'Roger,' she sounded worried. 'I just spoke to Molly. Who are these people?' She stared hard at Tab and me before addressing Wessex once again. 'And what is wrong with this man? What has happened, Roger?'

'Oh, nothing to worry yourself with, dear.' He struggled under the weight of the unconscious driver. 'Just a little accident.'

'An accident?'

'Just,' he replied quickly, 'a little one. Nothing much. Nothing much at all.'

'Mr Trott?' She turned to stare Trott directly in the face.

'Er . . . Nothing much, ma'am. Er . . .'

'Has my husband been driving that stupid car of his too fast again?'

'Er . . .' Trott looked about the place hoping for somebody to come and rescue him. 'Er . . .'

'It wasn't entirely your husband's fault.' I stepped forward.

The woman looked at me and then turned back to her husband. 'Oh, so it wasn't *entirely* your fault, Roger?'

'No, miss,' I carried on. 'This man here was driving just as fast as your husband.'

'Yeah. Only in the opposite direction, see?' Tab joined in, his hands wrapped around the dirty mess that was Mouse.

'So, if anything, they should both take the blame. Equally.'

The woman's eyes twitched between her husband and me. '*I'll* decide if my husband should be blamed for anything. Not two strange children I've never met before.' She was cold and tough and made Mr Trott look like a teddy bear. 'Roger, why have you brought these people here? You know what we said about outsiders . . .'

'Yes, yes, my dear. But look . . . they need help.'

'Because of your silly car.' She sighed. 'Really, Roger, I wish you would take things a little more seriously. You just can't bring outsiders into Ashdown.' Her eyes darted over me and Tab. 'It's dangerous.'

'Well, perhaps let's worry about that later, dear. Firstly, I think we need to take this poor man upstairs to one of the rooms to be cleaned up and put to bed. Molly should be sending someone down to the village to fetch Dr Buxton. With some luck, he shouldn't be too long. You might want to give our other two guests some food, eh?' And with that, Wessex and Trott lumbered towards the stairs, carrying the man between them.

'Guests? Huh!' Mrs Wessex looked disbelievingly at us before turning away and walking out through a door.

I looked at Tab and Tab looked at me. 'Should we follow her?' I asked.

'The man said summat about food. So yeah. We'd better follow her.'

We went through the door, down a long corridor and into the kitchen where the girl Molly was busy stirring a large pot and rocking a baby with her free arm. Mrs Wessex took the bulbous baby off the girl and cradled it protectively in her own arms.

'Molly,' she said, her eyes never leaving us, 'give these two . . . people . . . some of the soup you've been making. And perhaps a slice of bread.'

'Yes, miss.'

'And I suppose you'd better take some up to their father.'

'Oh no, he's not our father,' I said almost instinctively.

'Who is he then?'

Tab stepped forward. 'No one. He's . . . er . . . no one. Well, I mean he's someone . . . but he's no one to us.'

Mrs Wessex pulled the child closer to her and narrowed her eyes suspiciously. 'I don't understand.'

'Perhaps we'd better introduce ourselves,' I replied, sighing. 'This is Tab and his dog Mouse. And I'm Serendipity.' I held my hand out for her to shake.

'Oh my goodness!' Her face changed suddenly as she saw my hand. 'Your hand is burned.' She put the baby into a basket on the floor. 'Molly, a large bowl of water and towels please.' She came up to me and took me by the wrist. 'You must be in tremendous pain.'

To be honest, I had sort of forgotten the pain in the excitement of the moment. It seemed to have calmed down to a kind of dull thud and was probably more irritating than painful now.

'It's okay, miss. Nothing much.'

She gave me a hard glare. 'No, it's not okay. If you don't treat this burn straight away you could lose the use of your hand.'

'Really?'

'Yes, really. We need to clean it up and get it covered immediately.' Mrs Wessex looked up from my hand and stared deep into my eyes. 'My name's Lillibeth, by the way. Lily for short.'

Dr Buxton arrived late that afternoon with a bag stuffed to the top with herbs. He strapped some over the palm of my freshly washed hand before disappearing up the stairs to the room where the driver was recovering. After some time he came back down.

'He'll be okay, Lily. A bad cut to his forehead, some severe bruising and slight concussion, but nothing more. Apply the cold poultice to the cut every few hours, and brew him some of this.' He handed over a bag of what appeared to be leaves. They had a strong, sickly odour and Tab pinched the end of his nose with his fingers. 'He should drink it twice a day for the next couple of days. It will balance his aura.'

'Thank you, Jeremy.' Mr Wessex patted the doctor on the arm.

'Yes, thank you for coming out at such short notice.' Lily stood next to her husband. She was a good inch or two taller than him. 'Good of you.'

'Not a problem.' He stopped as he reached the front door, and turned ominously. 'There was . . . one other thing. I wasn't sure I should mention it but . . .' His eyes flicked back to where Tab and I stood. 'This chap upstairs. He was wearing a uniform?'

'Yes?'

'Well,' his voice slipped into a whisper, 'two men wearing exactly the same uniform were making enquiries in the village earlier today. They were asking about . . .' His eyes shot back to us. 'They were asking about a young boy and girl. And an old man. Wondering whether anyone had seen them.'

'Oh, yes?'

'They were walking from house to house. Knocking on each door. Naturally, nobody had seen anything . . . up to then. Er . . .' He looked awkwardly at the husband and wife.

'I think,' Lily started, 'it's probably best, Dr Buxton, that *still* nobody has seen anything.'

'Yes, Lily.' He nodded.

'Should these men come back to the village, it might be best to send them away. Yes? You know our views on outsiders.'

'Understood. Well, I bid you goodnight, Mr Wessex. Mrs Wessex.' The heavy door slammed to behind him.

The air seemed thick and sticky in the hallway as the silence fell and I thought it best if I stepped forward. 'I can explain,' I started.

'I'm sure you can,' Mrs Wessex said. 'And you definitely *will* explain everything to us – I shall make sure of it. But not tonight. Tonight I am rather tired and we've all had a strange and busy day, so it will have to wait until morning. Mr Trott will show you to your rooms.'

'What about Mouse?' Tab asked. 'Where's he gonna sleep?'

'I thought Molly might make him up a bed in the kitchen.'

'But I aint never spent a night away from him.' Tab looked like he might just be on the edge of tears. 'Tell yer what, missus. I'll sleep in the kitchen with him. On the floor, like. Yeah, that's what I'll do.'

'No, no. I'm sure Mouse can sleep upstairs with Tab, eh Lily?' Mr Wessex gave his wife a gentle nudge with his elbow. 'No harm in him sleeping upstairs, eh?'

Lily Wessex sighed, giving her husband a bit of a stare. 'No. I suppose not.'

Tab was taken aback. 'Oh. Thank you. Thank you very much, missus. Very kind.' Then he whistled. An ear-quaking sort of whistle that made Mr Wessex's tired eyes bound open, and Mouse came running, slipping, sliding around the corner and jumped up into Tab's arms.

Mr Trott was waiting for us at the top of the first flight of stairs and as Tab and I started ascending, he turned his back and trudged off ahead of us, around a bend and down a corridor. We sped up and ran alongside him, at which point he stopped dead and glared viciously at both of us.

'I don't knows what you're up to. Not yet I don't. But,' his finger jabbed towards us, 'I knows you're up to something. Knew it from the moment I set eyes on you. Untrustworthy. Thieves, more'n likely. Thieves and vagabonds. Here to take advantage of his Lordship. Out to get what you can from him. Mrs Wessex can see it too. Sneaky sort of raiders from Bristol, I'll bet. Been taught new tricks by your masters.' He scowled even harder, his voice dipped even lower and his eyes looked even nastier. 'But I tells you one thing. That man who's sleeping in the room down there, one day soon he's going to wake up and remember who he is. And just after he remembers who he is, he'll remember why it is he's chasing you. From what Dr Buxton just said, sounds like there are some of his friends floating around the place. If he can't remember, I'm sure they can.'

He straightened up and went back to his usual level of volume. 'You,' he stabbed his finger at Tab, 'in there.' He indicated a door. 'You,' he twirled his finger in my direction, 'there.' He gave a horrible sneer. 'Sleep tight now, won't you?'

23

Saddles and Books

I did sleep tight, as a matter of fact. It was nice lying in a bed not covered in the dust of a hundred years, and the sheets were slippery silky and cobweb light. I dreamt of nothing in particular and only woke when the sun was burning hard through the window, prising open my eyes.

I washed in the neat bathroom attached to my room before wandering down to the kitchen. The only people in there were Mrs Wessex and the baby. The baby was strapped in a tall chair whilst Mrs Wessex spooned a sort of grey gooey substance into his mouth. Most of it seemed to be on his chin.

She looked unsmilingly at me as I came in, before leaning close to the child and pulling a silly, pouty kind of face. The baby gurgled back appreciatively, dribbling more of the food onto its chest.

'Where is everyone?' I asked, looking around.

'The boy and his dog got up early and went with Roger to the train. They're bringing back the supplies they picked up yesterday.'

'Oh.' I suddenly felt a bit put out. What was Tab doing going off without me?

'They'll be back sometime this morning. That is if Roger doesn't get too distracted showing him an internal combustion engine or some such thing. Mr Trott is upstairs trying to give that man some breakfast.' My heart slipped. 'I suppose you'd better eat something yourself.' On the table sat plates dotted with the remnants of breakfast. Some crumbly toast, juicy sausages, streaky bacon and dark golden eggs all waiting to be finished up. I grabbed a plate and filled it. Mrs Wessex got up and charged a cup with milk from a jug before plonking it roughly down on the table beside me.

As I stuffed my mouth, I remembered the night before. The doctor looking over at us, Trott pointing his finger. A slight sense of guilt slowed my chewing so I could speak through my food.

'Mrs Wessex.'

'Hmm?' She'd given up on feeding the child – who, now I noticed him, looked like a tiny babyish version of his dad – and was wiping spittle and bubbles of breakfast from her own hands.

'Last night. I need to explain.'

'I was wondering when you'd start.'

I set down my knife and fork and began to explain. Everything. Well, nearly everything. I told her about Lahn Dan and the Minister and the Professor and the police men. I told her about Mordecai and Caritas and the *Au*s and *Pb*s. I told her about Mama and the map and the horses. The only thing I left out was about Tab being a smuggler. I thought it best not to give Mr Trott any more ammunition to fire him up.

After what felt like an hour, I shut my gob up, grabbed the fork and poked away awkwardly at the last few strands of egg white. Mrs Wessex drained the last of her tea.

'So you're not from Bristol, then?'

'What? What's Bristle?'

She gave a small smile. 'Bristol is a city, over the hills in that direction. The people who live there sometimes like to come over the hills and raid our stores. We grow our own food, you see. They don't. They prefer to just steal it. There's a lot less work involved in stealing it.' Tab once again leapt into my head. 'We have to defend ourselves against them. That's sort of why we grew the maze around the house. In case they ever try to attack Ashdown.'

I nodded and laid my knife and fork flat on the plate.

'After breakfast,' Mrs Wessex said suddenly, standing up, 'I like to take Lysander out for some fresh air. Would you care to join us?'

'I lost my mother when I was young too.' Lily Wessex watched where her feet were treading, the baby strapped to his mother's front in a sort of back-to-front rucksack thing, his little limbs dangling out and his head flopping from side to side. 'Younger than you, even. My father brought me up on his own.'

We had come outside of the maze and were picking our way across the grounds towards a small patch of trees at the rear of the house. The grass was dullish green and stony, and tiny, aggressive weeds knotted the way.

'What happened to her?'

'Oh, just sickness. You know. The Gases. People did that a lot back then – just die suddenly. Not quite so bad nowadays. Of course, having children,' she patted the bobbing baby on the bottom, 'is still difficult. We were lucky, though. Tried for ages to no avail and then, all of a sudden . . . Well . . . We were lucky, Roger and I. Lucky.'

I thought back to the smugglers and their tents. No children. Except Tab, that is. No children at all. Only adults.

'But in Lahn Dan there are lots of children,' I muttered, more to myself than to Mrs Wessex. 'In the storytelling sessions there are always lots of children.'

'I suppose,' she replied, 'there are probably more people, full stop, in London than there are out here. More chance of there being lots of children, you think?'

I shrugged as we made our way through the dark clump of trees. As my hand brushed the bark I noticed that they felt different to the trees I was used to in Lahn Dan. These felt more . . . alive. Not just brittle, peeling, barely breathing stumps. These were strong and solid. Trees that were still fighting to live. Tying the earth together with their roots.

Eventually the trees stopped. Suddenly. Like a brick wall that somebody had given up on building – and we stepped out into the brightness of the morning again. On this side of the wood the grass was slightly browner and obviously hadn't been cut for a very long time. We had to lift our legs higher to step through the clearing and, as we did so, I spotted a long, low construction a hundred yards or so away from us.

'What's that?' I asked, pointing. 'That building over there?'

'Those haven't been used for a long, long time.'

'Why not?'

'They're the stables.'

I had never smelled a horse before. Nor had Mrs Wessex. So neither of us knew if the scent filling our nostrils in that dark, wet outhouse was the smell of a horse or just something else. Years of rot or rat droppings, maybe. But as I stood there, sucking up the musty, chocolatey aroma, I told myself – persuaded my brain to believe – that it was definitely the smell of a horse. I imagined a big, velvety chestnut thing with a long, wavy mane and a neat, sweeping tail. A Whistlejacket. Trotting into his stable on the cold winter nights, nuzzling hay, dreaming of fields of praise. His master, a loving man with rough hands and a kind face.

'These were the reins.' She lifted some leather straps off a hook on the wall. 'You'd put them around the head so that you could ride the horse properly. And this,' she threw the reins down over a glossy black seat, itself thrown over a large wooden block, 'is the saddle. The seat, if you like.'

I ran my hand over the cracked, slightly gritty saddle. Who knew what horses it had sat on. Who knew what riders had slipped their feet into the silver stirrups that drooped below. I patted it like you'd pat a horse and it sounded dense yet hollow.

'Is it true?' Mrs Wessex repositioned the baby trussed to her chest. 'Do you think there are horses still alive somewhere?'

I nodded. 'I hope so.'

'Yes. So do I.' She looked sad all of a sudden and stroked Lysander's face with her finger. 'I imagine them to be beautiful things. Strong. Useful, too. A few horses pulling ploughs on the village farms would be more reliable than tractors that chew through diesel and constantly break down, needing new parts. Much more natural. Roger always has to go searching for them, you know? Tractor parts. That's what he was doing yesterday. Getting a sprocket or a shaft or a whizzybung or whatever the hell they're called.' She sighed. 'The people in the three villages all look to Roger, you see. Always have done. Even before Roger they looked to his father and his father's father before that. Looked to them for leadership.' She gave her head a shake as though clearing the unintentional thoughts out of her head. 'Anyway . . . Enough of that.' She picked the reins up from the saddle and slipped them back onto the hook like they should always be kept there. 'These horses wouldn't have been working horses. They would have been kept for pleasure. Roger's family used to hunt, you see.'

'Hunt?' I squinted at her. 'Hunt what?'

'Foxes. With hounds.'

'Hounds?'

'Dogs, if you like.'

'What? Like Mouse?'

'Well,' Lily smiled, 'perhaps not *quite* like Mouse. The hounds would sniff out the fox and the riders would chase behind. Then, when the hounds had cornered the fox, they would attack and kill it.'

'The riders?'

'No, no. The dogs.'

I weighed it all over in my mind. Hunters that didn't hunt. What was the point in that? Why not just ride without having to have something killed? Was

214

that the way mankind worked – always destroying, always killing?

I stood there in the silence for a second or two. 'It sounds horrible.'

'I know,' Mrs Wessex agreed.

'People in the old days were such idiots, weren't they?' I said, my voice quivering with anger.

'Perhaps,' she said softly, squeezing Lysander's hand. 'But we weren't there, so we don't really know. All we can hope for is that people in the future think better of *our* actions.'

They'll think better of *mine*, I told myself, still upset about the foxes. I'll make sure of it.

The bandages on my hand were bound tight and thick and I found it difficult to wiggle my fingers back and forth because of them. Twice a day they had to be changed, refreshed with a new smear of herbs. Mrs Wessex helped me to do it, gently unravelling the cloth, washing the burns with cool water and applying the herbs before wrapping my hand with a new dressing. It was after one such change that Mrs Wessex led me into a room tucked away in the corner of the building.

She pushed open the door and I was hit by an eruption of sunlight burning its way through the large, wide window. It took me a moment or so before my eyes grew accustomed to the brightness, then, looking around

215

the room, I could see books. Hundreds of them. Queued up on shelves that went right the way around the walls. I'd never seen so many of them. Even the ones in the Professor's office were nothing compared with this. There were big books and little books, thin books and fat books, stuffy-looking books with glossy leather spines and papery-looking books held together with creases. The walls were made of them.

'Do you read?' Mrs Wessex came alongside me.

'No.'

'You don't read?' She looked amazed.

'I'm afraid not. They never taught us properly in Lahn Dan.'

'Criminal. Absolutely criminal. Everyone should know how to read. It is a basic human right. How on earth do you manage?' I shrugged. 'It must make things very difficult.'

'I don't know. I just sort of get by – piece a few letters together. If you've never had something, I don't suppose you ever miss it.'

'But you are going in search of horses, are you not?' Her eyes narrowed and stared at me. 'And, of course, you've never seen a *real* horse before.' There was more of a question in that last sentence than a sentence.

She had a point.

'You've . . . er . . . you've got a lot of books.'

She pointed across the room. 'Third shelf down,

several books in from the left. A red-spined one. Do you see it?'

I wandered across the room to where she had pointed. 'There are a couple of them with red spines.'

'The one I am after has a gold embossed picture of a horse's head on the front.' She clipped over the wooden floor and joined me.

We tipped them out of the shelf individually. The third book I looked at had the horse's head. I pulled it out completely and turned to Mrs Wessex, who smiled.

'Can you read the title?' she asked.

I stared at the ornate lettering on the cover. 'Er . . . Bl . . . Black, is it?'

'Good.'

'Black . . . Be . . . Beau . . . I'm not sure.'

'Beauty. *Black Beauty*. Ever heard of it?'

'No, miss.'

'It is the most famous book about a horse ever written.' I held it out to her. 'No, I don't want it. It's for you. Take it.'

'What?'

'Take it. It's yours.'

'But –'

'No buts. It's yours. With the small proviso,' she gave me a solid glare that briefly reminded me of Mama, 'that you will learn how to read it, and you will then read it through from cover to cover. Yes?'

'Er . . .'

'Yes?'

'Yes,' I submitted. 'Yes. I will.'

'In fact . . .' Mrs Wessex thought for a moment or so. 'What if *I* taught you to read?'

'Miss?'

'I could teach you to read. It will be some time before your hand is fully recovered, and in that time I could help you to start reading. It'll be fun. What do you say?'

'Er . . .' I didn't really know what to say. In Lahn Dan, reading was always thought to be unimportant. A frivolity. Was it that much different outside the city? 'Yes,' I eventually replied. 'Thank you, miss. That would be kind.'

24

A Police Man's Tale

A few days later, bleary-eyed and puffed, I stumbled out of my bedroom to find myself head to head with the Minister's police man. He looked almost as exhausted as I felt. His forehead was creased and grey and his chin was covered in scritchity scratchity growth. The silk pyjamas he was wearing looked more crumpled than any silk pyjamas had a right to be.

I froze to the spot, my insides telling me to scream. But I didn't. I let the seconds pass like forever.

But the police man didn't seem all that interested in me. He put his index finger to his lips before creeping away from me towards the end of the corridor and the top of the stairs. When he reached the corner he squatted and leaned forward, trying to hear something.

I've no idea why I did it, but I followed him. I came alongside and crouched down, my ears straining to hear.

Voices. Downstairs. At the door. One of them was Mrs Wessex's. The other . . . I struggled to catch it. It was deep and hoarse like someone who'd forgotten to drink all day.

Mordecai.

My heart squelched. I steadied myself against the wall. Seeing my reaction, the police man reached out and grabbed me by the shoulder. His hand was soft and strong. Reassuring.

I listened as hard as I could.

'. . . a girl of about twelve. And a boy with a dog. You're positive you've never seen them? Taken them in? Helped them in any way?'

'As I said before, no. I've never seen them.'

'I'd like to remind you, Mrs . . .'

'Wessex. Lady Wessex.'

'I'd like to remind you, Mrs Wessex, that these people are criminals. They've broken a number of rules of –'

'How on earth did you get through the maze?' Lily sounded flustered, like she wasn't listening properly. 'Only a few people know the way through the maze.'

'Ha!' The laugh was bitter and self-satisfied. Almost mocking. 'If you can't get around something then just cut a direct route straight through it. That's always been my opinion.'

'You've cut holes in our maze?'

'Of course. We weren't going to waste our valuable time by negotiating it, now were we? Not when we've terrorists to catch.'

'Terrorists? But you say they're children. How can children be terrorists?'

Mordecai huffled a bit. 'Terrorists come in many sizes and shapes, Mrs . . . Wessex. These particular ones recently destroyed one of my men's vehicles, killing someone in the process.'

'Mr Mordecai –'

'Commander,' Mordecai corrected her.

'Mr Mordecai,' she ignored him. 'I find your tone rather disturbing. I have not seen either of these children, so I would be grateful if you would remove your trucks and your men from my drive.' Lily Wessex tried to sound tough but I could detect the slight wobble in her voice.

'Mrs Wessex,' Mordecai hissed. 'You have a very beautiful house. A *very* beautiful house. It would be a terrible shame if something were to happen to it.'

'Is that a threat?'

'No, no, Mrs Wessex. I don't make threats. I merely make promises. Promises that I intend to keep if I discover I have been lied to.'

'Get off my doorstep.'

'Good day to you.' The smirk on Mordecai's face was easily detectable in his voice.

The door slammed shut.

The police man and I quickly raced over to the window overlooking the drive, where we saw Mordecai

221

huffling back to the modpod, his head shaking in a tightly controlled way. One of the other men gave a sort of shrug before spitting coarsely on the gravel. Another more old-fashioned transporter, was parked nearby. A few of Mordecai's police men spilled out of it and they stood about for a few seconds, talking, glancing back occasionally at the house itself. After a while, they all climbed into the two vehicles and drove off through the freshly cut hole in the wall of the maze.

'He thinks I'm dead,' the man standing next to me announced. 'He actually thinks I'm dead.' I looked up at him. On his face was stuck a ginormously ecstatic grin. 'Oh, thank the God Man for that.' He laughed out loud then turned to me. 'I'm free. At last, I'm free.'

'I'm glad.' I managed to smile, though my insides were quaking. Was this how a hunted fox felt?

It was over a late breakfast that the police man told us his story. Mr Wessex was back from his trip into one of the villages; Tab had struggled to wake himself up; Mr Trott had come in from the garden, his spadey hands all wanting a sparkle; Mrs Wessex spooning grey lumps into Lysander's dribbling mouth, and me all hunched up footwise on my chair.

The man finished his smoky coffee, leaned back in his seat and began.

'My name is Saul Knottman. I was born in Lahn Dan

and I think I'm about thirty-two years old.' His eyes dipped to his coffee and he idly twisted the cup on its saucer as he spoke. 'My father was a police man under the service of two previous Ministers of Lahn Dan, eventually reaching the rank of Sturdy Inspector. He won a great many medals for gallantry and service to the Ministry and was well-regarded amongst the entire Police Force.'

From the corner of my eye I could see Tab stifling a yawn.

'Growing up, you see, ' Knottman continued, 'what I think I'm trying to say is that . . . well . . . my father was a hero. *My* hero. So it was only natural that I should want to join the Police Force myself. That's why, on or about my fourteenth birthday, I enrolled for training.'

He gave a little grin and leaned forward, helping himself to one of the pastries on the big plate in front of him.

'I did well. Flew through all the tests they put in front of me, ticked all the right boxes, listened to all the right people. And then, after ten years of training –'

'Ten years?' Mrs Wessex dropped a lump of the grey stuff in her lap.

Knottman continued as if he hadn't heard her. '– I eventually became a Constable in the Minister's Police Force. Proudest day of my father's life, I think.

'Then my mother passed away and my father became

ill. It wasn't good. Trying to juggle the needs of an ailing parent with my responsibilities as a *Cu* . . .

'My father struggled on for some months and then . . .' Knottman paused before going on. 'Then, on the day he died – literally just a few hours before he died – he pulled me closer to him and whispered to me.

'"Don't let them trap you," he said. "Don't let them trap you like they trapped me all these years."'

Like Mama. Just like Mama before she died.

Saul continued. 'It was scary, hearing my father talk like that. The loyal soldier, the decorated public servant. Scary. And it was then that I started questioning everything. The way Lahn Daners live. The isolation. The Minister. Everything. Like a time-bomb *tick-tick-tick*ing inside my head. It was bound to go off at some point.

'So I volunteered for this job.'

'What job?' Tab's yawns were still tumbling out occasionally from his mouth.

'This one. Finding you. Or more specifically finding *you*.' His finger was pointing straight at me.

'Me?'

'You.'

'Why me?'

'I don't know. The orders from the Minister were quite specific. Find the girl. Bring her back alive.'

'What about *me*?' Tab wasn't yawning now.

Knottman paused then sighed. 'The rest of the orders were to – and I quote – *execute the boy and the old man. Leave no trace of them. Dispose of the bodies.*'

Tab gulped. 'Execute? Me?'

Knottman nodded.

'I don't understand.' I could feel my brow all furrowed as I talked. 'I don't follow. Why kill the Professor and Tab but keep me alive?'

'Make you the scapegoat, possibly. I don't know. A police man never questions their orders, I tell you. The subservient rule. The only one who possibly does know why is Commander Mordecai.'

'The man who was here this morning?' Mr Wessex asked.

Knottman nodded. 'Mordecai is one of the Minister's closest confidants. He's bound to know why we've been chasing you.'

'So . . .' Mrs Wessex steered the story back on track. 'You signed up for this particular job. Why?'

'To escape. To get away. Life in Lahn Dan has become unbearable over the last months, the hypocrisy as obvious and ridiculous as an old clown.' He paused again. 'The Minister is not a good man.'

'That morning, when we pulled you out of the modpod.' I looked at him. 'You were escaping?'

Knottman nodded again. 'I had dropped everyone

225

else off at the local villages. They were asking around. Trying to find you. Suddenly I found myself alone in the modpod. My chance had come. So I took it.'

We all sat there silently for a while, weighing up all the information, allowing our minds to digest it.

Then Knottman gave me one of his tight stares and said, 'And then you saved my life.'

'Er . . .'

'And for that I will be forever indebted to you.' He waved a pastry in the air like a sort of salute before taking a bite out of it.

25

Black Beauty

The next few days passed slickly. Knottman, Tab and myself were shown around the villages that the Wessexes were responsible for. Little clusters of houses and farms and schools and churches that were home to little clusters of people. Everyone was sworn to secrecy, of course. No one was to tell Mordecai where we were, and I could tell they were trustworthy. Everyone respected Mr Wessex and everyone would happily do what he told them to. Mr Wessex was kind of the boss. Only nice with it.

Tab and I helped out in one of the fields, spooning up potatoes with mud-clumped forks. The potatoes here were much fatter and fuller than the squiggly little ones that didn't even struggle out of the ground in Lahn Dan, and as for the carrots . . . I had always thought that carrots were a dull yellow colour, finger-thin and rubbery. But these carrots snapped in two when you snapped them in two, and had sucked up much of the orange sun that was so obvious the further west we had come. Taking a nibble out of one, you could almost feel the sunshine on your tongue. Not like the tasteless, watery Lahn Dan carrots. These carrots were flavoursome.

Knottman was especially good with machinery, helping Mr Wessex and the other men fit blades on harvesters and buckets on diggers. He knew a fantastic lot about sprockets and shafts and pistons, and his face seemed to brighten as the days clicked by and his hands got dirtier. You could tell he was enjoying himself, finding his new role much more satisfying than chasing innocent children around the countryside.

Not that we were entirely without worry, of course. We were all aware that Mordecai and his men might be prowling the area still. I hoped that perhaps they had gone further on or had even given up the chase altogether, but secretly I worried that they might be just around the corner, about to pounce. Tab thought so too, I know, but we never talked about it. Probably in case we cursed ourselves by doing so.

One morning, Knottman took me aside.

'Something I haven't told you yet – I don't know why – but before I escaped we had news from Lahn Dan.' He seemed to be talking in a whisper, despite the fact that there was nobody else around. 'There is talk of unrest.'

'Unrest?'

'A revolution. They are saying that a revolution is imminent.'

'I don't understand.'

'*Cu*s and *Pb*s are protesting on the streets. Doing things they shouldn't. Not doing the things they should. General disobedience. Naturally the Minister is trying to crush it before it begins.'

The Professor? Could it be?

Knottman swivelled his head left to right to make sure nobody was listening in. 'They are saying the story-tellers are behind it. It all started with them.'

I felt like cheering.

But I didn't. I just gave a happy little nod and continued on my way.

In the evenings Knottman, Mr Wessex and Tab tried training Mouse while Mrs Wessex helped me with my reading. It was slow at first, painfully slow. But Lily Wessex was a good teacher, surprisingly patient and particular, and after a few nights I began picking things up quicker and quicker.

Two weeks later, it was time for my first recital. That evening, after dinner, Mrs Wessex coughed and, as agreed, I stood up from my place at the table.

'Serendipity has been preparing something for us all,' she said as I bent over and scooped the book up from under my chair. 'Some entertainment.' She grinned at me.

'Oh, fantastic!' Mr Wessex seemed particularly pleased about it. Tab looked up at me with a raised eyebrow before turning back to his pudding whilst Knottman put his spoon down and sat back in his chair to take in what I was about to do.

'Er . . .' I stammered. 'Mrs Wessex gave me this book and . . . er . . . she has been teaching me to read it. She's been helping me with the first few pages. And I'd like to read them to you.'

I cleared my throat and started to read.

'"Chapter One. My Early Home. The first place that I can well . . . re . . . remember, was a large . . . pl . . . easant . . . meadow with a pond of clear water in it. Some trees . . . over . . . oversha . . . overshadowed the pond, and rushes and water . . . lilies grew at the deep end."'

And so I read on. A bit stoppy-starty, not very smooth, but I read on. About the plantation. About Beauty's mother. About how Beauty's father was a very distinguished and important horse. About the rough farmboy who throws stones and sticks at the colts for fun. All words I'd been practising with Mrs Wessex.

When I reached the end of the first chapter, I thudded the book shut. Lily Wessex gave me a wink.

'Well done!' Mr Wessex clapped his hands together. 'Very well done, Serendipity. You read that beautifully.'

Tab was staring at me, his mouth so wide open I could see the last of his pudding disappearing. Knottman nodded and smiled.

I gave an embarrassed sort of shrug. 'It wasn't that good. Some of the words are hard. You know? Difficult to say.'

'That doesn't matter,' Knottman said. 'What matters is that you read it. You read it and understood it. I wish I could read like that.'

I puffed up a little bit.

'Do you want to know what happens next?' Lily Wessex was grinning at me.

I nodded.

'I could tell you, of course. I could tell you the story of Black Beauty. Tell you everything that happens from start to finish.' She gave a mischievous grin. 'I *could* tell you,' she repeated, 'but I won't.' A flicker, a flash of fire. 'That's down to you, Serendipity. You have to find out for yourself.'

26

Too Much Comfort

The problem was that, even though Ashdown lived under the constant threat of raids from Bristle, it was all becoming too easy. It wouldn't have been difficult to just stay here in Ashdown, or to clear up one of the abandoned houses in one of the villages and to move into it. It wouldn't have been difficult to help this community with the harvesting and the food preparation and the taking care of livestock. It wouldn't have been difficult at all.

No. Strangely it was all too comfortable.

My mind kept thinking back to Mama and the Professor. I was here right now because of them both, but I still wasn't where I was supposed to be. The Professor had stepped back into Lahn Dan, letting me escape with Tab, thinking we were heading for Whales and the horses. And as for Mama, she had told me to go outside, to get away from the wall and to breathe the freeness of the air. Hiding away behind the walls of the maze would be a backwards step, surely?

It was wrong. It would feel like a kind of betrayal to them both to sit here in this place of warmth and comfort, to feel wanted and useful . . . It wasn't right. So one afternoon, after returning from the fields, I took Tab aside and told him.

'But I don't understand. I like it ere. Don't you?'

'Tab, I don't expect you to come with me. It's something I've got to do. If I stay here much longer I'm going to forget why I left Lahn Dan in the first place. Also, if I'm here Mordecai'll come back someday and I don't want Lily and Lysander being put in danger again because of me.'

'Yeah, but –'

'It's good that you've found somewhere you feel wanted. You should stay. You and Mouse.'

'But I thought you might –'

'Who knows? After I've been to Whales and seen the horses or not seen the horses or whatever, perhaps . . . perhaps I might come back. But I have to try. First I have to try.'

Later, over dinner, I told the rest of the house.

'I mean, it's not that I'm not grateful for everything – really. You've been so incredibly kind to me, and I can't thank you enough. But I think the time has come.'

I couldn't read any emotion in the Wessexes' faces. I think they were a little shocked and I started to worry

233

that perhaps I had hurt their feelings. The whole room was quiet. Not even Mouse scratched himself.

Then Lily gave a smile and a wink and I knew that everything was going to be all right.

'We understand. We knew you would have to go, Serendipity. But please remember, wherever you are, you will always be welcome here. Ashdown needs good people like you. Remember that. Good, brave people.'

'Thank you, Lily. I will.'

Mr Wessex suddenly jumped into action, his brain whirring with a plan. 'We will take you as far as we possibly can on the train. Yes, that's what we'll do. Old Gussie isn't up to the roads beyond the immediate vicinity, I'm afraid. She'll just go and shudder herself to dust. But the train . . . Yes. Mr Trott!' His head whipped around. 'Mr Trott, we still have a good supply of coal, don't we?'

'Oh yessir, still got a good lump of the stuff left.'

'Good. Good. Now I know for a fact that we can get you north of Bristol. The line is pretty smooth up to there. We might not get much further though. We might have to abandon the train and set off on foot. So if we –'

'We?' I asked.

'Yes, we. We'll come with you. Some of us. Trott and me, certainly. So –'

'No.'

'What?'

'I said no.'

'No? But you can't go on your own. It's not safe.'

I shook my head. 'No. You all have other things that you need to be doing. Mr Wessex, you need to help run the farms and villages. They need you here. Your wife and son need you. So, thank you. I'll accept your offer of the train ride to Bristle. But after that I am going to do this alone.'

'No yer not.' It was Tab's voice, quieter and more subdued than normal.

'Eh?'

'I'm coming with yer. And Mouse. Can't leave Mouse behind.'

'Oh, Tab. No.'

'Don't argue.' He tutted. 'It's a foregone illusion. Can't have you runnin round on yer own. Yer won't last two minutes.'

'You can't –'

'Shut up. That's the end of the conversation.'

'I think Tab has definitely made up his mind,' Lily laughed. 'Looks like you haven't shaken him off quite yet, Serendipity.'

27

The Fear

I remember Mama talking to me about the fear. It was probably an awful rain-full day when we were trapped in our pod on the Lahn Dan High. The rain would blob up on the glass outside before getting too fat and finding itself having to run down in streaks, plopping off somewhere we couldn't see beneath. I realise now those days were lies – like most of the Lahn Dan life. We could easily have opened the door and climbed down our rope onto the pavement below. We could have stood, our faces up, sucking in droplets of rain, feeling them land on our tongues. We could have swallowed the water down and ran around in it, kicking up puddles and spraying each other with wetness. But we didn't. Because of the lies. Because of the fear.

The fear, Mama said, had been the biggest reason for unhappiness in the whole of the world. The fear stopped you doing something, kept you stapled to the spot like nails through your feet. The fear nuzzled away at you, making you doubt even your own feelings. The fear was a way of being controlled. That is what she said. Being too young at the time, I nodded and made nice noises to make her think I was listening, but basically I ignored her, letting the words pass through my ears but not into my brain.

I could live at Ashdown for the rest of my life, with people who would care for me and like me. People who would share dreams and secrets with me. It was warm and secure. What was outside of the area, past Bristle, nobody really knew. But I had to find out. I'd managed to step outside once already, I could do it again.

All I had to do was think about the horses.

This time we were travelling in the first of the two carriages that the steam engine pulled behind it. Me, Tab, Lily Wessex and Mouse spread ourselves across the plush seats that a couple of hundred years ago would have been graced by the bottoms of city-gent commuters and serious ministers. Meanwhile, Mr Wessex, Trott and Knottman were driving the locomotive ahead of us.

'I think I prefer it ere. S'more cumftable.' Tab nodded, his eyes half shut like he was a connoisseur of these things. 'Dirty and smelly up the front. And hot! Phew! I fought I was gonna cook me brain on the last trip. Mind you, I think I was a pretty good train driver, even if I says so meself.'

'I quite enjoyed it,' I chipped in, defending the dirt, noise, grease and heat. 'I found it kind of . . . exciting.'

Lily pointed up to a little red lever above the window. 'If you would rather ride up front, we can always let Roger know. He can stop the train and let you into the –'

'No, no. It's fine. I'm happy to sit here. With you.'

Lily smiled at me but the *tick-tock* of disappearing moments seemed to smother any joy or fun from the proceedings, so we all just stared out of the window and wondered how long the journey was going to be . . .

Eventually we felt the train slow down. It rumbled along for a good ten minutes until the brakes squawked and we all gave a jolt towards a standstill.

'This is about as far as we can get along the main line,' Mr Wessex said as we all stood on the grass verge to one side of the train. 'It's too overgrown to go any further.'

'Where are we? Exactly?' Knottman had a smashing great smudge of oil across his cheek.

'Few miles north of Bristol.'

'We need to find a road.'

Tab and I got our rucksacks down from the carriage and the men helped lower our bikes. We all struggled our way up the verge and across two overgrown whip-grass fields before hitting the first solid stretch of tarmac.

Setting his bike down, Tab hopped on and pedalled in a wide circle, Mouse scampering along behind him.

'Wheeeee. Nothing wrong with the action on this little beauty. Tyres might need a pump before the day's out though . . .'

Everybody looked at him and laughed. Me included. There was something over the egg about Tab. Over the egg but toasty, and I was secretly pleased that he had chosen to come along with me. Not that I would ever tell him that.

'Well. I suppose this is it.' Mr Wessex came next to me. 'Off on your big adventure, eh?' He crouched down and whispered in my ear, 'Wish I was coming with you.'

'Thank you, sir.' I held out my hand. 'For everything.'

He took it and squeezed it. 'Not at all, my girl. Come back and see us soon, you hear?'

'I will.'

Mr Knottman was next, patting me on the shoulder like a long-lost cousin or something. 'Commander Mordecai has instructions not to go back to Lahn Dan without you and he knows you're heading to Whales so, whatever you do, keep off the major roads as much as you can.'

'Okay.'

'Good. Be safe, my little heroine. Hope you find your horses.'

'What about you? What will you do?'

'I'll be fine, don't you worry. Now I'm free, the whole world has opened up so I may just do a bit of travelling around. Keep an eye on things, so to speak.'

Mr Trott stood slightly away from the group and I made a deliberate move towards him.

'Goodbye, Mr Trott.'

'Hmmph!' His face still held the suspicious frown it had acquired the first time he saw Tab and me. 'I still don't trust you, you know.'

'No. I know.'

'Never did trust you. Never will.' But as I turned away from him, I was certain he gave me a little wink.

Finally, Lily Wessex swooped up to me and threw her arms around me. She held me tight and kissed my hair. I could feel the tears trickling down onto my face and I wasn't too sure whose they were. We stood there for a minute or two, holding onto each other, not moving, not saying anything. Then –

'We'd better be getting off.' Tab was no longer whizzing about on his bike and Mouse was no longer chasing after him. 'We've got a long journey ahead of us, Serendipity.'

Lily and I pulled apart. She patted my cheeks and grinned through sore red eyes as I adjusted the straps on my backpack and picked up the handlebars from the ground.

'Come on then, Tab,' I croaked. 'Mouse.'

We hopped on the bikes and pushed off along the road.

28

The H H Bridge

We kept off the Emm Four like Mr Knottman had said, weaving near and around it as much as we could, keeping our little peepers peeled for Mordecai and his men. At the end of the first day, we had seen and met nobody. The land this side of Ashdown was as quiet as the land just outside of Lahn Dan. Fields were filled with a deep green grass and the houses looked weather-beaten and exhausted. But there were more birds. Many more birds. Seagulls seemed to boss the air like feathery kings and queens. Crows and blackbirds fought battles over worms and watched us pass by from the wires that strung themselves from post to post. Blue tits and sparrows darted in and out and up and down, diving and soaring like smears in the air.

And the air itself was filled with birdsong. Whenever we rested and could stop ourselves from panting, we listened to these sounds that boldly stated life was defin-itely all around us.

We spent that first night in another abandoned house,

and after the cosiness of Ashdown, it was strange to sleep in a cold bed that had not served its purpose for a very long time. I could hear Tab shuffling and moaning about in the next room, complaining no doubt that this was all my fault and what in the name of the God Man did I think I was doing. But the next morning, we ate some of the home-baked rations that Lily had made for us, and got quickly on our way without everything spinning into a squabble.

It was about halfway through the day when we saw the bridge for the first time.

'There,' I said.

'What?'

'The bridge.'

Two large letter Hs stood up against the sky and the hills beyond. Just as Miss Caritas had told me.

'The H H Bridge.'

'Looks normous.'

'Come on.'

Encouraged by the sight of it we pedalled hard for an hour, Mouse sprinting alongside us. In fact, it was fair to say that in the one day that we had been travelling, Mouse had managed to lose some of the weight that the rich food and leftovers at Ashdown had wrapped around his scruffity little body.

We freewheeled down a long winding hill, past long abandoned modpods and trucks, the tarmac sometimes

cracked and buckled. As we neared the bridge, something dawned on my silly brain and my brakes screeched
me to a stop.

'What is it?' Tab came alongside me, his brakes equally
screechy.

'The bridge. It's part of the Emm Four.'

'Yeah? So what?'

'Well, we've got to cross it.'

'Yeah?' He looked at me like I was stupid or
something.

'But we might get caught.'

'But we might not. It won't take long to cross it, will
it? What? Ten minutes? Then we can get off onto a
smaller road when we're on the other side. Yeah?'

'I suppose.'

'Of course you suppose. How the ell are we meant
to get into Whales otherwise?'

He had a point.

But as we got even nearer, it was Tab who applied
his brakes a little too roughly a second time.

'What now?'

'Sssh. Up there.' He whispered, even though there
was nothing near us.

'Why're you whispering?' I asked.

He pointed and I could see what he was getting at.
Way in the distance, at the place where the bridge seemed
to twist slightly over on itself, was a vehicle. I stared

243

hard – it was difficult to see with the sun glaring into my eyes – and eventually I could make it out. It was the unmistakable white-sided modpod of the Minister's police men. And it wasn't moving. It was straddling the lanes like a barrier. They were sitting there simply waiting for us to walk straight to them.

'Oh no.' Of course they were going to wait for us here. Why didn't I think of it before? 'We can't,' I said partly to myself. 'It's like walking into a trap.'

Tab pulled his bag tight over his shoulders and lurched towards me. 'I think we can.'

'Don't be ridiculous.'

'Look. You're right. If we go cycling up on the road – unless they're all really really tired and snoring away like the idiots they are and we can just tipsy-toe past them – then we've got no chance. But . . .' At this point he rolled his bike aside and it wobbled and clattered into the verge. 'But if we forget the bikes and just scoot along the hedges here – get ourselves a bit nearer to where the bridge actually starts, keep ourselves out of sight – then we might find a way.'

'It's no good, I tell you.'

'Cheer up, cheeky chops. I aint given up a nice warm bedroom and free food forever to pack up on this jus yet. If there is a way, I think we should find it. Come on.'

*　　*　　*

244

We crouched hard behind a long metal tank filled with slimy-looking water. Up on the top of the bridge, one of the police men was leaning over, staring into the distance. We were about a hundred yards from where this side of the bridge started to grow out of the ground. Tab held Mouse in his arms and, every now and then, we both peeked over the side of the tank.

'He's still there.'

'I know.'

'What's he doing?'

'Just lookin round. Bored probly.'

The man on the bridge did have an air of boredom about him, even from this distance. He was sort of huffling and puffling to himself. You could tell.

'Right.' Tab leaned towards me. 'Next time he moves away from the edge we need to make a dash for it.'

'A dash? Where to?'

'Well, there of course.' He pointed to the base of the bridge. 'Get in under there for a starters.'

'Why?'

'Why dya think?'

I gave a sort of shrug and Tab shook his head. 'You're opeless. I'll show you when we get there.'

We waited for a couple of minutes, watching the police man leaning over the barrier on the bridge. He tapped out a rhythm on the metal poles running alongside, gave a couple of yawns and then suddenly disappeared from the edge.

'Now!' Tab ran out, Mouse gripped in his hands, and sprinted away from the metal tank in the direction of the bridge. A moment later and I was close behind him, my legs pushing hard over the uneven ground, my rucksack banging away on my aching back.

Tab got to the bridge and climbed through a gap in the rusting fence.

'Quick. In here.'

I scrambled in through the hole, catching my bag on the spiky wires as I did so. Pulling it free I fell onto my face and landed in a puddle of mud.

'You awright?' Tab helped me up and I wiped the thick black muck off my trousers.

'Yeah.'

I straightened up and looked around. It was dark underneath the bridge with shafts of light poking in through the sides. Over in a far corner I could hear the squeal and *pitter-patter* of rats. Mouse had obviously picked up on it too and he scampered over to where the noise was coming from and began to bark.

'Mouse you stupid git! Shut it! Come on. Come ere.' Tab waved at the dog and clapped his hands. But Mouse ignored him and skittered around the writhing mass of vermin, letting off the occasional yelp. 'Oy! Mouse. Come ere.'

This time Mouse noticed his young master's voice and backed away with a slight growl before trotting back to Tab.

'Good boy. That's a good boy, that is.'

'Okay. What now?' I asked.

'Now we start climbing.'

Tab pointed a little further along to where the bridge started to lift itself away from the earth. The rickety fencing we'd just squeezed through gave way to a more solid, hefty-looking construction – part of the underside itself. A never-ending mish-mash of rods and girders, zig-zagging and double-crossing, that supported and stretched all the way across to the other side.

'Hold on.' I shook my head. 'You expect us to climb all the way over to Whales from here?'

'Yep.'

'It's miles.'

'Well, I think you'll find that it's not technically *miles*. More likely a mile, praps a mile and a bit. So not even two miles, which makes it not technically *miles*.'

'We'll get exhausted.'

'Nah, we won't. We can do it. It'll be easy.'

'Easy?'

'Yeah.'

'What about Mouse?'

'What about him?'

'He can't climb.'

'I've already thought of that.' Tab tapped the side of his head with his finger to demonstrate just how clever he was.

'Oh yes?'

He nodded before lowering the grubby rucksack from his back. He opened it up and pulled out some of the sandwiches and cakes that the Wessexes had given us only the day before. Unravelling some of the brown paper the food had been wrapped in, he fished out a large cheese roll and started stuffing it into his mouth.

'Er . . . What are you doing?'

'Wha duh i loo li ahm doon? Ahm eehen.' I could barely understand what he was saying through his over-packed gob. 'Ere.' He tossed over an unopened packet. 'Tuh in.'

I caught it and knew instantly that it was a slice of the rather heavy sponge that Molly had baked only the other morning.

'I don't understand.'

Tab swallowed down his current mouthful. 'You probly can't get any more in your rucksack, can yer? So I'll have to dump the rest for the rats.' He got out some more food and, after feeding a handful of some tasty treat to Mouse, threw it over to the wriggling nest in the corner. His hand dived into his bag a few times and he flung the remaining parcels of food in the same direction.

'What are you doing? We might need that food.'

Tab gave his head a shake. 'I need Mouse more.' He bent over and pulled the top of the rucksack open. 'C'mon, boy. Get in.' Obligingly, Mouse crawled into the bag, turning himself around so that his head was sticking out of the top. Tab lifted the rucksack up, straightened the straps and pulled it onto his back. Mouse peered around Tab's head at me, his tongue lolling out of his panting face like some sort of puppet. We began to climb.

At first, it was easy going. The beams and girders were close together and simple to get hold of. Tab was ahead of me with Mouse jutting his little head out of the rucksack, and I followed close behind. We kept to the edge of the bridge where we could see what we were doing. But as we made our way slowly across, the distance between us and the ground increased. Soon the ground disappeared altogether and hundreds of feet below us was a muddy sludge not unlike the Tems in Lahn Dan. Grey and pitted, the sun sparkled across its shiny surface.

The wind was making things difficult too. Now and then it would whip angrily at us like that nasty troll trying to stop the goats from crossing his bridge in that silly old story Mama used to tell me. When it did, you had to grip tightly onto the metal and wait for it to stop. Sometimes it caught you out, blowing itself up from nowhere, and it was a struggle to stop yourself flipping away backwards.

We forced ourselves slowly over the girders and beams, pulling our bodies through the tight squeezes where they criss-crossed, stepping carefully over the wild open spaces beneath our feet. After an hour or so, my arms and legs were aching like fiddlesticks, and we weren't even halfway there.

'This is tiring,' I cried over the blustering wind to Tab.

'What?'

'I'm tired.'

'Yeah.' He puffled across at me. 'It is a bit harder work than I thought it was going to be.' He repositioned Mouse on his back. 'But we can't stop. Gotta keep going. Can't just lie down and have a rest up here. Too far to fall into bed.'

We forced ourselves on, and about ten minutes later, Tab put his finger to his lips again and pointed upwards.

'Minister's men,' he mouthed at me. 'Listen.'

It was hard to hear. The wind whistled around the framework and you had to sort of ignore it to hear. But there were two voices. Talking to each other.

'. . . problem with those old modpods. Need petrol. Won't be long now, more's the pity . . .'

Buffeting winds knocked the voices out for a few seconds before slipping down and easing them back in.

'. . . goosechase.'

'Tell me abaht it. Rather be back in me old home with the missus. Lahn Dan might be miserable, but at least there are people around. I mean, look at it out there. Gives me the flamin cobbleywobbles, I tell yer. Sends shivers up me derriere. Nobody to see for bleedin miles and miles.'

'Dunno what he wants with her anyway, do you?'

'He don't tell anyone anything, old Morbid Mordecai. He gives me the creeps an all. Puts the fear of the God Man into yer. Like he could go nuts and just shoot yer at any time over a scrap of bread. He knows why we're chasing her but he won't tell us. Rather die than divulge anything to us scum. It's like that time . . .'

I gripped on as the winds flew past us again. I pulled myself tighter to the girders and let the tunnelling winds flick my hair all about my face. I suddenly realised that the sweat was flowing from me and that my aching arms weren't going to be able to cling on for much longer – I wasn't going to be able to climb much further. Realising that was one of the scariest things that could happen to me at that moment. I was trapped under the Minister's men and hundreds of feet above the mud. I didn't want to give myself up to the police men, but I also didn't want to find myself falling to death. No matter how I looked at it, I was stuck. Stuck here with just a couple of choices of how to lose in this game.

It was then that my body began to choose for me. My arms started to shake and my legs weakened beneath me. The whole landscape turned black and white and my eyes desperately wanted to shut themselves tight. It had never happened to me before but I knew precisely what was going on. I was starting to faint.

Suddenly, a dull thud came from my left, and back on the Grey Britan side of the bridge, a ball of fire seemed to roll vertically up into the air. The noise smacked me awake again and I gripped on tighter than ever.

'Blimey! Whassat?' one of the men above called to the other. 'Come ere. Gimme those.'

Tab turned to look at the fireball slowly burning itself out before looking at me with a squinting puzzley expression. I shook my head back at him.

'There's someone there,' the first man continued. 'Someone down there.'

'Who is it?' the second man asked. 'What they doing?'

'Dunno.'

WHOOOOMPH.

Another fireball, much bigger and more ball-shaped than the first, filled the eastern sky and I swear I could even feel its heat from this distance.

'What's happening, Stu? What's going on?' The second man's voice had a wobble of panic wrapped around it.

'Er . . . I dunno.'

'What we going to do, Stu?'

'Er . . .' The first man seemed to be weighing up the odds. 'Come on.'

'What?'

'Let's go.'

'But the Commander told us not to leave our post.'

'Yeah, but what if that's them down there? Do you want to be the one to tell him we stood here while they prannied about in front of us?'

'But –'

'No buts. Get yer stuff in the pod and let's get down there.'

'I don't think this is a good idea, Stu.'

'Oh shut up and get in, will yer?'

'Not a good idea at all.'

The modpod's engine started and we could hear the squeal of its tyres as it pulled away.

'Weird,' I said.

'Weird or not,' Tab shouted excitedly, 'this is our chance. Quick. Let's get up there.'

We rushed ourselves over to the outer edge of the framework and started scrambling up the side. The metal here was more decorative and flimsy and felt as if it might snap as you grabbed it. Bolts appeared to loosen as my weight yanked on them. My hands got scraped and sore pulling myself up over the barrier, but

I kicked hard with my legs and got to the top, throwing myself onto the pavement beneath.

Tab was still climbing when – *CHUNG* – a bolt ripped out from the metal girder making one of the more fragile pieces of barrier spring out at one end. He slipped and his hand came away as he toppled to one side. Luckily his other hand shot out and latched onto another part of the bridge.

'MOUSE!'

The rucksack on Tab's back had spun upside down and Mouse was starting to slither slowly out of it.

'MOUSE! NO!'

Jumping to my feet, I stretched my arm out through the barrier, standing on tipsy-toe to reach, and managed to grab hold of a clump of Mouse's fur just as he began to sag out of Tab's bag.

It was enough. I pulled him through the barrier onto the bridge before he slid out of my fingers for good.

Tab righted himself and sprang over the last few rungs and onto the pavement in front of me.

'Thank you, Serendipity. Thank you. I thought I'd lost him.' He wiped a droplet of wetness out of his eye with the back of his wrist. 'I thought . . . I thought he was going to fall.' He sniffed and bent down to stroke the dog – who appeared not to have noticed just how close to death he had come – and kissed the mangy mutt on the top of his scabby little head. 'I thought I'd gone and lost you there, boy. It was a close thing.'

'We don't have time for this, Tab,' I said. 'We've got to get moving. Before they come back.'

He raised himself up. 'Yeah. You're right.' Tears had vanished in that cold bare second. 'Let's get shifting.'

We set off at a fast run – Tab and I alongside each other, Mouse a smudgen behind. We had already climbed beyond the first H and we quickly passed under the second one, our feet pounding the concrete, our back-packs slapping up and down.

The bridge seemed to start casting downwards, bringing itself in to land on the opposite side with a gentle – almost unnoticeable – slope. Whales was coming into clearer view with every blister-popping stride.

'Not far.' I strained towards Tab who just ignored me and kept on running. 'Nearly there.'

At last the mud beneath us turned into solid earth once again and the bridge was edging closer and closer to the ground, to the place Whales would start. The large steel barrier gave way to a smaller steel barrier and joy was starting to become something real in my chest.

But then . . .

In the distance, a truck came into view, heading towards us on the Emm Four.

'It's the others! Mordecai. They're coming back!'

Tab and I rushed to the barrier and scrambled over it, Tab scooping Mouse up as he did so. Looking down to the ground beneath, I could see it was at least a fifteen foot fall.

'We have to jump,' I said. 'They'll see us any second – we have to jump.'

I launched myself off and fell for what seemed like forever. My legs buckled under me and I rolled over onto my side, cushioning the blow. Beside me Tab hit the ground with a terrible thud, and Mouse gave a squeak.

'Aaargh.'

I pulled myself up off the grass and ran over to Tab. 'You all right?'

'No.' His face wrinkled in a spasm of pain. 'My ankle. I hurt my ankle.'

He struggled to his feet and we tucked ourselves in closer to the foot of the bridge. We listened hard, and a minute or so later the roar of the modpod passed overhead.

Part Three

Across

29

The Wizard on the Hill

'It keeps hurting,' Tab said, his strides nothing more than stumps. 'Hurts more than ever.'

We weevilled our way down from the main road to a small blob of a town – almost a village – at the bottom of a sweeping street. It had taken us hours to get anywhere with Tab's ankle – every step seemed to make him cry out in pain – and avoiding the major roads slowed our progress even more. But at least we had, for the moment, lost Mordecai and his men. Wherever they were. We had slipped past them and found our way into Whales without them even noticing.

It felt good.

'OwwwWww,' Tab moaned for the squillionth time that day.

'We need to get you help,' I said, Tab's arm pulling my shoulders down.

In the centre of the village there were people around. Men and women. Children and babies. Most of them seemed to ignore us, or just give us a bleating glance.

Some of them, though, probably spotting how differently we were dressed and hearing how differently we talked, rushed up to us and asked us where we were going, where we had come from. Whenever I questioned them about horses, none of them knew what I was talking about.

'Is there a doctor?' I asked, remembering Tab's ankle. 'My friend finds it hard to walk.'

'No doctor. Not round here. But . . . there's a wizard,' a young boy told me. His accent was roly-poly and hard to follow. 'He lives on the hill.' He pointed vaguely along a road and up a slope. 'I've never seen him, though. We don't go up there. No one goes up there. Not now. Not for a long time. He lives on the Terrace. You have to be careful . . .' He left the sentence drooping in the air, and arched his eyebrows knowingly before walking away. Across the road another young man goggled us.

'Don't like the sound of tha,' Tab moaned, his leg a minute or two behind him. 'Don't like the sound of tha at all.'

Up the hill we went, Tab limping all the way, Mouse scratching and yawning every few steps or so. Following the signs to the Terrace, we passed an overgrown children's park with long deserted swings and a faded pirate-ship slide. As we turned a corner, a large wooden sign stood to the side of us.

260

'What's it say?'

'Hold on. "Keep Out. Enter At Own . . . er . . . Risk. Beware Guard Dogs. This Is A CCTV . . . er . . . Zone. Turn Around And Go Away. Now! Signed, The Wizard."'

'Don't seem very friendly.'

'No.'

'Specially tha bit about guard dogs. I don't think guard dogs'll take too kindly to Mouse. Eat him up, they will.'

'I can't see any guard dogs, can you?'

'Not yet, no. Can't we just go back? My ankle feels a bit better now. Honestly.'

I stared at Tab. 'If you keep walking on that ankle without getting it sorted, you're going to find yourself walking on your bottom. We need someone to look at it.'

Tab huffed.

'Wait! Look!' I spotted it lying on the ground next to the signpost, smothered in the long thin grass.

'Wha?'

I ran over and picked it up. It was weather-worn and scuffed with patches of greeny moss.

Tab squashed up his face again. 'A star?'

It was large – three or four times bigger than my head – and painted a fading goldy-yellow. A long thick rod had been stuck on the back of it at some point, before snapping in half, the star falling to the earth.

'Wha's tha about?' Tab asked.

'The Professor told me that in Lahn Dan stars were

261

sometimes used to show a safe place. Somewhere you could hide away from the Minister.'

'This place don't seem all tha safe to me.'

I reached down to the locket and unclicked it, before pulling out the map. I opened it up and jabbed a finger at the paper.

'There!'

Tab winced his way over to me and looked at the star on the map.

'Another star.' He shook his head. 'Nice.'

'Don't you see?' I couldn't believe he couldn't see. 'This is that place. We're here on the map.'

Suddenly there was a whirring sound followed by the heavy clank of metal upon metal. A large creature stood in front of us. It was at least ten feet tall and had red glows where its eyes should have been. Its skin was shiny and hard and its muscly arms straightened out with bunched up fists as it took loud earth-shaking steps towards us.

'It's a gorilla!' Tab screamed. 'Run!'

But I couldn't. My legs were sprouted to the spot as the creature stomped its way closer to me.

And then it spoke.

'WHO DARES TO TRESPASS ON THE WIZARD'S LAND? I AM THE GUARDIAN OF THE TERRACE AND I INSIST YOU LEAVE NOW. OTHERWISE . . . I WILL CRUSH YOU.' Its jaw worked mechanically as it spoke and it lifted one of its arms and squeezed its fingers in and out to show us just how crushing its hands were.

'Serendipity! Come on!' Tab had limped some yards already, Mouse whimpering alongside him. 'Sorry, Mr Gorilla! Didn't mean to intrude, like.'

The creature took another step towards me. 'LISTEN TO YOUR FRIEND, LITTLE GIRL. GO BACK DOWN TO YOUR VILLAGE AND NEVER COME BACK HERE AGAIN.'

'Serendipity!'

The monster was bearing down on me, its red eyes glowing even brighter than before. But there was something about its voice . . . Something that made me fix myself where I stood.

'Serendipity!'

'No. I'm not going anywhere!' I shouted.

The creature stopped about five feet from me, and bent forwards, its face level with mine.

'FOOLISH GIRL! THEN I WILL CRUSH YOU AND EAT YOUR INNARDS FOR SUPPER.'

'No you won't,' I replied as calmly as I could. 'You are a robot. Not a gorilla. You can't eat me.'

'BUT I CAN STILL CRUSH YOU.'

'I don't think you will, though, will you?'

The monster went quiet for a few seconds as if weighing it all up.

'Serendipity! What're you doing?'

'I'm staying here.'

'Why?'

'I haven't come all this way to be scared off by a hunk of metal, Tab. Besides,' I whispered, 'this place is on the map and I want to know why.'

The creature stood dead still and silent for a while, the only sounds coming from its robotic insides. After a while, it started talking again, this time with much less aggression and certainty in its voice. 'GO ON . . . SHOO . . . CLEAR OFF.'

'I've told you, no.' I stood my ground. 'I'm not leaving until I've seen the Wizard.'

The robot seemed to sigh. 'YOU ARE VERY IRRITATING, YOU KNOW. VERY IRRITATING. USUALLY THE CHILDREN WHO COME UP HERE AND ANNOY ME RUN OFF. SCARED. PETRIFIED, USUALLY. THEY DON'T TEND TO COME BACK. THEY LEAVE ME ALONE IN PEACE – WHICH IS HOW I LIKE IT. BUT YOU . . .' It sighed again. 'YOU ARE VERY, *VERY* IRRITATING. WHAT DO YOU WANT FROM ME?'

'Well, firstly I would like to talk to you in person. Not through this . . . thing, here.'

'THIS THING HAS A NAME, YOU KNOW. HE TOOK ME YEARS TO BUILD AND REQUIRES A LOT OF LOOKING AFTER. I HAVE TO DISMANTLE THE JOINTS AND LUBRICATE EVERY COUPLE

264

OF MONTHS OR SO, AND WITH THE WET
WEATHER UP HERE THE RUBBER SEALS HAVE
TO BE REFRESHED MUCH MORE OFTEN THAN
I WOULD LIKE.'

'What's goin on?' Tab muttered behind me.

'So what *is* this thing's name?' I asked, still staring into
the robot's eyes.

'BRAN.'

'Bran?'

'IT STANDS FOR 'BIOMECHANICAL ROBOTIC
– WAIT A MINUTE. I'LL COME OUT AND –

'– talk to you. Take this silly thing off my head.' One
of the doors to one of the houses had opened up and
a smallish man wearing a strange wiry sort of helmet
and holding a bulky metal box had walked out into
the street. He fiddled with the straps around his chin
and pulled the helmet off the top of his head. 'That's
better. As I was saying, it stands for "Biomechanical
Robotic Anti-Nuisance Device".'

'Er . . . That's BRAND, isn't it?'

'Yes, it is. But I prefer BRAN. He was a king.'

'Why should I help you?' The Wizard sat in his armchair
and watched us. 'I fail to see a reason why I should
help you.'

Tab and I were scrunched up on the sofa opposite
him, Mouse on the floor between us.

265

'Um . . .' Tab's eyes rolled around the room, looking for a reason. 'Because . . . it's a . . . nice thing to do?'

'Nice? Huh. Such a meaningless word. Nice.'

He wasn't what you would think a wizard would be like. He was grey and thin with hopeless, floppy hair and what appeared to be luggage stored under his eyes. And he was a miseryguts. Definitely a miseryguts.

Oh, and he didn't have a big pointy hat and a wand.

'You really a wizard?' Tab asked expectantly. 'A real, proper wizard?'

'Of course I am,' the Wizard spat. 'You saw BRAN out there, didn't you? You saw how magical I'd made him.'

'Yeah, but . . . but you didn't make him from magic, did ya? Not real magic.' Tab was grinning like he'd worked out the big joke and was wanting to be let in on it.

'Depends on your interpretation of magic.' A flash of hurt shone in the Wizard's face. 'If you want me to levitate right now, I wouldn't be able to. *No one* would be able to. But give me a couple of days in my workshop and I'd work something out.'

'Levi . . .?'

'Sir,' I started, deciding to be a little more polite than I'd just been on the pavement outside. 'Sir, Tab's ankle is hurting badly and he's slowing us down. We were hoping that you would help us. We still have a long way to go and—'

'Where are you going exactly?'

266

'As far as we can. Until the land stops at the sea.'

'You are heading west?'

'Yes.'

'Pembrokeshire, then. And why,' he intertwined his fingers and goggled over them at us, 'are you going to Pembrokeshire? What is it that Pembrokeshire holds to make you walk so far that your ankles and knees and thighs are worth damaging?'

'We're looking for horses, sir.'

'Horses, eh?' He straightened himself in his chair.

'Yes. Horses. Not that we've seen any so far. We were told that there were still horses in Whales, but we've seen nothing yet. I'm starting to wonder . . .' My voice trailed off the path.

'Yes?'

I coughed. 'I'm starting to wonder if the stories I've heard aren't true. That there really aren't any horses any more. That horses don't exist.'

The Wizard pulled himself forward and gripped his knees with his hands.

'Oh, they exist, all right.'

'What?'

'Horses most definitely exist.'

I think I sat there with my mouth all sort of O'd.

'How . . . how do you know?'

'I've seen them.'

'Where? When?'

267

'Many years ago. In Pembrokeshire, funnily enough. Back then I wasn't such a recluse. I travelled around Britain. The two of us did. We worked our way up to where Scotland once sat and down the east coast of England. Then we headed west, crossed the Severn Bridge and pushed on until – as you said – the land stopped at the sea. We spent weeks investigating and documenting the flora and fauna that still existed. That was when we saw them.'

I couldn't trust my ears.

'Really?'

'Oh yes. Running wild. A whole cloud of them galloping past in the distance, over some dirty fields and into a wood. Only lasted a few seconds, but we saw them.'

'But, if it was only for a few seconds, and it was far away . . . perhaps you were mistaken? Perhaps they weren't horses at all.'

'No,' he said. 'They were horses.'

I could barely tin my excitement. 'There were two of you? You said there were two of you?'

'Hmm.' His mouth twitched and twittered and his fingers leaned across to the coffee table before us. On the table sat little toys – tiny robots not unlike BRAN outside. He flicked the back of one of them and it started walking across the table, dials and gears whizzing and whirring as it went. After a couple of seconds it stopped, did a backwards somersault and then hopped on one leg before coming to a halt.

'Wow. Cool,' Tab laughed. 'S'cool.'

'Tell me,' the Wizard had managed to gain control of his twitching, twittering mouth, 'where are you both from?'

'Lahn Dan.'

He leaned forward in his chair, suddenly very interested. 'Lahn Dan, eh?' I noticed that he said it the same way I did. 'So how did you find out about the horses in West Wales? I really wouldn't have thought that people in Lahn Dan would be aware of such things.'

'A map.' My hands dug deep down into the bottom of my rucksack where I'd shoved it roughly not an hour before. 'I was given it by . . . someone I knew.' I found the curled, battered sheet of paper and pulled it out. Squatting alongside the Wizard, I unravelled it and showed him. 'This is Lahn Dan. That's the road we've been following.' I pointed. 'The H H Bridge.' And finally, 'The horses.' I handed the map over to the Wizard and he silently took it from me. 'And I think the place with the star . . . I think that's here, isn't it?'

He sat there for quite a while, just staring and running his fingers over the crinkled piece of paper, not saying anything. Then I noticed that his hands were shaking and a single, lonely little tear ran down his face and dripped onto the parchment.

269

'Sir?'

The Wizard pointed to where Shy's signature sat.

'Come with me. Both of you. There's something I think you should see.'

We went out through the kitchen, through the garden, across a stony lane to a field directly behind the house.

'There.'

A headstone jutted out from the earth, rough and coarsely chiselled. On it were the words:

Shy Elinore
The most beautiful woman that ever graced
the universe
'We met under a shower of bird-notes'

'Shy?' I sucked in air almost too quickly to say the word.

Tab stubbed his finger towards the stone. 'She drew the map?'

'Yes. A long, long time ago.'

We all just stood there not saying anything for ages, the sparrows and blue tits in the trees singing away above us like an orchestra filling the gaps in the sky.

'"*We met under a shower of bird-notes*"?'

'It's from a poem she loved. About growing old and accepting one's fate.'

I looked around. The hill behind the field was rich

270

and green and squeezed full of life. Trees were thick with leaves and the air hung heavy with the scent of creation. I thought I saw squirrels and rabbits, and butterflies danced around each other like petals in the breeze. Bees buzzed past and small white flowers sacrificed themselves under our feet. There was not even a hint of Lahn Dan violet in the sky.

The Wizard eventually turned to me. 'What is your name?'

'Serendipity, sir.'

He smiled an enormous smile.

'Of course it is. Of course it is.'

The Wizard wrapped a large bandage soaked in herbs around Tab's leg. Round and round it went, up and down, until there was only a little bandage left with which to tie a knot.

'Ow! Not too tight.'

'It has to be fairly tight. It won't work otherwise.'

'But me leg'll drop off.'

The Wizard looked up at him with a bit of a pitying face.

'Your leg will *not* drop off. Trust me.'

Tab wriggled about a bit on the sofa while the Wizard pulled the bandage even tighter whilst telling us all about himself and Shy.

'I was a *Cu* in Lahn Dan. I used to invent things.

Modpods, telebracelets, announcement monitors, you know? That sort of thing.'

'You invented modpods?' Tab momentarily forgot about the bandage being pulled tightly around his ankle. 'Woah! Cool.'

'Well . . . improved upon the old concepts of vehicular travel, I suppose. Made them better.'

'Cool.'

'All those little and not so little things that kept the *Au*s entertained and their lives running as smoothly as possible. It was a tedious and thankless task, to be honest. No one really cares about the builders of such things. As long as their monitors are plugged in and working, anyone could have made them. But then I met Shy.'

'An *Au*?' I asked.

'Yes, she was an *Au*. But a different sort of *Au*. She understood that for the world to work properly everyone has to interact and get on with everyone else. It was no good building walls or glass towers to keep everyone apart. Bringing people together was much more important.'

'She knew my mother, did you know?'

The Wizard turned and burned a look straight into my face. 'Oh, we both knew Oleander.'

I thought back to what the Professor had once told me. 'How did you know her? Is it true? Were they best friends? Even though Mama was a *Pb* and Shy was an *Au*?'

He nodded. 'They were the greatest of friends. The thickest of friends. Of course, this rather upended the apple cart. It was not allowed. The social conventions were being tossed aside and many of the *Au*s spurned Shy over it. There was one older *Au* in particular who desperately tried to befriend Shy and turn her against Oleander. It didn't work, of course.'

A sudden flash of a face in my head. A face jolted into shock after seeing the map. A plan being quickly formed in her mind.

'Miss Caritas.'

The Wizard looked surprised. 'You know her?'

'Well . . .' I told him about my meeting with Miss Caritas. From the moment I saw the telebracelet on the ground, through the dresses she let me try on, all the way to how she betrayed the Professor and me at the Emm Twenty-five.

The Wizard snorted to himself. 'As soon as she worked out who you were, she was going to try and trap you. No doubt about it. You see, Caritas was bitterly jealous of your mother. Bitterly jealous. For a number of reasons.'

'OOOwwwww, me ankle!' Tab cried out in pain again.

'I really wish you'd stop screeching like that,' the

Wizard huffed, deliberately pulling the bandage just that little bit tighter. 'You sound like a buzzard making off with its prey.'

He adjusted some of the wrapping before patting Tab gently on the leg and handing him one of his boots. Tab forced it on over the white legging before standing up and trying it out, walking over to the window and back again. 'S'awright. I think. S'awright.'

'You need to keep the wrappings on for at least two days. Give the herbs a chance to work.'

Tab nodded.

I bit my bottom lip in frustration. I was desperate to find out about Mama and Miss Caritas, but I knew I had to stay calm and wait for the Wizard to tell me when he was ready. Mama always got annoyed with me when I rushed her. I could almost imagine her saying – as she often did – *'Possess your singular soul in patience, Dipity.'*

The Wizard gave us soup for lunch. A strangely rich, red tomato soup that peppered the tongue as you fed it between your lips. As we slurped and dribbled, the Wizard talked to us about this, that and a bit of the other.

'Before the Gases,' he said, stopping then to spoon some of the hot liquid into his mouth, 'people had stopped walking. They had forgotten how to walk.

They drove in their cars from their homes to their places of work, and then drove in their cars from their places of work to their homes once again. They lost all contact with the outside world. The outside world was just a tunnel through which to get from A to B. Changes in the weather passed them by; the rain was something to hate – something unreal to them. Dirt was something dirty. They liked their lives all clean and antiseptic. In the evenings they plugged themselves into the wall and did pointless things with each other. They lived through technology that none of them understood. Before the Gases, people had stopped being organic, breathing, moving creatures, and had become static, unthinking, blinkered automata. A bit like BRAN. Only more stupid.'

The Wizard tossed Mouse a hunk of bread. 'They sent messages to friends they didn't have and told perfect strangers the detail of their lives. Everyone was simply pretending to everyone else. The truth was just a matter of opinion, and opinions could change on a rolling pin.' He reached across the table and took another slice of bread for himself. 'And then the wars happened. The Gases came and all technology ground to a halt. The people who knew what to do with it died and everybody else fluffed about, waiting for it to be turned back on. Except it didn't. And nobody knew what to do. So they fought amongst themselves until they too died out. And here we are today. An empty world with empty hopes.' He dunked the bread into the remains of the glowing red soup. 'Which makes your plight all the more honourable. Reminds me of Shy and myself.'

We finished our meal in silence before I sat back in my chair and asked the question that was burning my mind.

'Why did my mama have the map, sir? I don't understand why or how she had the map. It doesn't make sense to me.'

The Wizard sighed, his eyes dancing about, trying to piece the pieces of the story together. 'When we left – Shy and I – it was in a hurry. She had no time to tell Oleander. And over the years – the years of travelling – it ate away at Shy. She was actually quite a delicate creature, you know?' He smiled to himself. 'That was when she decided to go back into Lahn Dan.'

'Go back in?' I asked, a tad dumbfoundled.

'Yes. To see if she could help Oleander escape too.'

'But how could you get back into Lahn Dan?'

'With the help of smugglers, of course.' The Wizard looked over at Tab, and straight away we both realised that he knew exactly what Tab was. 'Smugglers know all the ins and outs and ups and downs of Lahn Dan. So we employed their help.'

'Musta charged you an awful lot.' Tab grinned.

The Wizard laughed. 'Lots. So we got in late one

276

night and Shy went to the Lahn Dan High to see Oleander. Only . . .'

'Yes?' I was sitting on the edge of the chair now.

'Only, she had a baby. She had you.'

My heart was clanging in my chest.

'Oleander was overwhelmed at seeing Shy. Ecstatic. They both were. But she couldn't leave. She had you to take care of, Serendipity, and risking capture . . . well, it just wasn't worth it. So Shy scribbled down the map on a piece of ripped-up paper and told her to hide it away so that nobody could find it. And if one day she felt the time was right to find a way out of the city walls then . . .' The Wizard paused. 'Well, obviously that eventually fell to you.' He stared hard at me. 'You know, you rather remind me of Oleander. A flaming fire in your eyes.'

So Mama was supposed to be the one to escape, but she gave up her freedom for me. My beautiful mama. Sacrificing any life she may have had for me. Just thinking about this, just hearing about her again, made me feel as if she was in the room with us, and I wanted to reach out and hold her one more time.

We stayed two nights with the Wizard. He let us sleep in his spare bedroom and told us things that he'd learned from his travels – like how the men in Scotland used to dance over swords and hurl lumps of wood at each other, and how the people in the borderlands would roll big round cheeses down hills and chase after them. Strange, unbelievable facts that he swore were the truth. He also told me tiny little things about Shy and Mama. Little things like the games they played and the stories they'd make up. For the first time since she died, I felt close to my mama.

On the second day, while the Wizard hunched over the dining table and tinkered with one of his tiny metal machines, I brought up another subject that had been pestering my brain.

'I was wondering,' I started. 'Did you ever . . . meet my father?'

The Wizard stopped what he was doing and turned to face me. 'Did your mother tell you anything about your father?' His eyes were doubtful and questioning. 'What did she tell you?'

'Nothing,' I replied honestly. 'She never told me anything.'

'And why was that, do you think?'

I looked around the rickety clutterbuck room that desperately needed dusting. 'Because she thought we could manage without him – because she thought we were better off without him. We could live our lives alone and we didn't need him.'

'But that's no reason not to *talk* about him, don't you think? Was she worried you might want to find him? Be with him? Go away from her?'

'No,' I quickly replied. 'No, that's not right. She would never think that.'

'Then why did she never tell you about him? Think hard.'

I did think hard. Eventually I said, 'Because she wanted to protect me?'

The Wizard gave a hardly noticeable nod. 'And if she didn't want to tell you because she wanted to protect you, what sort of a friend of Oleander's would I be if I started spilling out the beans the moment she dies?'

'So you met my father!'

He sighed. 'Yes. I've met your father, Serendipity.' He twisted back to the metal toy he was fiddling with on the table. 'And that's all you need to know. Now I think it's probably best if you never ask me about it again. As a mark of respect for your mother, you understand?'

I suddenly felt incredibly frustrated – pulled back and forth like a rope in a tuggle war game. Here was a man who knew about my father, but he wasn't going to tell me anything about him! Not because he didn't want to. Not because he didn't like me or because he wanted to hurt me. But because he cared about Mama.

'Must you go?' the Wizard asked. 'So soon?'

'You've given me a burst in my heart,' I told him. 'I was starting to doubt that there were any horses left alive.'

279

Tab pointed to his bandaged leg. 'Thanks for this. Feels better already.'

'Here.' I pushed the scrunched-up map into his hands. 'Keep it.'

'No, no,' the Wizard protested. 'It is yours. Shy would –'

'Keep it,' I insisted. 'I don't need it any more. I know exactly where I'm going.'

He nodded, grinned and took the map. 'You know, the sea is a very beautiful thing. Whatever you do, keep going until you see the sea. See it and smell it and feel it on your skin.'

We went out back onto the pavement where BRAN was lolling in standby mode.

'One more thing,' I said, turning to the Wizard. 'Why do you scare people away with BRAN? Don't you like people?'

He laughed. 'It's not that I don't like people. Not at all. But I have a role to play. "The Wizard on the Hill". That's what they all call me. The children in the village expect me to play that role, and they play theirs – daring each other to get as near as they can, running away like frightened rabbits whenever I turn on BRAN.'

'But you scare them.'

'Do I? I'm not so sure I do. A little fear is essential for growing up, I believe. Without moments of controlled fear, how can you possibly learn anything about the incredible potential and possibilities of life? How can you judge between right and wrong? When do you see the outline of your own character? True bravery can only grow from being scared.'

I thought about Mama staying in Lahn Dan because she was scared about hurting or losing me, and I realised she must have been the bravest person I ever knew.

30

A Debt Repaid

We'd gone maybe a mile or so when I noticed Tab smiling.

'What you so pleased with yourself for?' I asked him.

'What? Oh, nuffin.'

His grin didn't do anything to persuade me that it was nothing.

'No. Go on. What is it?'

He gave a sort of wink before stopping and pulling something out of his pocket. He bent down on the ground and flicked whatever it was with his finger. A tiny whizz sounded and he straightened up.

'There,' he jibbered. 'Tha.' The tiny robot that had somersaulted and hopped along the Wizard's coffee table was now somersaulting and hopping along the buckled tarmac on the road. 'S'cool, yeah?'

I froze.

'You . . . you stole it? You took it from the Wizard?'

'Yeah.'

I fought with myself, trying to find words that fitted this odd moment.

'But . . . You can't just take things, not from anyone! And he trusted us, Tab. He helped you.' Tab's eyes flickered guiltily before hardening. 'And you stole from him.'

'Yeah . . . well . . .' His shoulders squared against me. 'You were happy to steal those bikes from that bike shop, weren't you? Yeah?'

'I wasn't really, no. But that was different. Like you said, the man who'd made the bikes is dead. But the Wizard isn't. You shouldn't have taken it.'

'Listen to you, Little Miss . . . Little Miss . . . I dunno.' There was a bubble of anger in his voice. 'With yer . . . up-yer-nose ideas. Too good to steal, aincha? Too . . . big and . . . big and *important* to steal. Well, I'm a smuggler. Right? Stealing's what we do.'

'Stealing's what you *used* to do,' I corrected him. 'Stealing's what you did when you were with the smugglers. But you're not a smuggler now. You walked away from them.'

'Yeah, to help *you*,' he shouted. 'To help *you* get away. Wish I hadn't now.'

I stopped talking. It was obvious that if I kept on talking, Tab would talk right back, and then I'd talk back at him and we'd keep right on and on and get ourselves into a rolling stew of fury. So I stood without moving and looked at the ground.

'Wish I hadn't . . .' His voice was faltering. Cracking.

'Wish I'd . . . let the King take you back to the Minister. Wish I'd done that. I'd be okay, then . . . I'd be awright. Nobody . . . nobody wanting to kill me.'

I looked up at him. Suddenly, within just a couple of seconds, he'd gone from red-in-the-face mad to pitiful. I reached out and patted him on the shoulder.

'No one's going to kill you,' I said.

'Yeah? Old Mordecai hasn't given up on you yet, has he? Soon as he's found you he's gonna wanna ram me bones under the turf. That's what Knottman said.'

'But you're Tab the Magnificent,' I joked. 'Tab the Incredible. Tab the Miraculous with his trusty sidekick Mouse the Super Dog.' Tab kind of smiled through his sniffles. 'What sort of a match for you is that moron Mordecai? Mordecai the Moron, eh?'

'True. Very true.' He was entering into the spirits of it. 'Don't stand a chance, do he?'

'Not a dicky-bird.'

'Course he don't.'

We stood there for a few seconds before I started once again.

'We'd better take it back, though, don't you think?'

Tab paused before nodding. 'Yeah. I spose. Yeah. We'd better take it back.'

'For the best, eh?'

'Yeah.'

'Anyway,' I continued, 'Modecai the Moron hasn't got a clue where we are. He's not going to come after us now, is he?'

I couldn't have been further from the truth.

As we cornered the road where the Terrace began, we came across a vicious and horrible scene.

'Tell me where they are!' Mordecai shouted at the uppermost end of his voice. 'They came up here – WHERE ARE THEY?'

In front of him was the Wizard, kneeling uncomfortably, his lapels gripped tightly by Mordecai's fists.

'I . . . don't know . . . what you mean,' the Wizard said, his words all dry and forced. 'Nobody's been up here. Nobody. Not . . . recently.'

'Liar.' Mordecai smiled. 'You lie! Someone down the hill told us they were here.'

'I don't know . . . what you mean.' The Wizard kept up the act.

'Your face.' Mordecai sounded momentarily puzzley. 'It looks . . . familiar. Are you a traitor to the Minister? Are you an escapee?' Behind them, some of the Minister's police men were standing around awkwardly, looking like they'd rather be somewhere else. 'Tell me. Or I'll –'

'Let him go!' I shouted.

Instantly Mordecai dropped the Wizard, who fell clumsily to the pavement. 'There! There they are.'

The Minister's police men stirred, turning their heads to take us in.

'Leave him alone!' I screamed. 'Leave him alone. What harm has he done to you?'

Mouse starting yelping and rushed towards the Wizard.

'Get them!' Mordecai shouted.

Anger suddenly filled me to the brimful. I stretched out my arms. 'Go on then! If those are your orders, here I am! What are you waiting for? Come and get me!'

The police men all turned to one another, questioning.

'Go on! Get them!'

The police men did nothing.

'But . . .' one of them started. 'But they really are . . . just kids.'

'Yeah. Kids,' another one agreed.

'So what?' Mordecai answered. 'Get them. On the Minister's orders. Get them.'

'I've got kids of me own, back home.'

'Me too.'

Mordecai twisted his head. 'I don't care! Kill the boy. Get the girl. The quicker we do it, the sooner you can all see your children again.'

The Wizard was still lying on the ground, his head raised, taking it all in. Mouse was barking and *grrr*-ing at Mordecai, a nervous stutter twitching his feet.

One of the larger police men stepped forward. 'I aint killing no kid. Not even on the orders of the Minister.'

'Me neither.' A slightly smaller one came alongside him. 'It's not right.'

'What?'

'Yeah, Commander. You're on your own.'

Mordecai turned to us. 'Then –' he smiled again – 'I'll do it myself.'

His right hand flicked down to his side and a flash of steel appeared in the early evening light.

'No!' I shouted, throwing myself in front of Tab. 'You can't!'

Mordecai raised his hand and it twisted quickly in mid-air. Metal sliced through the sky between us and, at exactly the same moment, Mouse jumped up. Whether he thought it was some sort of game or whether he was trying to attack Mordecai, I didn't know. A small part of me likes to think he did it to protect us – to stop the knife from hitting Tab or me. Whatever the reason, Mouse sprang up from the ground into the air and –

Clump.

The dog squealed as he fell to the ground, the knife jutting out of his side.

'Mouse!' Tab screamed from behind me.

'Get them!' Mordecai called in vain.

The next few seconds were filled with far too much. I crouched, scooping Mouse up in my arms as the sounds of a machine whirring into action smothered the horrible gaps in the air. The Minister's men backed away in fear as BRAN rotated himself towards them.

'Look out!'

'It's coming to get us!'

'I said GET THEM!'

'Quick, Tab. Run!' I said as the blood gushed out from the poor dog's side. 'RUN!'

Our feet hit the ground hard and fast. One of the modpods started up behind us.

'Come back,' Mordecai ordered.

'No fear,' I heard one of the police men call.

Thump. Thump. Thump. BRAN was stomping.

'No!'

Crash.

'Stop it!'

Crash. Crunch.

I didn't turn to see what was happening. We just kept running. Running and running and running. We skirted down a little patchy path with tripping-up roots of trees and muddy smudges, our legs throwing us forward, away from the Terrace. Mouse's limp chest puffed and gurgled, the blood trickling warmly down my arms and onto my legs. My head was dizzy and my eyes were wide, and we ran and ran, who knows for how long.

'In here!' Tab's voice snapped me out of the fug and I spun around to see him, his face a mess of confusion and horror. He was pointing at a tree, the huge trunk all hollowed out leaving a sort of shelter.

He crawled in first and I got down on my knees and pushed my way in behind him.

We sat there quietly for a few seconds, listening. Listening for the sounds of following footsteps and madman yells. Guns and modpods. But there weren't any.

Eventually Tab reached out and touched Mouse. 'Is he . . . ?' he asked. 'Is he . . . dead? He's not, is he?'

And then I started to cry.

I cried for Mouse. Brave little Mouse who took the knife instead of me. Scruffy little Mouse with his stiff, rough fur who'd sleep anywhere and eat anything. So easy to ignore, so easy to dislike, but so very very brave when bravery wasn't even asked of him.

But most of all I cried for Mama.

Mama. My beautiful mama. Mama who'd brought me into this world, who'd filled me full of herself, who would toss me into the sky with happiness and who'd set me free from the walls of Lahn Dan with her last ever, hopeless breath.

My mama.

I cried so easily.

So easily.

'Is he . . . ?' The tears were riveting down Tab's cheeks too.

My hand stroked the dog's thick, dullish fur, sticky with blood. Mouse's chest rose slightly, barely there.

'No,' I answered. 'No, he's still alive.'

'Oh, Mouse!' Tab leaned across me and laid his head on Mouse's side, careful not to go anywhere near the knife that stuck out of his body. 'Oh, Mouse.'

We sat there for a forever, a tree trunk full of tears, waiting for Mouse to die. But his tongue kept lolling, his breath kept breathing and his tiny ribcage kept twitching up and down.

'I don't understand,' Tab whispered eventually. 'What happened back there? The Minister's men – they didn't want to kill me. And then . . . and then that robot thing started up. I don't understand.'

'Me neither,' I said.

'How did it start up? The Wizard was on the floor. He wasn't controlling it. It just started up on its own.'

I shook my head, but the thought of Mama kept swooping in. 'Angels,' I answered. 'Must have been angels.'

The day was slowly dying outside the tree when I heard the crunch of footsteps getting closer and closer. My eyes must have gone all wide open because so did Tab's. Once again his stubby little finger shot up to his lips to silence me.

'Mordecai!' he warned in a whisper. 'He's found us!'

I hugged Mouse closer to me. Mordecai had as good

as killed Mouse, had wanted to kill Tab. But I wasn't going to go back to Lahn Dan with the Commander. He was going to have to kill me too.

Crunch. Crunch.

The footsteps stopped frighteningly near us. A sort of *swish* noise as the someone outside spun on their feet. And then –

Quick as a slash, a face swept down into the trunk of the tree, blocking out the slowly ebbing blue of the early evening sky. Tab and I jumped, and braced ourselves for whatever was about to happen to us both. I noticed Tab's fists were clenched hard and my hand was resting on the hilt of the knife, ready to pull it out of Mouse and plunge it into Moron's head.

'Hello? Serendipity? Tab?'

The voice was soft, familiar. It was not Mordecai.

'Mr Knottman?'

'There you are. Thank the God Man.'

'Mr Knottman? What are you doing here?'

'Don't worry about that now. Are you both okay?'

'Mouse,' I cried. 'He stabbed Mouse.' I thrust Mouse forward so he could see. His hand slipped over the dog and he felt for his heart.

'He's still alive. But he might not have much time. We need to be quick.' He took Mouse from my lap, cradling him in his arms, and stood. 'Come on. Come with me.'

*   *   *

We made our way back to the Terrace, all of us under a sort of half-run hypnosis. As we neared the Wizard's house, I could see that one of the modpods that Mordecai and his men had come in was completely smashed up, its side caved in and its wheels carbuncled beneath it. Nearby stood BRAN with strips of shredded steel hanging from his fists.

The Wizard waved us through the door and Mr Knottman carried Mouse into the kitchen. He cleared a space on the worktop and placed the dying dog onto it. After explaining to the Wizard – who filled a bucket with water – he grabbed hold of the knife's handle and pulled it straight out of Mouse's chest. Mouse squealed in agony as a sudden rush of blood spurted out from the wound. Mr Knottman threw water over it, packed it over with a bag of herbs that the Wizard handed him and then quickly wrapped a large, longish piece of cloth about Mouse's torso and tugged it ultra-tight.

'This'll stop the bleeding.'

'The herbs will take away any infection and help the healing,' the Wizard added.

We managed to dip some sugary water into Mouse's mouth, and were relieved to see his little tongue darting in and out to catch the drips. Then the Wizard made up a cosy bed next to the fire that was glowing away, and we tucked rugs and blankets around the dog, who was puffing and panting like a bellows. Tab squatted on the floor next to him, curling his body around Mouse and gently stroking his head.

'I'm sleeping here tonight,' he said.

The rest of us sank onto the Wizard's chairs.

'So what happened?' I asked. 'After we ran off? I heard BRAN, but –' It suddenly hit me like an arrow. 'You!' I turned to face Mr Knottman. 'It was *you* who got BRAN to attack Mordecai.'

Knottman nodded.

'He got too close. *Far* too close to catching you both.'

Tab shuffled. 'And it was you who got that explosion to happen when we were on the bridge, weren't it?'

Knottman nodded again. 'You needed the distraction. I watched you from the other side. It looked as if you were struggling so I rigged up one of the half full gasworks and . . . Boom.'

'Hmmph. We were doing awright without yer, thank you very much.' Tab seemed to shrug his shoulders in protest, but nobody paid any attention.

'Where's Mordecai?' I asked. 'Is he dead?'

'Unfortunately, no.' Knottman frowned. 'But he's on his own now. The rest of the police men have headed back to Lahn Dan without him. They all hated him as much as I did, it appears.'

'He'll be off trying to find some new transport, heh heh.' The Wizard smiled. 'Did you see the damage that BRAN did to his truck? Polished it off good and proper.'

The fire crackled, snapping loudly as the wood in its heart burned itself to cinders and each of us kept checking Mouse to see that his little body was still sucking in air.

'Mordecai won't be able to do much on his own,' Knottman reassured us. 'He's really only brave behind his men.' His eyes looked solemnly towards me. 'Still . . . might be time to bring this journey to a close, Serendipity. Might be time to go back to Ashdown.'

'No.' I half stood. 'No way! I've come this far and I'll carry on until the very end. I'm not going to let Mordecai scare me off. Not now. Not ever. I set out to get to the edge of this country and I'm going to do it. With or without your sneaky help. If there *are* horses – which according to the Wizard there are –' Knottman looked at the Wizard and the Wizard nodded – 'then I'm going to find them. I owe it to Mama, I owe it to the Professor, I owe it to Tab and I definitely, definitely owe it to Mouse.'

Knottman stared at the ground. 'I know,' he said quietly. 'I know.'

'You won't stop her.' Tab grinned. 'Bit mad if you ask me.' He twirled his finger around in a loop-the-loop fashion right next to his forehead. 'Crazee.'

Over the next few days I'd catch Knottman looking at me. Every now and then I'd see him staring at the outline of my nose, or the way my chin rounded itself off, or the gap between my ear and my neck. And each time his face was covered with a confused, questioning sort of frown.

And I knew that he was starting to think what I'd started to think.

'I need to know,' I said, as the Wizard finished up watering the small flowers that were growing up around the edge of Shy's grave. He turned and looked me in the eye. 'I mean, I think I already know . . . but I need you to tell me. The truth. All of it. For my sake. Not for my mama's. Mine. It's my turn now.'

He straightened himself up and walked right past me, head down, along the garden path and back into the house. I followed as he made his way to the sitting room where Tab and Knottman were feeding slivers of bacon to Mouse.

'Please. I want you to tell me about my father.'

The Wizard stopped and pointed to an armchair. 'If you want me to tell you, you'd better sit down.'

I lowered myself into the chair as the Wizard folded his arms, scrunched up his face and paced back and forth, thinking it all through. Tab and Knottman gave up on feeding Mouse and watched the Wizard as he pieced everything together in his mind, reconstructing it. He reminded me a little of the Professor.

'The other day . . .' he eventually started. 'The other

day you told me that Caritas was responsible for your capture. And I told you that Caritas was jealous of Shy and Oleander's friendship. Yes?'

'Yes.'

'Well, that wasn't the only reason that Caritas was jealous of your mother. You see, Caritas was also madly in love with your father – probably still is. Obsessed with him. Not that he would ever have anything to do with her, of course – she would have been far too old for him. Quite wrong for a man of his position. But she had her little dream that perhaps, one day, they would be together.' The Wizard looked oddly nervous. 'So to find out that you were Oleander's daughter would have been horrific to her.'

I saw from the edge of my eye that Tab was looking at me.

The Wizard continued. 'If she could ruin your hope, crush your spirit, then she would willingly do so. Without further thought. Stop you from doing anything as a form of revenge on your mother.'

I got the impression that the Wizard was trying to avoid facing this thing head on, so I forced him to.

'Please, sir . . . tell me. I need to hear it. Who is my father?'

The Wizard sighed loudly and looked to the ceiling in hope that the angels would spare him this particular job. But no angels came.

He stared me in the eye and tried to smile.

'Your father's name is Easterbrook.' He paused. 'But you know him better as the Minister.'

I seemed to stop breathing. My whole body stuck like mud to the chair. The wisps of questions and thoughts that I'd been having had now been frozen into fact.

The Minister. My father.

'Your mother loved him very much, you know. Loved him greatly. But then he changed.'

All of a sudden I didn't want to know. Didn't care for the facts that just moments before I'd craved so badly. Why had I been so stupid? Why couldn't I have just left it all alone and kept the thoughts inside my head? What was the point in knowing any of this stuff? It wouldn't do me or anybody else any good. None of it was worth anything. It was all pointless.

I found the strength to stand up, walked around the sofa and opened the front door. I needed air.

'Serendipity?' It was Tab. But I didn't care. I couldn't speak to anyone right now. My head was full of noise and my eyes were full of tears.

I walked along the road and opened the rusting gate into the children's park. There I sat myself down on a worn away swing and cried, catching the drips in the palms of my hands.

* * *

'Serendipity?' It was Tab's voice again.

I didn't know how long I'd been sitting there, but all of a sudden Tab was rocking gently forward and backward on the swing next to mine.

'What?'

'You awright?' He was soft and gentle and so unlike Tab that just hearing him made me want to smile.

'Think so,' I replied, my throat all sore and croaky.

'I think Mouse is getting a lot better,' he said. 'Don't you?'

I grunted.

'When old Moron threw his knife the other day . . . I thought Mouse was a gonna, I can tell yer.' The wind blew across us like dust and the sun fought a losing battle with some puffy white clouds. 'Thought he was gonna die, I did. I was definite he was gonna die.' His voice paled away for a second before coming back stronger than ever. 'Cos without Mouse, I might not be ere right now.'

'What do you mean?'

'Well . . .' He thought. 'I don't know who my parents were. Never knew em. But whoever they were, they didn't want me. That's a fact.'

I wiped the drying tears from my hands and turned to look at him. 'They didn't want you?'

'No. They dumped me just outside the smuggler's camp. In a box, apparently. A beaten-up old cardboard box. Wrapped me in a blanket and left me alone. It was Mouse who found me.' He grinned a sad sort of grin. 'If he hadn't been out tryin to find some scraps to nibble on, he might never have heard me crying and I'd probly have died in the night. From the cold or summat. No one would ever have known.'

I reach across and squeeze his hand. 'I'm glad he found you.'

Tab nodded. 'Yeah. Me too.'

It was another week before Mouse opened his eyes fully, lifting his head and wagging his tail when he spotted Tab. Knottman loosened the bandages and checked the wound again – not without the usual growls and whimpers from Mouse himself – before applying a new herb bag and weaving fresh gauze around the dog's tiny body.

The day after that, Mouse stood and hobbled over to a bowl of food that the Wizard had prepared for him, complete with extra oils and ground minerals. He gobbled and drooled and looked positively pleased to be stuffing his face.

It was the day after that that I thought we should be leaving.

The Wizard shook each of our hands in turn and patted Mouse, who was strapped snugly into Tab's backpack once more.

'Well,' the Wizard said, a tad sadly, 'good luck. I do hope you see the horses. They were very beautiful from what I can remember. Tickle one on the mane from me. And from Shy, of course.'

'We will,' I replied, my arms clamped around his waist, showing him more affection than he'd had in ages judging by his reaction. 'We will. Thank you. And thank you for telling me about my father.'

'Yes,' his voice quivered. 'I'm . . . er . . . sorry I did that. Perhaps it would have been better if I'd not said anything. Kept it all under wraps. Like your mother wanted.'

I shook my head. 'No. I'm pleased you told me. Sometimes I think it's best to just goggle the truth in the face no matter how ugly it looks.' I gave him an extra squeeze. 'And I'm old enough to handle it now. I think.'

The Wizard patted me on the shoulder. 'Good. Good.' We stood there in silence for a while, the only noise the shuffling and snuffling of Mouse in the backpack.

'Er . . .' Tab was fidgeting like his feet were on fire. 'There was summat I wanted to do.' He reached into his pocket and pulled out the tiny leaping robot that had brought us back to the Terrace. 'I want to apologise, sir. I took this. From yer table. It was wrong of me. Sorry.'

The Wizard took the small toy from him. 'Thank you, Tab. I can understand. It's easy to be tempted by such remarkable workmanship as this. You know, if you had

300

asked me, I would have let you have it.' He held it back out to Tab. 'You can keep it, if you'd like.'

Tab shook his head. 'Thank you, sir. But no. Because I took tha, I nearly lost my Mouse ere, and, no offence, but my Mouse is worth more than a million squillion of anything – even clever little robots like yours. So thanks, but no thanks. I learned me lesson. And sorry.'

The Wizard suddenly looked sad again. 'Promise me you'll visit again one day, Tab, and I promise I'll make one specially for you. Yes?'

Tab grinned. 'Oh yeah, sir. Ta very much, sir.'

It was Knottman's turn.

'You know where I'm going, don't you?'

I nodded and smiled at him. 'Ashdown.'

'I think I'm needed there. I mean, nobody back at Ashdown has any idea how to change a flange sprocket.' He grinned. 'Mordecai has gone now, I'm pretty certain of it. And anyway –' he pulled his bag tighter around his shoulders – 'I think you need to do this last bit alone. Finish it the way you started it. The two of you.' It went through my head that I hadn't started this journey with Tab but with the Professor, but the thought whistled itself away quickly. 'Also,' Knottman went on, 'I promised Molly I'd show her how to make a proper apple crumble.'

Molly? The sparkle in his eye made it all clear. Molly. Of course.

31

The End of the World

We ticked days off like naughty children and the blisters on our feet helped to fill our socks and slow us down. One morning, the sun burst through the clouds and the heat fed all the way through to my bones, piling on the hope. We straightened our rucksacks and pushed on.

We were surrounded by lush countryside that seemed to level itself off the further we trudged. Wild and un-dapper with scruffity bushes and pokes of trees, the sky live with dust clouds of birds.

Suddenly, Tab stopped.

'What is it?' I asked.

He sniffed. 'Can you smell that?'

I sniffed too. It was true, the air smelled different.

'The sea,' Tab said. 'I fink it's the sea.'

We pushed on, the hedges either side of us twisting with the road. Left then right, right then left again. Small lanes leading off in all directions, signposts flailing with their names. On we marched, Mouse and Tab hobbling like wonky toys. We eased up another hill and then, at the top –

The sky had never looked bigger. The whole world had never looked bigger. It was like staring into another universe. Everything just stretched and pointed away into a distance my tiny brain could never have imagined.

'The sea.' I smiled.

The land that we stood on tumbled down for about a mile to the mud and the mud seemed to slip away and into the grey of the sea. For the first time ever I could see, hear and smell the sea.

'That's it,' said Tab. 'The end of the world. We made it, Serendipity.' He patted me on the back of my rucksack. 'You made it.'

We took the road down to the houses that seemed to cluster about the bay. Just above the tiny town, we passed a field full of men dragging and pushing old-fashioned farming machinery. Some were digging, whilst others were on their knees, prising vegetables out with their hands.

'Hello!' we called over to them. The ones who noticed us stopped their work and looked, smiling and waving back at us. An oldish guy hobbled over, his hat all faded and crumpled on his head.

'Shmae. Dydd hyfryd. Sut alla i eich helpu chi?'

'Er . . .' The two of us looked at each other. Perhaps the man was drunk.

'We . . . was . . . wondrin –' Tab spoke louder than he normally did – 'if . . . there . . . was . . . orses.'

The man stared blankly back.

'Yer know. Orses?' Tab did a little skip about, pretending he was riding a horse.

The man nodded. 'Saesneg, eh? Arhoswch funud. Rhodri!' He seemed to be calling over to a younger man. 'Saesneg!'

The man dropped the plough thing he was pushing and ran over to us, pulling the gloves off his hands.

'Hello,' he said, leaning over the trimmed hedge and holding out his hand to us. 'My name's Rhodri. It's not often we get English people in this part of the world.' His voice sounded normal but with a slightly strange, strangulated back-of-the-throat warble.

'English?'

We shook his hand and introduced ourselves.

'Everyone around here tends to speak Welsh. There are only a handful of us who speak proper English.'

'Welsh?'

'Yes. Come with me. I'll take you down into the village.'

'You in charge round ere?' Tab asked as Rhodri climbed over a gate to join us.

'Me? In charge? Good heavens, no.'

'Then p'raps you better take us to the person who *is* in charge? I fink we need to talk to them.'

'Oh, there's nobody in charge. Not here.'

We stumped on down past the first of the houses. A sign covered in moss revealed the last part of the town's name to be *Haven* – the first part being too thick with slimy green fuzz to see.

'No one in charge?' Tab seemed amazed. 'Wha? Not even a Mayor or a Minister? A King or a Lord?'

'No. None of those.'

'Aint there someone who makes the decisions? Someone who controls everything that goes on here?'

'No. Nobody. We all take care of each other.'

We leaned hard back against the steep hill as it staggered down towards the bay, our ankles straining.

'We work for ourselves and we work for everyone else. Seems simple enough to me.' We steered right onto a road behind the mudflats and Rhodri pushed open a door on the front of a creamish-coloured house.

'Llinos! Mae gennym westeion.'

A pretty woman came out from the kitchen area drying a plate with a tea towel.

'Oh. Helo.'

'Maent yn Saeson.'

'Really? Hello.'

'Hi.'

'Yeah. Hi.'

'This is my wife, Llinos,' Rhodri said proudly. 'Llinos, this is Serendipity, Tab and . . . er . . . Mouse.'

'Lovely to meet you all,' the pretty woman said, grinning. 'I've some cookies just out of the oven. Would you care for some?'

32

Bishops and Clerks

'Have you seen,' I ventured eventually, my belly full stuffed with six loganberry cookies. 'Have you ever seen any . . . horses in this area?'

The husband and wife looked at each other.

'No.'

'Me neither.'

I couldn't believe it.

'What? Never?'

'No.'

'I'd remember if I had.'

I sat there dumbfoundled. Surely they were wrong? They *must* have seen horses.

'Perhaps there are other people who've seen them? Yes?'

They looked at each other again.

'I don't think I know of anyone who's seen horses, do you?'

'No, I'm certain no one in the village has seen horses. Even though there have always been the rumours. But you know what rumours are like. Not very often true.'

It couldn't end like this, could it? Had the Wizard and Shy been mistaken? Had their map sent me on one enormous goosey-goosey-gander chase? Was it all just one big, unfunny joke?

'We'll ask the whole village tonight,' Rhodri said, seeing my reaction. 'At the village concert. We'll find out then.'

The village hall was filling up. Young men, old men, young women, old women, children and dogs seemed to take up the seats that were laid out row upon row. We sat up at the front and everyone's eyes burned into the back of my neck.

'Ope they're not gonna eat us,' Tab whispered in my ear.

'What do you mean?'

'I dunno. Just get the feeling they might wanna eat us. If they do, can I just say it was nice knowing you.'

'Tab,' I sighed. 'Despite having travelled so far and seen so many things, you can still be the number one idiot in the world, you know?'

He nodded in agreement.

'But if they do eat me, try to make sure that Mouse don't end up in a kebab or a fricassee or summat.'

The burble and gurgle of noise settled down and a man took to the stage. He looked like he'd put on a fresh shirt for the occasion, but his face was sunburned and leathery and his chin unshaven. He addressed the

308

crowd. In Welsh. At one point the audience laughed, but Tab and I didn't understand so we just looked at each other like we were all lost. He carried on talking for a while, sounding to me like he was listing things.

Rhodri leaned over to us and said, 'That's Mr Llewellyn. He keeps an eye on all the farming and the livestock and gives us advice on which areas we should be putting our efforts into over the next few weeks.'

'Sounds like he's the boss,' Tab replied.

Rhodri smiled. 'Like I said, there *is* no boss. We all pull along together. Mr Llewellyn understands numbers, that's all.'

After a while, Mr Llewellyn left the stage and the crowd clapped him as he returned to his seat. Then Llinos stood up and climbed the steps.

'Good evening, everybody,' she said. 'I hope you don't mind if I do most of the talking in English tonight as – I'm sure you are all aware – we have some guests in the village.' She waved at us to get up so we did. Tab and I straightened and turned to face the people gathered in the hall. To my surprise they looked a friendly bunch, grinning and fluttering fingers at us, and I found myself grinning right back, nodding towards some of them. Llinos introduced us – including Mouse – before waving for us to sit back down again. 'Before we get to the main reason for Serendipity and Tab's visit, a small matter of housekeeping. Mine and Rhodri's house only has the one spare bedroom, so we can only put up one of our visitors. Serendipity, will you stay with us?' I agreed with a nod. 'Good. Now, is there anyone else willing to give up a spare room for Tab and Mouse?'

'The boy and his dog can come and stay with me,' growled a man in a threadbare cap, sucking on a pipe. We all turned round to get a good look at him. The beard that sprawled out of his face looked like a living breathing animal as he chewed on the pipe's end, and his other hand reached down and patted the head of a slobbering dog with large bloodshot eyes that flopped exhausted at his feet. 'Be nice for my Toby to have a bit of company.'

Tab stared at me. '*He's* going to eat me. I just know it. Look at him. Look at his beard. That's the beard of a cannibal if ever there was one.'

'Sssh,' I warned.

'Da iawn,' Llinos eventually said as the muttering subsided. 'So Serendipity will stay with us, and Tab and Mouse, you will stay with Morgan the Nets.'

'Morgan the what?' Tab scrunched his eyes up to me.

'And now, something I need to ask of all of you. Serendipity has travelled from London to be with us, and she is with us for a reason. She has come to West Wales in the belief that horses still exist in these parts. I for one have definitely never seen a horse – of that I'm certain. Rhodri has never seen one. Is there anyone in this room who has ever seen a horse in the area? Seen a horse or even heard of someone who has seen a horse?'

Everyone chattered between themselves, Llinos repeating herself in Welsh to those who didn't understand. I watched as they frowned and shook their heads and mumbled and scratched their brows. Nobody responded.

'Anybody?' Llinos asked again. 'Anything?'

'There were the man and the woman, of course,' Mr Nets called out. 'Years ago now. They said they'd seen the horses, remember? The lady wanted to paint them. I don't know if she ever did. That was a long time ago.'

The Wizard and Shy, I thought to myself. That would have been them.

'But the only horse *I've* ever seen is the Marie Llwyd,' Mr Nets finished.

'What's that?' I replied. 'What's the Marie Llwyd?'

'Oh, nothing,' Llinos said, casting a look at the craggy old man. 'It's just a tradition we do once a year. Someone dresses up as a horse and knocks on people's doors, asking them questions and trying to be let into the house.'

'Sounds daft,' Tab said.

'It is,' Llinos agreed. 'Has *no one* ever seen a horse? A *real* horse? *Ceffyl go iawn?*'

The room just went silent and my heart felt like it had died on the spot.

311

'Don't mean there aren't any?' Tab whispered. Then, in a quieter voice, 'I don't think this bunch'd know a horse if it stood on their foot.'

But it wasn't any good. My legs felt suddenly heavier than they had in a long while, and as Llinos came down from the stage and rested her hand on my shoulder, I tried shutting my eyes and wishing myself away from this place. Back to the dirt and fear and misery of Lahn Dan. Back to where hope didn't exist and disappointment was just a matter of everyday life. Back to where everything had always *been* awful, always *is* awful and always *will be* awful. Especially now Mama wasn't there.

I found myself cursing the hopelessness of hope. Everything was pointless and I didn't know whether to scream or cry, so I just sat there, dumb.

The evening passed by in a blur. People took to the stage and sang songs, played guitars and violins and strange trumpety things, and everyone clapped and sang and foot-tapped along.

The day dipped into darkness as we left the hall and everyone made their ways home. Tab and Mouse went off with the beardy man and I was buoyed along by Llinos and Rhodri. I guess I got changed, crawled into bed and fell asleep.

But I didn't really notice.

*   *   *

The following morning I met up with Tab.

'He's awright,' Tab explained. 'I was a bit worried at first. I thought perhaps "Morgan the Nets" might be a way of saying how he caught people in nets before cooking them and eating them. But it's not. He's a fisherman. He goes out and puts nets in the water and drags home any fish he catches. The people in the village buy them and eat them. And his dog is pretty cute too. Mouse spent most of last night running around and chasing him. I could barely get him up this morning. The house smells a bit, mind.'

'You'll be right at home then,' I chucked back at him.

'Ha! Aint you the witless one?'

'I think you mean witty.'

'Maybe I do and maybe I don't.'

'You're over the egg, Tab, d'you know that?'

'Yeah, but I'm toasty with it!'

'So what do you think?' I said at last, after we'd both stopped giggling. 'Do you think these people know what they're talking about? Do you think they've never seen horses?'

'Dunno,' Tab said, giving Mouse a quick tap on the head. 'Couldn't really tell yer.'

'Well,' I asked, 'shall we go and see for ourselves?'

Tab nodded.

'Let's head out of this town,' he started. 'Then praps we can spread out, split up. Go across the fields and

313

see.' He gave me a very glaring look. 'If there *are* any horses, Serendipity, *we* will find them.' He winked.

We met up just after lunchtime.

'Anything?' I asked, hopefully.

'I went south and a bit further inland,' Tab said, Mouse panting at his feet. 'The grass was so green and lovelier than any I'd ever seen around Lahn Dan . . . but . . .' His eyes told me the truth. 'But I didn't see any horses. Not one.'

My heart was sinking faster than a pebble in a pond. 'I went back towards that market town and skirted north and south. I didn't see anything either. No horses. Nothing.'

We stood on the edge of the village in silence for a while.

'S'nice ere, innit?' Tab said as the sea breeze blew over us, bringing with it a particularly salty waft. 'Fresh. Like just being ere does yer some good.'

I had to agree, although my sorrow tried to drown out any sense of joy that might have been struggling to surface. Eventually I left Tab and Mouse to it, wandered down to Llinos and Rhodri's house, rolled out onto my bed with four fresh rowanberry cookies and a glass of elderflower water and read some more chapters of *Black Beauty*.

*   *   *

314

The day after, Morgan the Nets invited Tab and me to go out fishing with him. We dragged ourselves to the harbour before the birds had cleaned their beaks even – the stars had just twinkled themselves out and the sky was summoning up the strength to put on a really blue burst later that morning.

After the Gases, the seas had all retreated from the shores, pulling themselves back away from the edges, scared to touch the land that man was desperately trying to destroy. That's what they used to teach us in story-telling, anyway. And down on the harbour you could see it was real. The sea started a long way out and the people of the village had built a long wooden walkway over the muddy sand to the place where the sea began and the boats sat bobbing. We met Mr Nets and his dog at the start of this wooden bridge.

'Ever been on a boat before?' he asked, his pipe firmly wedged into his face.

'No, sir,' I replied. 'Never even seen the sea before we came here.'

His jaw dropped open and he nearly lost control of his pipe.

'Never seen the . . . Well, bless me. Never seen the sea!'

We creaked our way along the pier, Mouse and Toby chasing about under our feet. I may have walked an awfully long way from Lahn Dan, but that walk out to the boats felt like it was going on for days. After quite a while, the sea started lapping and slapping at the struts and beams of the wooden walkway. Alongside, boats filled with baskets and nets and sails were trussed up, swaying with the swell of the waves.

'Now Toby, you and young Mouse need to run along – no room for you on this trip, m'lad.'

Toby gave a sharp bark as if he understood exactly what Mr Nets was saying, before turning around and walking slowly away.

'Arf!' he called back to Mouse, who promptly forgot all about his master and whizzed away to catch up with his new friend.

'Well. Of all the –'

'C'mon. Smells like a good day for fish.'

'Smells?' I said.

'Oh yes. Good smelling day, this one.'

I felt sick. The constant up-and-down, up-and-down was making my stomach do a cartwheel; it was slowly working its way up my oesophagus and into the twitchy part of my throat. Any moment soon I was going to spill the beans. It was all I could do to hold onto the side and shut my eyes, persuading my brain that I wasn't on a boat, oh no, certainly not on a boat. Definitely not on a boat.

Tab, on the other hand, was loving it. Despite my

tightly squeezed eyes, I could hear him jumping around, swinging the sail to Mr Nets's orders, casting out the ropes, dragging them back in, all the while fish flipping about in the bottom of the boat.

'Great, innit, Serendipity?'

'Yeah. Great.'

'Mr Nets, sir . . .' I'd never heard such enthusiasm in Tab's voice. 'Mr Nets, what are they?' His silhouette through my eyelashes was pointing into the distance, so I allowed one eyelid to open.

'Those?' Mr Nets nodded towards some rocks jutting up out of the water. A long regular line of them, like the fingers of a slowly drowning man. 'Bishops and Clerks.'

'Eh?'

'Bishops and Clerks. That's what they call em. Don't know why. Must look like some bishops and some clerks, I suppose. Whatever they were.'

'And what's that?'

I turned my head a little – not too quickly, of course – to see a long, flat-topped island, craggy rocks leading up through mossy green to a grassy level.

'That's the Invisible Island.'

'Invisible? But I can see it.'

'Ah yes, but you couldn't. Before the Gases. Used to be submerged. And then the waters subsided over time and – there it was. Rising out of the waters like a phoenix. Apparently. Before my day, of course.'

'Do people live there?' Tab was overspilling with questions.

'No. We tried using the land for farming – good land for growing stuff, that is – but it's just too far offshore for regular use. We even put a couple of houses on there and some workshops with all the tools. But it's been abandoned now for a couple of years. No one there any more. Probably a whole load of vegetables ready for the picking just gone wild.'

The trip seemed to go on forever and I clung to the side of the boat with white fingertips. The fish flapped and the sea splashed and slapped the vessel, giving me mouthfuls of salty water every now and again and making my hair sticky and wet.

I thought back to that first train ride with Mr Wessex and Mr Trott – me all excited and excitable, and Tab refusing to budge from the safety of his pole. Today it was me who was fixed in place while Tab whooped it up and leapt about like a cat with a rat. Part of me wanted him to shut his face and sit down and stop rocking the boat while another part of me . . . well . . . I was pleased that Tab was feeling happy. Pleased that *someone* at least was feeling happy.

33

The Invisible Island

A couple of days later, Tab disappeared. We'd split up to look for the horses again, and I'd wandered the fields and villages, up and over the hills and mountains, but still I'd seen nothing. No horses anywhere.

I was first to return to Haven. An hour passed. Then another. And then Mouse scampered into the village, puffing like his lungs depended on it.

'Mouse,' I said. 'What is it, boy? Where's Tab?'

Mouse just ran around in circles, barking madly.

'What's wrong with him?' Rhodri asked.

'It's Tab. Something's happened to Tab.'

We searched the edges of the village, calling his name and listening closely, just in case he'd hurt himself. Meanwhile, Mouse skittered about like electricity filled his skin.

'Something's very wrong.'

We gathered at Rhodri's and Llinos's house – me, Rhodri, Llinos, Mr Nets and some of the other villagers.

It was as we were planning the search parties that we heard the voice.

'Come out, Serendipity Goudge.'

'It's Mordecai!'

'I have your friend, Serendipity Goudge. Come out now and he won't get hurt.'

I stood up, but Rhodri pushed me down again.

'Stay here.'

'But he's got Tab.'

'Stay here! And keep out of sight. I'll deal with this.'

Rhodri got up and went to the door.

The rest of us moved near the window and peered out. Mr Nets pulled me to the side and I was forced to look through the crack between the curtain and the wall.

'"Keep out of sight," he said.' Mr Nets frowned at me. 'Don't let him see you.'

Outside, Mordecai was stood in the middle of the road. There wasn't any sign of Tab.

'Serendipity Goudge! I warn you. If you don't come out soon I will kill your friend, the ugly little smuggler boy. His life is in your hands, girl.'

'Who are you?' It was Rhodri's voice. 'What do you want from us?'

'What do *I* want from *you*? I want nothing from *you*. What have you got that I haven't got? That I would need? What do you know of the world, hidden away from everywhere in your secret seaside pit? All I want is the girl. Give me the girl and the boy will live.'

'Leave these children alone. Let the boy go free and go back to your home. You are not wanted here.'

'Not without the girl!' His voice was increasingly angry.

'Never.'

'Then the boy will die.'

'You will *not* hurt that boy. If you do, I'll –'

'You'll what? Kill me? Ha! I don't believe you could kill a damned chicken.' The mood went silent for a few seconds before Mordecai spoke again. 'You have until tomorrow morning. Bring the girl to me and I shall release the boy unharmed. My modpod is on the road out of the village. The boy isn't there, so no heroic ideas about rescuing him or I'll simply leave him where he is to starve to death. Tomorrow morning.' And with that he turned and walked straight back out of the village.

'I've got to go,' I barked as Rhodri came back into the house. 'It's my fault that he's got Tab. I have to go and get him.'

'You're going nowhere, Serendipity,' Rhodri said, his hands on my shoulders.

'But he's got Tab! The Minister wants *me*, not Tab. If I go to him now he'll set him free.'

'I don't understand,' Mr Nets began. 'Why does this

Minister bloke want you? What have you got that he wants so badly?'

I thought back to the Wizard, standing in his sitting room, wondering how to break the news to me that the Minister was my father.

'I must go,' I insisted.

'No.' Rhodri gave me a little shake. 'That man out there won't give Tab back. Not that easily anyway. He doesn't deal in fairness. Doesn't understand the word. I can see it in his eyes. Walking right up to him won't do Tab any good, I can tell you.'

'But what can we do? None of this is Tab's fault. It's all my stupid fault for thinking there might be horses here. It's my fault he's in danger now. It was all my idea.'

'Ahem.' It was Mr Nets again. 'Sorry to interrupt but may I say something? I wouldn't fret too much about the boy. He strikes me as resourceful and as sharp a young man as I've ever met. A night or so of imprisonment won't harm him. Anyway,' he leaned in with a sort of wicked glimmer in his misty eye, 'I have a plan.'

Before the day had pushed itself up over the horizon, I found myself being ferried over the sea in Mr Nets's boat once again, but the feeling in my stomach had nothing whatsoever to do with the bobbing of the waves. My concerns were for Tab.

The night before, Mouse had snuggled down at the

foot of my bed, but he didn't rest. Occasionally he'd get up, swivel himself around and grumble and whine. His master had disappeared and he didn't understand why.

The whoosh and splash of the sea against the boat and the flicker of the dying stars on the water were nothing to me now. I felt numb as Mr Nets carried me and Rhodri over to the Invisible Island. Behind us I could see the second boat.

As we approached the small jetty on the island, the pilot of the second boat waved at us and carried on past to the other side of the raggedy rocky mass of land.

'He'll be waiting on the other, smaller landing spot. There are rough steps down to it – Rhodri will show you when you get there.' Mr Nets jumped out and tied the boat to a pole. 'Now remember, use the binoculars. The sun will catch on them. Make sure you are obvious when Mordecai looks across the bay. He needs to see you on the island otherwise he won't trust us.'

Rhodri and I got out and Mr Nets pushed off again. He nodded all dead duck serious and pulled the sail around to carry him back to the shore.

The island was even greener than the mainland. The grass that grew along its edges was toppling over with its luscious weight – ideal for horses, I thought as we made our way across to the two brick houses. As we walked, we passed vegetables and fruits growing wild and uncontrolled in the ground, on bushes, in trees. Seagulls circled and dived above our heads.

'It's possible to live off this island, there's so much stuff that's been left to grow on it.' Rhodri looked around. 'I haven't been here for years.'

We opened the door to one of the houses and were hit by a wall of cobwebs.

'Could do with a clean-up,' Rhodri said. The rooms were barely furnished and dust had taken over what had once been the sitting room. He brushed his hands over the walls. 'Dry, though. Not a bit of damp.'

We went back outside and walked towards the cliffs that faced the mainland. The sun was finally making its way out of bed as we unpacked the binoculars and pointed them in the direction of the Haven. Rhodri used them first.

'I can see Mordecai's van. It's going down into the village.'

'Let me see.'

I held the binoculars against my face. Suddenly I could see the detail of the village. The smoke whirling its way out of the chimneys; the birds tittering on the rooftops; the blooms in the window boxes. And then there he was. Commander Mordecai, in the rusty, creaking van. And there was Mr Nets waiting for him near the bay.

The van pulled over and Mordecai jumped out. He opened the back of the van and dragged something out.

'Tab!'

Tab had his hands tied behind his back. His hair looked even more bedraggled than it usually did, and he was stumbling as he walked. He saw Mr Nets and tried running to him, but Mordecai grabbed Tab by the shirt and yanked him back. Mr Nets shouted something at Mordecai and Mordecai shouted something back. Mr Nets pointed towards us and Mordecai took out his own binoculars, his eyes burning across the water towards us.

'He's seen us,' I said.

'Good. Now perhaps he'll come across to get you.'

Mordecai was angry; I could see him yelling. Shouting and screaming at the old sailor. Suddenly Mordecai pulled out his revolver and held it to Tab's head.

'No!'

Mr Nets stretched out his hand; he obviously started talking in a calmer way because the shape of his body changed within seconds. He was trying to soothe it all over. But Mordecai was still spitting out venom, pushing and pulling Tab about. Nets pointed over to us again. Finally, Mordecai seemed to cool it, but kept the gun aimed at Tab's head.

Seconds later they were all heading towards the water.

*   *   *

Watching the boat sail through the waves towards us made me realise what a slow, drawn-out way of travelling it was. It also made me realise what a beautiful thing the sea was. The Wizard was right. Always rolling. Always moving. The waves could smother and snap you in two in a snitch. But using the sea as a way of getting around? A way of getting from one place to another? Not the best.

Mr Nets was controlling the sail, pulling on ropes and swinging big beams round. Mordecai had positioned himself as far back as he could possibly sit without falling into the water. Still he held the gun to Tab's head and none of them seemed to be talking. In fact, Mordecai was looking a bit seasick.

'Nearly here,' Rhodri said. 'We'd better take up our positions. Remember, we have to wait until he lets Tab go. We can't move until that happens.'

We went further inland and waited for Mordecai to arrive. The wait seemed to sludge on forever; the wind whipping over the land a reminder that the world was still turning. After some minutes we heard voices and then Mr Nets came over the brow of the hill, his eyes wide and strained. About ten yards behind him were Mordecai and Tab. Tab looked exhausted and confused, his face a bloodied mess.

'He's been beaten.' I glanced up at Rhodri. 'Mordecai's beaten him up.'

'The man's a monster,' Rhodri replied, his fists balling. 'Deserves all he gets.'

Mordecai's harsh, sharp voice cut through the peaceful, silent air like a cheese grater.

'. . . ridiculous place. I tell you, if this is some sort of a trap –'

And then he stopped, jerking Tab backwards so that he nearly fell over. Mordecai had spotted me. 'Serendipity Goudge. Good of you to turn up today.' His smirk seemed to ooze itself out of his face. 'As you can see I've taken good care of your smuggler friend here – piece of scum that he is. Tried to get a good night's sleep but . . . er . . . he kept falling down some . . . ahem . . . stairs. Didn't you, scum? Terribly clumsy.' He smiled a smile to no one but himself. 'Step forward, girl, so that I can see your face.'

I walked away from Rhodri and shortened the distance between myself and Mordecai.

'Out of the way.' He waved his gun at Mr Nets who eased himself backwards so that he was standing to the side of us. I stood straight and tall and as proud as I could muster. This bully needed to see that I wasn't frightened of him. And to be honest, I wasn't frightened of him any more. He was weak and stupid and pointless. So what if he waved a gun around and pointed it at people? So what if he would happily smash his fists into your face as soon as look at you?

There was nothing worthy in his soul, and that made him pitiable.

'Nobody here to help you, Commander? All your men gone?'

'Traitors, the lot of them. Should all be hung, drawn and halved.'

He stared hard at me, like he was checking my face wasn't too dirty or something.

'What's wrong, Commander? Can't believe you've found me at last?'

He ignored me.

'The Minister wants you back in Lahn Dan, Serendipity Goudge.'

'Why?'

His eyes narrowed. 'You *know* why.'

Yes. I knew why.

'So we can play happy families?'

'Not quite.' Mordecai smiled thinly. 'First you'll be made an example of – sent to the prison camp in Hen Field. That was my idea.'

'I bet it was.'

'Stamp on your own flesh and blood, I told him, and see how they respect you. Imagine that leaden bunch of idiots thinking, *If he can do that to his daughter, what can he do to me?* After a year or so – if you prove worthy – you return. Rehabilitated. Remorseful. Ready to rule the people. Father and daughter united. A family.'

Like sunlight on water I had a glimpse of our lives as they might have been – me with my mama and my father before he became the man who became the Minister . . . Then it was gone.

'Ha. What good did the Minister do my mama when she was alive? What good has he ever done me? He didn't even know I existed.'

'Your mother kept you from him. It was all her fault.'

'None of this is my mother's fault! Don't you blame my mother!'

'Your mother was just a ridiculous *Pb*, which is what *you'll* always be if you stay out here in this backwater.'

'Did he love her?'

'What?'

'Did he ever love her?' I realised suddenly that my cheeks were wet with tears.

'How should I know? What does that matter?'

'It matters to me!'

Mordecai's eyes narrowed. 'Why don't you come back and find out for yourself?'

'And what about *me*? Does he really want to get to know *me*? Or just use me to keep his career going?'

He hesitated. 'I suppose . . .' His voice seemed softer, but his eyes were still cold. 'I suppose you *are* his . . . flesh and blood. I think . . . perhaps . . .'

And in that moment I saw it all. As clear as new spun rain. One day I would make the trip back to Lahn Dan and speak to the man who became the Minister. The man my mama loved. I would ask him why he did the things he did and find out who he really was. But not yet. My loyalty didn't lie with my father. It didn't even lie with my mama at this point.

My loyalty lay with Tab.

Tab. My good, kind, brave friend who'd stood by me through everything. Now it was my turn to stand by him.

'Come back to Lahn Dan. Embrace it.' Mordecai's voice was like a snake. 'Try not to fight against it like your mother did. Share his power.'

'Like you've always done? No. I don't think so.'

Mordecai gave a sort of growl. 'You don't understand. You *will* come back to Lahn Dan with me.' He gave Tab another shake. 'You have no choice.'

'I have every choice. That's what someone like you doesn't get. *I* choose what I do, where I go, who I see, where I stay. *I* choose. Nobody else. Not you, not the Minister. Not any more.'

'Then you'd better *choose* whether or not your smuggler friend here lives or dies, because if you're not coming with me he's as dead as those horses you've been looking for.'

I cast a quick look over at Mr Nets and then back to Mordecai. 'I. Am. Not. Coming. With. You.'

He shoved Tab roughly forward and started to turn the revolver at him.

'You've made your choice. Wave goodbye to your friend, Goudge.'

Clunk.

'Now! Run, Tab!'

The rock that I had been holding in my hand had spun through the air and hit Mordecai flat on the side of his head. Mordecai stumbled to the ground, stunned for a second or two, his eyes glaring. He tried shaking the sense back into his head before – *clank* – the rock Mr Nets threw smashed into the side of his nose and he fell back to the earth.

Mr Nets turned and bumbled quickly away back towards his boat.

Rhodri used a knife to slice through the rope around Tab's wrists.

'Come on. We need to get out of here.'

We ran as fast as we could, leaving Mordecai to pick himself up. Rhodri led the way down some awkward dunes and over a field of the green, wind-swaying grasses. We soon came to the top of the cliffs on the opposite side of the island. Peering down I could see the second boat waiting for us at the bottom of a long line of steep steps cut into the rock.

'Let's go,' Rhodri said and we began to pick our way slowly down the first few, difficult steps.

Bang.

A shot rang out somewhere above our heads.

'Come on. We've no time to lose!' Rhodri pushed me and Tab in front of him, our feet moving quicker now.

We were about halfway down when I made the mistake of looking up. Mordecai had appeared at the top of the steps and was staring down at us.

'Wrong decision, Serendipity Goudge,' he shouted. 'You made the wrong decision. If I can't take you back alive, I will take you back dead and suffer the consequences. Either way I am not going to the Minister empty-handed. Time for you to die, *Goudge.*'

I froze. As scared as I was, I stood rock still and glared at the monster of a man. If I was to die, I was going to die with my cold eyes fast on his.

Click.

A tiny far-off noise.

Click. Click. Click. Click.

Mordecai checked his gun then pointed it back towards us.

Click. Click. Click. Click. Click. Click.

The gun wasn't working. Something had happened to it.

'Angels.' I smiled to myself.

Mordecai swore and threw the gun down at us. It bounced off rocks, shattered and curved its way into the sea. He started bounding down the steps, two, three at a time.

'You can't get away, girl! I've followed you to the ends of the world and I'll follow you over its edge too.'

332

The three of us ran faster, skipping over the slippery steps. We were most of the way down when Tab's legs slid away from under him and his body rolled and bumped itself down the steps and into the gorse that clung onto the side of the cliff.

'Tab!'

He pulled himself up and looked at us bearing down on him. 'I'm awright. Don't worry. Keep going.' He tore his way through the weeds and brambles and back onto the steps, Rhodri holding out a hand to help him. 'Gotta watch yer step,' Tab said. 'Slippy.'

We kept on, all the time aware of how fast Mordecai was gaining on us.

'I'm going to get you, Goudge. And once I've got you, I'm going to finish you.' His voice found its way over the roar of the sea.

Finally – at last – we came out on the small wooden jetty.

'Yma. Yn gyflym. Mae e'n dod.' The pilot was waving us on, his face twisted. Mordecai was close behind, only twenty or thirty more steps and he would be upon us.

'Serendipity Goudge!' he screamed as we clambered into the boat. 'Serendipity Goudge!'

Slap.

His feet hit the wooden pier as the pilot pushed the boat away from its mooring and pulled the rope lifting the sail. Mordecai sprinted as hard as his legs could manage and at the end of the jetty launched himself into the sky.

'Aaaaargh!'

His legs kept kicking and his arms kept pounding as he flew through the air towards us, rising up, before –

Splash.

He fell straight into the water, three or four feet behind the boat.

He went under. A few seconds later his arms and head reappeared, frothing up the sea with their uncontrollable panic.

'He can't swim,' Rhodri realised.

He flailed about for a few seconds before managing to grab hold of one of the shiny rocks that bordered the bottom of the cliff. Mordecai's little white fingers pulled him up and out of the water, his clothes drenched, his hair flattened against his head. He turned and watched us as the wind blew up and filled the sail, taking us further and further away from him.

'Toodle pip, Moron!' Tab yelled as Mordecai's damp body dwindled into the distance like a tiny, steaming dot of loneliness. 'Toodle pip.'

Nobody said anything. We sat there in silence as the boat fought its tiny way against the pull of the tide. Tab snuffled and rubbed the cuts and bruises on his arms and legs. It was difficult to tell which ones the gorse had made and which ones Mordecai had made. Rhodri sat staring into the distance.

The wind brought us around the side of Invisible Island and the spray from the sea landed on my face, adding more salty tears to those that were already there.

'I can't believe . . . I think he shot Mr Nets.'

As we rounded the island we could make out the Haven, a small cluster of rectangular buildings nestling in the crook of the hill's arm.

'Look!'

Tab spotted him first, cutting through the water like a knife through fog. It was Mr Nets.

'He's alive!'

The old sailor gave us a happy sort of wave followed by a thumbs up. Everything had gone exactly to plan. Everything.

'It's lucky that he was such a lousy shot,' Mr Nets laughed as we guzzled ourselves senseless over a late breakfast. Mouse and Toby poked about our legs, searching for scraps, Mouse nudging us with his nose in the hope that we'd take pity on him. Tab took pity more times than was necessary. 'It's a wonder he even knew which way round to hold the thing.'

'Can he get off the island?' I asked. 'Couldn't he just make a boat and sail across to us?'

'Listen, my dear,' Mr Nets answered, bits of toast

hanging onto his beard. 'These waters are difficult to sail. Even if he did have the wit to make a boat, it would probably break up before it left the jetty. It takes a special type of seaman to cope in these parts.' His eye momentarily flashed over to Tab. 'No, he's stuck there for good. And good riddance, I say.'

'But won't he starve to death, like?' Tab asked. 'Or freeze to death?'

'There's a whole load of fruit and vegetables that grow on that island. At the back of the houses, there are more dried logs in a shed than there are trees in the world, I'd've thought. And some bits of coal. Anyway,' Mr Nets picked the bits of toast out of his fuzzy face mop, 'we'll see him right. We'll drop packages of food and provisions every now and then. When he's not looking. Fresh water – that kind of thing. And he can fish and trap birds. In a way he's got his own little paradise island.'

After breakfast, Llinos tended to Tab's wounds. They weren't as bad as everybody had feared, although that didn't stop Tab from screeching out in pain every time Llinos dabbed a bruise with cotton wool.

'He'll be fine,' Llinos said to me before squatting alongside my chair. 'How about you, Seren?' Her hand was warm against my shoulder and for the first time I noticed the freckles on her nose and the way her orange-gold hair tumbled down. 'What about you?'

'I'm okay. I think.'

To be honest, I didn't really think I was okay. Mordecai had come close to killing me and that thought made me shiver to my boots. My mind was running away with all the what-ifs and what-nots of possibilities. What if the stone I threw hadn't hit its mark? What if Mordecai's gun hadn't jammed? What if he'd managed to catch up with us on the wooden jetty? I suddenly knew exactly how Tab had felt knowing that the Minister wanted him dead. And it was a scary, lonely sensation.

Llinos could see the pain in my eyes so she leaned in and kissed me on the head. I quickly found myself hugging her and holding on tight.

In the evening, Tab and I walked to the top of the hill above the village and looked across the bay to where Invisible Island jutted out from the water. We sat on the grass and watched as the sun died. Tab took the binoculars that Rhodri had lent him and pointed them at the island.

'He's got a fire going in the house. And he musta found some candles.'

Smoke was coming from the chimney and lights flickered in a couple of the windows.

'I hope he'll be okay.'

'You what?' Tab sounded shocked. 'You ope he'll be

okay? That bully! The trouble with you, Serendipity, is that you're softer than a soft-boiled egg.'

'And the trouble with you, Tab, is you're right the way over the egg.'

'Maybe. But I'm so toasty it hurts.'

After we'd both stopped laughing, he said seriously, 'You know what this means, doncha, Serendipity?'

'What?'

'It means yer free. Nobody's going to come after yer now. Yer free to go where y'like. Free to do what yer want. Yer undred per cent free.'

I looked up at Tab and patted him on the arm.

'Thanks, Tab. But I think I always was. I think we always were.'

34

The Haven

The days passed like moments and the autumn nights drew in like they couldn't even have thought about doing back in Lahn Dan. Leaves on the trees became yellow and brown, and the air turned to smoke whenever you breathed.

Tab was spending his time finding his sea feet with Mr Nets. He'd taken to the water like a duck. In the evenings we'd meet up and he would tell me about the day's catch and the biggest haddock he'd ever seen and how Mr Nets would knock his pipe clean on the side of the boat and how he thought he'd seen a whale and the ins and outs of handling the rigging and the sail. He would chatter on for ages until his jaw ached. Then he would tap Mouse on the head and ask me about my day before daydreaming of the sea while I told him.

Tab had come home.

It wasn't long before I'd finished *Black Beauty* so I went in search of another book, and then another and then another.

Over the weeks I found I was spending more and more time at the village school. Mrs Rhys, the teacher, needed a helper and I would go around the children showing them what to do. The fact that neither Mrs Rhys nor the children hardly spoke a word of English made my job all the more challenging. Twice a week I took over the class for English reading lessons. I would write words on large sheets of paper – nothing too demanding. Words like 'up' or 'down' or 'inside' or 'outside' or 'across' or 'later' – easy sorts of words that everybody should know. I would hold them up and say the word and Mrs Rhys would work out what I meant and tell the class the same sort of word in Welsh. I would do it several times, then mix up the sheets before testing them. I would test them again in the following lesson. Some would remember, but some wouldn't. So I'd keep on at it until everybody understood.

At the weekends I would pack my rucksack and wander the hills and moors and coves and bays. Alone. Still looking for the creatures I'd come to see. My travels took me up mountains and right the way along the stretches of coast in both directions. I scanned the horizons with my binoculars. I dug about in muddy forests. I fought my way through walls of brambles.

But I found nothing.

And I realised my journey had really been about the journey, as much as the prize at the end of it. I had wandered through unknown lands, travelled in ways I'd never ever dreamt about. I had seen the sky turn itself slowly from dull violet to a blue you could row across in a boat, seen the grass change from fake to the real bean green thing. I had seen the trees come alive with each step further west, and flowers just begging to be sniffed.

I had met many people. Most good – the Wessexes, Mr Knottman, the Wizard, Mr Nets, Rhodri and Llinos. A few bad – Miss Caritas, the Minister, Mordecai.

I had met them and coped. And here I was now, the wind blustering through my hair as I took peaceful, thoughtful walks over the lands of West Whales.

I mean Wales.

My life had gone on. It hadn't just stopped still. I hadn't just stood there and waited for things to wash across me like the pebbles on the beach. I had marched into the sea and dived in – turned over by some waves, yes, but I had surfaced; I had swum. My thoughts sometimes went back to Lahn Dan – I mean London – and there were moments, I'll admit, when I missed the tall buildings and people like the Professor and Gry and Bracken. And my mama, of course. Always Mama. But my life had slipped on. For now, this was where I belonged.

And the horses?

I slowly came to believe that there were no horses.

341

That they had truly died out when mankind had been so consumed by its own ideas and principles that they had released the Gases. Man had stamped its hefty foot across everything else and hadn't cared what lived and what died. The Wizard and Shy had been mistaken. They had seen something else. Wind blowing leaves in the distance. A sudden burst of midsummer rain. Whatever. Whatever it was, it hadn't been horses.

There were no horses.

Or at least that's what I thought at the time.

Years Later

I awoke one morning to the faint *chug-chug-chugging* from a car. I stepped out to find one of the Minister's modpods pulling into the centre of the village. A sudden rush of panic whooshed in my chest. Had the Minister sent new police men to come and get his daughter after all this time? It couldn't be true. Surely he had given up all hope of catching me now?

I held my ground as I watched the door swing open and a young woman jump out. She was tall and thin with sticky-up spiky hair and the way she stood reminded me of somebody.

'Gry?' I asked cautiously. 'Gry? Is that you?'

She turned to look at me and her whole face sparkled.

'At last! Serendipity. We found you.'

I ran up to her and threw my arms around her. 'We?' I questioned.

'Yes, my dear,' came a voice from the modpod. 'We.' The opposite door opened then slammed shut and around the front of the vehicle came a bent-double old man with a stick, finding it hard to walk. 'I hope you don't mind us landing upon you like this, but you really are a difficult person to track down, Serendipity Goudge.'

The tears seemed to spin from my eyes and I lost my grip on Gry.

'Professor?'

He struggled and straightened, holding his arms open for me. 'So very good to see you, my dear. So very good indeed.'

London had changed, he told us. Everything in London had changed. There was no such thing as an *Au* or a *Cu* or a *Pb* now. The crowds had spoken, led by the storytellers, of all people.

'Everybody's calling it the "Storytellers' Revolution",' the Professor mumbled over his stew. 'But to be honest, we humble tellers-of-tales and recounters-of-history merely helped to start the process. It was the people of Lahn Dan who took it all to their hearts so valiantly.' I could still spot his pride even though he tried to disguise it the best he could.

'So what about the Minister?' I asked. 'Is he . . . dead?'

'No, no. Goodness, no. We are not barbarians.'

'What has happened to him then?'

The Professor stared me fixedly in the eye. 'You know, don't you?'

'What do you mean?'

'The Minister. Your mother.' His eyebrows moved closer to each other. 'You.'

'Yes. I do.'

He sighed and sat further back in his chair. 'She tried to keep it from you, Serendipity. Tried to hide it. Did a good job too, if I'm being honest. But I think she always knew that, one day, you might find out.'

'Is he safe?'

'Oh, yes. He's safe. Safe and free. Which is more than could have been said for the people of Lahn Dan during his Ministry. He lives in an apartment at Bucknam Place –'

'In prison!'

'Not any more, it's not. He lives in an apartment in Bucknam Place and is free to come and go when he chooses. Within reason.'

We sat there silently for a minute, dipping rye bread into our stew.

'You know, Serendipity,' he said, a moment or two later. 'None of us can choose our parents. Neither our mothers, nor our fathers. We simply are who we are.'

The sun was low in the sky as the Professor hobbled along the wooden jetty in front of us, his stick *tip-tapp*ing away. The sea rolled beneath and the boats jounced up and down.

'Strange, isn't it?' he said, turning back to look at Gry and me. 'The way you picture things in your head.' He waved his stick across the horizon. 'This, for example . . . I hadn't realised just how . . . just how *big* the sea would be. Look at it. It goes on forever. Remarkable. Quite remarkable.' He lowered his stick to his side and stood there, staring at the water lit suddenly red by the sun.

'He's dying, you know?' Gry said quietly.

'What?'

'Three months. Six months. That's what they said.'

I couldn't reply.

'He was determined to find you, though. Kept saying how finding you was to be his last, great adventure. His last, great dream.'

I smiled to myself, the Professor's words at the Emm Twenty-five Wall flushing back to me – *This is your dream, Serendipity. Dreams are things that you have to reach and stretch for.*

'He's definitely dying? There's nothing anyone can do?'

Gry shook her head.

We both watched as the Professor saluted the sun as it faded gently into the sea.

Gry returned to London a few days later. There was urgent work to be done, wading through the Ministry's

348

records of political prisoners – families to be informed, children and parents reunited. Bracken had joined a team of archivists, scouring documents and cross-referencing names, and Gry – having just acquired her modpod licence – was needed to transport and store all this material at the British Library.

Soon Professor Nimbus's strength started to fail – even Llinos's amazing caraway seed cakes couldn't sustain him – and Tab and I resorted to pushing him around the village in a wheeling chair. As his eyesight worsened, I read him books.

'You can read!' he said, the first time I took down a book. 'Goodness me, Serendipity. You can read.' The smile on his face spoke to the moon and back and I knew he was so proud of me.

I told him stories of our journey and of all the people we met. All of it. Every last single bit of it. Even of Mordecai and his lonely new life on the island. But at the very end, when the Professor was bedbound and silent – everything on the verge of stopping – I would simply hold his hand and wipe the sweat from his forehead just before wiping the tears from my own face.

When he did pass, we found a sweet spot on the hill above the village to bury him. Tab made up a headstone of a wooden cross and I told him what to carve into it. It read:

Here lies
Horatio Napoleon Nimbus
Scholar
Storyteller
Liberator of London

It was a Sunday, and sometimes on Sundays I venture into the fields to the north where the wildflowers bloom particularly well. Taking a basket with me I collect as many of the purple cornflowers, yellow flags, Solomon's seals, red valerians, lilacs, brooms, sweet woodruffs and forget-me-nots as I can possibly manage, to bring back for the older ladies in the village who fill their vases and coo at them all week.

I set off before the rest of the village had surfaced and made my way along the sweeping roads before climbing the rotting stile into the boggy moorlands, through the patches of oak forests and over the acres of old farmland.

The flowers were especially full this morning, so I cut them carefully and lined them up gently along the length of the basket.

It was just as I was about to set off home that I heard the sound. It was distant and unlike anything I'd ever heard before. A strange high-pitched stuttering.

I swivelled around to see where it was coming from.

And there they were. Two of them. Trotting up from

350

the wood, coming to see me. They moved slowly, but not uncertainly. Large, beautiful creatures plodding their way up the hill towards me.

Horses.

The one in front was a chestnut colour, his eyes open and wide as his tail swished. The one to the rear was a greyish white, with a long mane that fell gracefully over her neck. They whinnied and snorted as they got nearer.

I watched them calmly, my heart filling with a glow that melted away the years like ice. Suddenly I was that little girl in the Gallery Market again, staring at Whistlejacket. Thinking and wondering and hoping.

And now here they were.

I thought of Tab and wished that he could have been here with me to see them. But Tab's journey hadn't ever really been about the horses. He had come looking for somewhere he could call home. Something he could reach out and touch and know it was his. And in the Haven, on the sea, he had found it.

I put the basket down and pulled out the apple I was saving for my lunch. I cut it into pieces, and waited for them.

'Hello, boy.' I held a chunk of apple out to the chestnut as he came alongside me. He sniffed at my hand before snaffling it up with his rubbery lips, so I placed another chunk on my flattened palm. The white soon joined us and was just as greedy as her friend. In seconds my apple had gone.

'All gone, I'm afraid. All gone. No more apple.'

But they didn't seem to mind. It was as though they knew and they understood that I had been waiting for them; that I had travelled to this very point to be here at this very moment to see them. Their heads nuzzled closer and I could smell that warm musty smell that I had vaguely caught in the old stables at Ashdown. Rich and reassuring.

I reached up and wrapped my arms around their muscular necks, and pulled them nearer to me. They were real. They were alive. I wasn't imagining them. I wasn't dreaming.

They existed.

I cried and they watched me, allowing me to wipe my cheeks in their magnificent manes. They didn't move. Didn't pull away. They stood there as proud and as beautiful as I'd always imagined them to be, creatures with souls as deep as the deepest seas and as wide as the skies. These most majestic of beasts. These Whistlejackets.

My thoughts filled with Mama and that bashed-up wooden toy she'd bought with her last few pennies once upon a long ago.

It was night-time. Mama had spent all day carving an ear for the horse from an old wooden clothes peg. It was larger than the other ear and rougher-looking and it had fallen off three times already, but I told her it was wonderful.

'So,' she started with a laughing wheeze in her voice, 'have you decided on a name yet?'

I looked out. The other pods were shut up now. Mrs Ludovic's lamp had just come on. In the old days the Lahn Dan High had turned, the people flown like birds, soaring over city streets and the boats on the river Tems.

'We've had Magic and Fairy, Firefly and Velvet. I think we've had all the names under the moon and the God Man.'

The sky was prickled with stars. One star in particular was trying its ever-so-hardest to shine before a big purple cloud faded it out. I drew the curtains, my fingers trembling and my heart nearly slipping its ribs at how hard that star was trying.

'Hope.'

I turned and smiled at Mama, propped up with pillows, her skin so thin, her eyes all red and tiredy. She smiled her warm wide smile right back.

'I've decided on Hope.'

I don't know how long I stood there. It may have been minutes, it may have been hours. I wished it could roll into days or weeks. But I do know that at some point

I nestled my head into their necks one last time, gave them both a final sturdy pat before stepping back and letting them go.

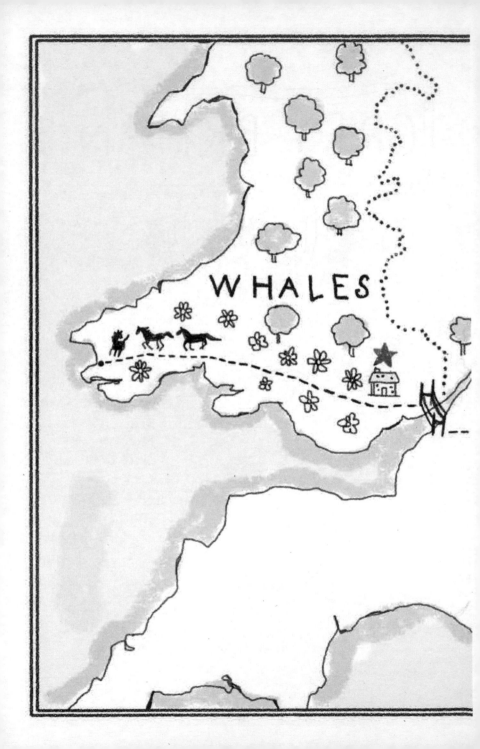

GREY BRITAN

LAHN DAN

Shy